CW00833291

A Dove Descending

By the same author

FRANCESCA

A DOVE DESCENDING

and other stories by

ROGER SCRUTON

SINCLAIR-STEVENSON LTD

First published in Great Britain by
Sinclair-Stevenson Limited
7/8 Kendrick Mews
London SW7 3HG, England

Copyright © 1991 by Roger Scruton

British Library Cataloguing in Publication Data
A CIP catalogue record for this book is available from the British Library.
ISBN: 1 85619 068 4

Typeset by Rowland Phototypesetting Limited
Bury St Edmunds, Suffolk
Printed and bound in Great Britain by
Butler & Tanner Limited, Frome and London

Contents

Author's Note

THESE STORIES share a theme, for which I have no simple word, although loss and self-deception are both involved in it. The first story is a kind of prelude to the second. The others stand alone. Two of the pieces are being sold under the wrong label. *A Dove Descending* is really a novella, while *The Seminar* is a mystery enfolded in a ballet, within an opera enclosed by a dream.

London, April 1990.

Departures

A s THE second vacation came to an end, Michael Ashley began to spend his afternoons in the shopping centre, sketching the loiterers in the covered concrete hall. He did not like the drawings and one day he sold them for five pounds to a one-legged American in a coffee bar. The American's other leg lay somewhere in Vietnam, and for several years now its owner had limped about Europe, spending the small change of an army pension. He explained to Ashley how to live without money in Italy, and gave him the address of a sculptress in Rome. As he left the coffee bar, Ashley made up his mind to visit her, travelling overnight if necessary.

His course was clear. First he must cross the garden and enter the house without speaking to his father. Then he must break open the box that lay beneath the bed where his mother died. He knew the box contained money, for once he had caught sight of Mr Ashley kneeling before it, counting out bank notes from the packet in his hand. Finally he had to slip out of the front door and make his way to the station. The plan was quite straightforward. But the first move, on reflection, seemed fraught with difficulty. He had never avoided an encounter with his father. Even now, when he was eighteen, and had been two terms in the Haydon School of Art, travelling every day on the train to Broad Street and coming back sometimes late at night, Ashley was not allowed to carry his own front door-key, but must creep into the house through the back garden, where his father kept unceasing vigil. He thought about this as he walked through the demolished streets, so that, standing in the roadway at the back of the house, he was too anxious to consider the details of his plan. When at last he made a move he found himself falling heavily through the gate; a blackbird shot away across the garden, shrieking like chalk on a blackboard.

But his feet continued to move, first left, then right, and as luck would have it he got across the tussocks of the upper garden and was soon within reach of the apple trees. His success was breathtaking. Then his father leaned on the fork with which he had been digging and clucked four times rapidly with his tongue. The feet began to stagger and disobey. Ashley looked down at the right shoe, a black canvas envelope through which a pink patch of flesh peeped vulnerably.

Mr Ashley's hips jerked against the fork. He straightened, and placed his hands in the stretched pockets of his canvas jacket, where seeds and tubers were kept from the rain. He clucked, and then cocked his head to one side, the long strand of crinkled chicken-flesh tightening and quivering. Ashley watched the coruscated edges of his father's ears as they caught the sunlight from behind. They were waggling furiously.

'You have not been out in those clothes,' Mr Ashley stipulated.

His son was obliged to assert the contrary, which induced in Mr Ashley a crisis of disbelief.

'No; seriously. Have you been out in those clothes?'

His forehead crowded hopefully with purple-tinged wrinkles; his eyes groped in their cavities. One hand disengaged itself from the pocket as if to bestow a blessing or illustrate a maxim. All would be well, Mr Ashley's gestures confided, so long as he had been obeyed in this one smallest thing.

'No,' Ashley tried this time.

'Don't lie to me please. You just came through the gate. Therefore you have gone out – looking like that.'

'So why do you ask?'

'Are you trying to provoke me?'

The father lifted the fork, embedded it, and then stood with both hands agitated.

'Of course not.'

'Then don't mock me. And answer my question if you would be so kind. I would like to know if you have had the audacity to go out dressed in those rags.'

'Well, I came back in them.'

'You mean then,' Mr Ashley proceeded bluntly, 'that you went out in some other clothes and changed into those expressly to annoy me on your return? Or what do you mean?'

'I mean that I went out dressed like this, for Christ's sake!'

'Is there any need to blaspheme? I ask you a reasonable question. You could give a reasonable answer, and so avoid unpleasantness.'

He spoke precisely, sucking at the words and letting them drop out one by one.

'Well, since it's unpleasantness you want . . .' Ashley stopped, distracted.

'I beg your pardon?'

Mr Ashley had been instructed to make a note of every word. Orders were orders. He was not to blame.

'Nothing.'

'No. There was something. What was it you said?'

'Nothing important,' Ashley repeated. But his mind was jelly and all other thoughts had dissolved.

'Nothing *important*. I see. In that case it will hardly matter if you repeat it.'

'Nor if I don't.'

'Will you repeat what you said?'

'No.'

'You won't repeat what you said?'

'No.'

'Then that's the end. You had better leave this house. There is no point in our continuing to live under the same roof if we cannot speak openly to each other.'

Ashley said: 'It struck me that you were wanting a quarrel.'

'What's that?' Mr Ashley paused and looked searchingly at his son. 'Do you realise what you are accusing me of?'

'Of what you are accusing me,' said Ashley, and set in motion the apparatus of flight. But Mr Ashley no longer wished to be alone.

'Come here. Don't go away when I am speaking to you.'

'Oh, what's the point . . .'

He watched the two feet shuffle back, obedient only to his father. Ashley stared down at a patch of lettuces, beginning to calculate in miles per hour the steady movement of a slug.

'I'll tell you what's the point. You have been trying to humiliate me and I resent that. I resent your going about like a layabout when I have made every effort to provide you with suitable clothing. I resent your addressing me as some kind of underling.' Mr Ashley paused to review the extent of his grievances. 'You do not wish to understand me. You take no account of my existence. You regard yourself as too educated to notice a worm like me. That's what I resent. But my wishes are every bit as important in their humble way as yours are, my work . . .'

'No, more important,' Ashley interrupted, but still watched the slug as it moved along the surface of a lettuce leaf. Luckily there was some misunderstanding, for his father continued:

'And anyway, when are you going to play your part? That's what I want to know. Am I to stay here slaving in the garden, our garden, just so that you . . . I don't know!'

Ashley took the fork. It was smooth and dry and set his teeth on edge. He began to dig. His father's face cracked slightly open, and then sealed itself again. Its expression suggested some unimaginable extreme of human virtue. Ashley reminded himself never to lose sight of the fact that he was a creature without initiative, who would submit immediately to any sign of moral strength.

'Do you realise,' Mr Ashley murmured, 'that I have been working here for a whole hour, not to speak of the day at the office? Do you realise that? While you were lazing about the town like an out-of-work burglar. Would any father accept it? Would he? Would he?'

He muttered for several minutes, and then they dug together in silence for another hour. Or almost in silence. For as time went on, Mr Ashley became slowly more ready to communicate. He began now to stumble across things in the earth (a potato, a bulb, a worm) as though retrieving objects he had buried against the eventuality of his son's presence. He picked them up and brought them across in slightly trembling hands, rubbing the earth from them gently with his thumb so that it slid off in moist brown flakes. The potato he explained away mildly:

'Here – see this? Beautiful, yes? A fruit of the earth, nature's gift.' He looked at his son, a long, urgent look. 'Do you understand? A gift. There. I imagine this is all more or less beyond you. I imagine you are unable to enjoy the way things grow. That seed potato I planted – you remember? And now a whole plant, the roots splitting away to start again. Can you not see what it is,' he roared, 'to live from the work of your own hands? Ah, yes, I understand, yes. You are blind,' (his voice dropped to a whisper) 'you are blind. Could you even tell me what kind it is? No? No? Then I'll tell you: it's a King Edward.'

He pronounced the words in a hushed voice, as though they contained the whole cause of his emotion.

'Cruel hands,' said Ashley.

'Cruel hands!' his father chortled. 'On the contrary. Hands for planting; hands for harvesting!'

He hobbled away gnomishly, leaned on a spade, and watched his son throw in the fork with slow, sullen swings.

'Aaaaaah!'

He ran back to wrench the tool away and apply himself to the task.

'Here's how you should do it. Christ Almighty! I hate to think of the damage.'

A smeared iris-bulb offered itself to his red-eyed gaze, split open and revealing a crisp white interior: an aperture in the humus through which only Mr Ashley could enter and share in the general pain.

'Oh God!' he moaned, clicking his tongue, and caressing the injured root. Ashley stared. 'Was it you who did this? Didn't I tell you to be careful? You must have known. To think . . .'

He clucked on for several seconds. Then, catching sight of a worm, he held that up too. It wriggled stoutly in his palm like another cracked red finger.

'Beautiful creature.' He smiled on it blissfully. 'Where would we be without you? Wonderful thing . . .'

He went on to explain the function of worms, their essential part in the cycle of nature, how they made the air-tunnels, turning the earth, allowing it to breathe. He explained how they were born, how reproduced, and how they died; he carefully demolished many popular superstitions about worms, and at the end of it all laid the creature in a safe place, with the words, 'For your own sake, don't let me see you killing one of these.'

Ashley spoke at last: 'Well, I'll be going.'

The words sounded hollow, irresolute, and he was not surprised when his father chose to ignore them.

'Carry on now,' said Mr Ashley genially. 'And remember to shake the soil from the weeds. Every bit is precious. Our life-blood.'

The sloping sunlight picked out his features in bloody affirmation. Ashley said: 'I don't think I *can* carry on. I have to go out.'

The physiognomy melted, flowed into a pool, shrank, became troubled, and then froze in a different form. Once more its mouth was hard, unyielding, and the eyes cavernous, without a glimmer.

'You what?'

'I have to go out,' Ashley replied. Looking down, he watched the worm as it revived and wriggled away. Its severed end, which his father had neglected to see, lay lifeless, rolled up in a balm of brown earth.

'But you've just been out. I don't understand you.'

The effort of not understanding his son held Mr Ashley tense during several seconds.

'I have to go into town. To a party.'

'You *have* to go. To a party.'

'Yes,' said Ashley, breathless at the chance to say something true. 'I've been invited.'

'Invited,' said Mr Ashley, and paused to shake the earth from a tuft of uprooted grass. 'Ridiculous.'

'I have I tell you. I've been invited to a party. By one of the people at the Haydon. I said I'd go.'

'Oh. One of your art school parties. Well then, you won't be missing very much.'

'But I promised I'd be there.'

'I see. You're the guest of honour. They're all desperate to meet you. Your arrival has been announced. I see.'

'I promised someone I'd meet him there.'

'Well then. She'll be disappointed.'

'I said *him*.'

'Look. Don't lie to me please. You know that this party, even if it existed, would not be very significant. Your duty is here, in this house, my house, your house, the house where your mother died. You know that. If you're making excuses it's because there's some other reason why you want to get away. And you know that's true. I can see it in your face. So not another word about that party.'

Mr Ashley began to dig again, and his son stared round at the garden. The blackbird was singing now, laying habitual claim to the territory where they stood.

'Why are you standing there?' asked Mr Ashley after a while. 'Have you given up?'

'I have decided to go to this party.'

His father stopped, looked at him, and then spat from the corner of his mouth.

'Good. Well then. You've made a decision. The next thing is to carry it out.'

Ashley stared down at his wrists, not to be opened until the final banquet.

'Off you go,' his father repeated, jubilant. 'I don't want to see you in this house any more. It's the end so far as I'm concerned.'

Ashley watched as his feet began to move, backwards at first, then turning, staggering, advancing in a grotesque cakewalk towards the house. He felt the excoriating eyes behind him, stripping layer after layer from his counterfeited form.

II

In the kitchen he found a loaf of bread, cheese in a plastic box, and a tin of pilchards, laid out in readiness on the sideboard. Ashley stared at them, and then filled the electric kettle from the kitchen tap. He spread out the oilskin cloth on the white-painted table, and began to gather plates and cutlery from the dresser. Soon there appeared at the window an expressionless redness like a child's drawing of a face. Ashley looked at it, and it seemed very strange. He knew it was his father's head, that it demanded words, apologies, explanations, but for a moment it was more interesting just to look at it and wait for it to speak.

'I thought you were leaving.'

'I decided not to.'

'I see. This is very confusing. What does it mean?'

Ashley felt weary. He looked at the bottles of sauce on the sideboard and imagined himself lying on the floor with red ketchup on his shirt.

'I though I'd better prepare supper. Are you coming in?'

'Not while there is light,' said Mr Ashley, who nevertheless stepped through the door and began to take off his rubber boots. 'I might sit down for a while, however. Perhaps we could have a chat.'

Mr Ashley left his boots on the kitchen floor and went fidgeting into the living room where his papers were kept. He extracted one from the middle of the pile – a copy of the *Guardian*, three years old – and began to read, sniffing disdainfully at the items which displeased him. After a while he reached across to the old brown radio and switched it on. Mantovani was playing, and Mr Ashley began to sway gently to the music.

'Where did you put the . . .'

'That was Mantovani and his strings, playing "Springtime". The weather forecast follows in a few moments at five to six . . .'

'The what?' asked Ashley, who had prepared the table and was beginning to unwrap the cheese from its greaseproof paper.

'The gun. You know, the nickel gun which you used last week to shoot me.'

'I didn't. It was an accident. You know it was. Surely . . .'

Ashley stood with the cheese in his hand. In the front room they battled on eternally. He could not remember now why they had quarrelled, or what he had hoped to achieve through his gesture. The gun was no more than a nickel air-pistol, slim and ineffectual. It was primed by pulling a handle at the base of the butt and fired tiny silver darts, each with a flight of coloured hairs behind it. There were six darts – a red, an orange, a green, a violet, a yellow and a blue. On the barrel was engraved his maternal grandfather's name, 'Martin Sylvester Holmes', in ornamental letters; it was the only heirloom that the house contained. In the midst of his father's shrill denunciations, Ashley had gently taken it from the drawer of the sideboard, opening the velvet case and lifting it out. It was certain to be loaded. All he needed to do was to pull at the handle in the butt and turn it through a quarter-circle. Suddenly his father had hissed, leapt up, and fallen back in the armchair, holding fingers to his wounded brow. A tiny drop of purple blood was all the life that issued.

'The dry weather will continue over the South East until the evening, when . . .'

'I wanted to make sure that it was in a safe place you see, before we started. By the way, I have tested the darts. It was bad luck it contained the red one, you know. The blue is very much sharper. Also it flies more straight. However . . .'

'I don't want to discuss it,' said Ashley, 'I don't want to discuss anything.'

His father suddenly roared with laughter. It was an interesting sound, ranging from middle C to F three octaves above, and containing indistinct gong-like resonances which came and went at intervals like the sound of church bells carried on the wind. The radio was trying to announce something of great importance. Was it a war? An invasion? A general strike? With a sudden farting noise the announcer was extinguished and the laughter stopped. Mr Ashley had stood up, his hand still on the brown plastic knob of the radio.

'I think it needs another battery,' his son said.

'Never mind the battery.'

'Nor the assault.'

'Ha ha!' Mr Ashley shouted. There was a silence.

'The food is ready now,' Ashley said. His voice trembled slightly. 'There's cheese . . . and horrid pilchards, and lettuce from the garden; ever so natural.'

'I said ha ha!'

'Yes, I thought that was what you said.'

'How long is it going to continue,' said Mr Ashley, not pronouncing the question mark, since he was speaking from a prepared text and neither of them needed to be reminded of the inflections, 'that's what I want to know how long is this game going to continue how long are you going to hide the truth from me and why don't you leave in any case if you find it so unbearable you would probably be happier you creep you probably would I daresay.'

After a silence, during which Mr Ashley stood chewing as though some particle had lodged in his teeth, but remaining otherwise inactive and staring at the volume of Kipling's poems that he had put down the day before on the mantelpiece, Ashley finally lifted up the salad and put it on the table. He was certain now that, if his thoughts had not been disturbed by his father's outburst, he would have formulated a brilliant plan of action, the first glimmerings of which had been rising on the horizon of his mind.

'Well,' he said at last, 'here's the food. I suppose we could eat.'

Mr Ashley rubbed his cheek with one hand.

'Eat. Do you really think that I could eat.'

Ashley forked a pilchard out of the blue striped bowl and let it flop onto the plate, where it lay, oozing red liquor from its sides.

'You could always try.'

'Christ! Why did I let you go to that damned place, eh? That's all you learn there: bloody sarcasm. Makes a man sick to bloody hear it, right bloody sick!'

'Stop hissing; it gets on my nerves.'

'What?'

'I said it gets on my nerves.'

Ashley had a distinct memory of saying that before, perhaps when his mother was alive and he a child, for an image came to mind of a white pinafore with pink and blue flowers scattered in squares across its surface, his father a tall red god thundering and with a pen or whistle in his hand. He felt as though a woman's tears were scalding him. It seemed to hurt terribly, far more than fire or steel. He pushed the plate away, and stared from the window. It seemed for a moment as though his whole childhood were welling up inside him, crying to be let out into the world.

'How can you speak of nerves who haven't got a nerve in your body?'

Ashley hardly knew whether it was hatred or sorrow that he felt. His father too seemed uncertain, for he was watching his son from the corner of one eye, and his face wore an apologetic expression as though he regretted the words which were rising against his will to his lips. It had been like this the day before, except that Ashley had tried to cook supper then and now he could only manage to open a tin. Something else had changed, something which he found difficult to identify. He looked at his father's check shirt, one degree greasier round the collar now. It bore a strange relation to the pinafore that fluttered in his memory. He felt there was something new in his father's voice.

'I think if you don't mind I'll put on the radio again,' said Ashley. 'Perhaps there's a concert.'

'I do bloody mind. Can't you bloody understand? I want to speak to you. I want to have it all out.'

'But perhaps I'll put it on all the same.'

Ashley got up and began to cross the room, concentrating all his thoughts on the sound of a Beethoven overture that was soon to blaze triumphantly forth. He put on his gangster face, pursed his lips and narrowed his eyes. Soon his father would go pale, drop his hands to his sides, spin on his heels dizzily, and then slowly and gently collapse like a punctured dummy.

It will not exactly happen that way, was his thought as the radio went crashing on to the carpet. Now there was screaming everywhere in the room, hands and fingers flying, and a feeling of reddened eyes and ears.

'Stop that will you? Stop it!'

'Ha ha!' his father shouted, aiming blow after blow at Ashley's face. 'Ha ha! Ha ha!'

'Stop it, you madman! Just stop it will you?'

Somehow a pilchard managed to lodge in the collar of his father's shirt, and a smear of oily tomato widened across the front. The fish wriggled against the dry rills of flesh as though newly out of water. Mr Ashley's face wore a light smile, and his eyes were half-closed as he beat the air – less purposefully now – with his dry red fists. Ashley backed quietly towards the kitchen and out into the garden. Only when he reached the cabbages did he at last begin to run.

III

The sun had set and all the corners of Broad Street station were gathering darkness. Ashley walked down the little stairway of arches and polished porphyry columns towards the street. A panic had seized him in the train. He had stood in the corridor, clutching his stomach and staring from the window. Now he felt better. He turned towards Spitalfields. In his pocket was the piece of paper that a girl had given him on the last day of term.

COME TO SUSIE FAIRFAX'S FROLIC
WHOEVER YOU ARE
AND BRING A BOTTLE

The paper gave the date, and an address in Stepney Green. Ashley stared at it, and then folded it carefully. He began to walk, and his progress was good. Soon he was making nearly ten yards a minute, stopping only when absolutely necessary to lean on a lamp-post and stare at the passing cars. He saw a telephone booth and made towards it. When he was fifty yards short he sat on a public bench, and took from his pocket a dry ham sandwich that he had bought at the station. But no sooner was the stale wedge of bread between his lips than he was overcome by nausea. He got up and squeezed his arms against his stomach, bending forward and taking in gulp after gulp of air. The feeling passed, and he sat down again exhausted. Nothing came before his mind save the image of his father's face, tormented and unforgiving, and the thought of the long, cold future to which he had banished himself. He could not understand this feeling; perhaps it was fear, perhaps it was love or guilt.

He forced himself towards the telephone, dialled the first few figures of his father's number, and dropped the receiver. Then he picked it up and dialled again. The telephone began to ring back at home; there was no reply. But Ashley did not replace the receiver; he kept it in his hand and slowly moved the earpiece towards the crown of his head. Now the monotonous ringing came faint and distant from the centre of his skull. He stood this way for some time, listening. He fancied he could detect in the sound all kinds of subtle variations, as though it were a companion distantly speaking to him. And then it seemed as if he had become the noise, as if he had retreated into the cavity of his skull, with his gentle complaining cry, and buried himself carefully in a grey pulp of brain, awaiting the end.

After a while Ashley felt better and stronger, and when he had replaced the receiver he began to walk off briskly towards Stepney Green. The streets he passed through were broken-backed and sprawling, often walled in on one side by the long flanks of factories. The occasional clumps of houses were dark, shapeless and miserable, like tramps huddled in sleep. And from time to time there would be a flashing high up of gaudy vermilion and blue, where a new block reared above the grovelling throng and stared blankly, as though waking from a nightmare.

He entered a pub. A man called Josephine was singing *falsetto*, rustling his sequined woman's skirt, tapping on the platform with high stiletto heels, and raising painted hands continually to the high fluffy wig which he wore like a crown. A short-haired girl in glossy trousers and with a smudged ciga-rette drooping from her lip accompanied Josephine on the piano, while a boy plucked at a bass guitar. The song was sentimental, brimming with nostalgia and aimless tenderness. Ashley felt the tears start to his eyes as he listened. Some door in him opened a fraction and stood ajar, so that his mind was filled with a strange and musty perfume, wafting from he knew not where. And then, when the music ended, he turned his attention to the crowd of onlookers and the door slammed shut, crushing some little fingers that had just emerged. All were standing, the women with dyed hair-styles and heart-shaped lips, the men shrunken and desiccated in their old baggy suits, peeping out like goblins from the skirts of their glistening paramours. They were shrieking and clapping; one or two of the men began to climb on to tables, slipping as they did so in pools of yellow beer. Josephine raised to his lips his rugged workman's hands, stuck kisses to the fingers, and flung them out like confetti over the heads of the crowd. But his eyes were cloudy and hopeless, and he looked yearningly at Ashley with a strange expressive sadness. Suddenly, meeting those eyes, Ashley saw his father. It was Mr Ashley's face, remodelled in a soft and spongy substance. Ashley made for the door. Outside he fell among a group of little girls, all puffy-eyed in their glossy paraphernalia. They leaned against the wall of a boarded church, jittering their bare legs nervously and sucking at the butts of thin brown cigarettes. Falling silent at his approach, they suddenly all answered together when he asked the way.

Most of the houses had been cleared to make way for the new hygienic towers. The few that remained were dark, with perhaps a single bulb glowing in a garret room, or a red glow behind dusty glass above the door. But one of them, towards the end of the street, surrounded by bomb sites, was alive with sound. Through the open door Ashley glimpsed the movements of people inside. He walked up the steps and stood for a moment in the porch. Then, having meticulously persuaded himself that it was not his own decision, he found himself inside, amid a seething crowd of bodies. The music was very loud, and he could hear no voices above it, only a confused wail of human sound.

In the centre of the downstairs room a girandole of stainless steel hung spinning from the ceiling, caparisoned in fairy lights. Ashley stood by the door, recognising no one; yet someone here must help him, with money, sympathy, even a ticket to Rome. The lights winked hilariously on the waxy faces of the dancers; he felt his footling self-involvement swell into genuine despair. Big with the future, he turned towards a girl who was leaning against the wall.

Long copperbrown hair lay fallen over her shoulder. Her head also drooped as she vainly tried to roll a cigarette. Ashley picked up a chair and took it to her. Unblinking preoccupied eyes eventually fell on him, and their light, which had hovered in mid-distances of grey and lichen-green, cleared to a hazel colour, mild and beautiful.

She continued to study the confusion of tobacco and cigarette-paper between her fingers, as Ashley sat down beside her on

another chair. She paid no attention to him, while he, unhinged
by her detachment, could not quite bring himself to speak.
Instead, he peered through the translucent fronds of hair. Her
neck shone in a faded shadowgraph; her cheek was ricey and
pale. Suddenly she held out her hands.

'Can you do this?' she asked.

Her hands lay open untremblingly. The lines were faint,
with no stains from smoking. Perhaps there was nothing there
to be ashamed of, nothing at all. Ashley snatched the unmade
cigarette and began to fumble with it. He chuckled nervously.

'Why do you laugh?'

'I have to laugh. Otherwise I'd go mad.'

'Don't be boring.'

There was something mournful in her eyes that persuaded
him to ignore what she said.

'No, but you see,' he confided, leaning forward, 'there's no
reason why we should speak to each other at all, no reason at all.
It just so happened that I've found you, at the end of a damned
tunnel which I've been digging, digging with my own hands,
digging and digging. It took an awful long time, I can tell you.
Where are you from? What are you doing here? No, don't tell
me, it won't change matters. I don't think I even want to know
what you do. I suspect you of reading Tennyson, however. It is
clear from your ears that you like Tennyson.'

'My ears?'

'Yes. Don't you see? The ears are always the most revealing.'

He handed her the cigarette, clumsily made and moist with
his saliva. She placed it between her lips, kissing his tongue's
mark with indifference, and then leaned away as he tried to put
his arm around her shoulder. He managed to catch hold of her
nearside ear and stroke it for a moment between thumb and
forefinger.

'You obviously have a thing about ears,' she said.

'Oh, not particularly. I mean there are other parts I like just
as well. But we are now at a turning point in history. We've
met at last, so we've got to throw ourselves in together and swim

for it, right? Let's swim away from them, away from them all.'

'What on earth are you talking about? Swim away from whom?'

'From everyone, from him, from her, from them,' he shouted, pointing about him furiously, 'from all the scarecrows, the parsons, the ostrich gobblers, the muddled middlemen, from everything, from trade secrets, from fathers, from the prospect of safe employment, cabbages, law and order, shit, moral turpitude . . .'

He buried his head like a hatchet in her neck and snorted wildly. She squirmed away.

'Christ. Talk about being fresh!'

'Don't worry about it,' he said, beginning to panic, 'it was only by way of introduction.'

'Charming.'

'So what's your name?'

'My name? Anne Wilcox.'

'Oh,' said Ashley bashfully. 'Are you related to Mr Wilcox by any chance? I mean the one who teaches us painting?'

'I'm married to him, if you call that related. And what's your name?'

'Oh well, you see, my name's Martin, Martin Sylvester. I don't really belong here, I mean I don't really know anyone here.'

He stared at her. Her expression was calm, clear, shallow, like a pebbly pool. And then she smiled, touching his hand.

'Don't look so sad. I didn't mind what you did. Not in the least.'

'Oh I see.'

Someone put on a record and the noise was suddenly shattering. Black spheres seemed to drift out from the centre of the room, bouncing from person to person. He wanted to get away, but she had gripped his hand, dragged him to his feet and was dancing with him. He could think of nothing to say as they swung back and forth, wrenching against each other's hands and gasping like caught fish. Eventually he shouted:

'What did you do with the cigarette?'

She looked up, but did not answer. The dance was mon-otonous, with neither pattern nor movement, only a mindless agitation that grew from nothing and withered at once away. Then the noise suddenly stopped and all other people seemed to stand for a moment in their last dying postures; Anne Wilcox fell instantly into repose as if something else had been dancing in her, something which had usurped her body and now discarded it. She squeezed his hand and fell limply towards him, pressing her pale parted lips to his. They withdrew into darkness, exchanging fretful comfortless kisses. Ashley avoided her eyes, and hid his face in her hair, smelling its almost no smell. He began to whisper, telling her to come away with him, to be his love, for he was mad and needed her. It was only a few days ago that he had shot his own father . . .

'Shot your father?' She drew away and studied him ad-miringly. Then suddenly her expression changed.

'What's the matter?'

'My husband has come.'

Ashley thought for a moment, and then: 'Here,' he said, 'quick, write your address on this bit of paper. I'll get in touch with you. God strike me pink if I don't.'

She did as he asked and then looked at him with a gay laugh.

'You idiot. Go away before I slap you.'

'Tata,' he said, with a wink and a mime of a kiss, snatching the paper.

Ashley walked away, and at once regretted everything. A short bearded man, with electrified hair and black obsidian eyes, stood to confront him, seeking redress for unnumbered crimes. Ashley stared at the hairy and familiar belly, gos-samered over by a thin silky shirt. His little crown of lies fell and splintered.

'Don't I know you?' the man asked.

'No. It's your wife I know.' Ashley gulped.

'Yes.' The man laughed, a red rag of dog's tongue panting from his jaws. 'But aren't you one of ours? Aren't you the one who came to college a bit late, instead of going to Oxford or somewhere? I've seen you in my life class. John Wilcox is the name.'

'Michael Ashley.'

'That's right. You're the one who paints girls in cinnamon and sepia; little doe-eyed ballerinas, conscripted circus waifs, that kind of thing. I like it. Come and have a drink. See you in a moment duckie,' he shouted, as the music thundered in the room. Sir Michael, pale paladin, saluted his queen, who giggled. Mr Wilcox, taking Ashley by the arm, administered an inexplicable pinch of fellowship as he steered him through the door.

A trestle table stood in the hall, bearing enamel bowls of punch. The liquid was served by a brassy girl with high made-up cheeks, green plucked eyebrows, and plump breasts popping at the lip of a cotton dress. She smiled at Ashley a lustreless smile and held back his glass, so that his hand groped emptily for several seconds as he and Mr Wilcox spoke. They drank. It was impossible not to splash the liquid over the hands and faces that pressed into them from every side. Mr Wilcox, spouting cockney and hippy in a friendly brew, swaggered and swanked. Ashley synchronised his admiration, feeling absurdly fragile. Often he did not hear what his teacher was saying, but laughed or was grave as if following an involuntary impulse.

'Why you here?' Mr Wilcox asked. 'How come you know Susie Fairfax, the wicked old brass? She pick you up somewhere?'

Ashley simpered immoderately. He wanted to confess everything to Mr Wilcox.

'I don't know Susie Fairfax. I'm almost a gate-crasher. I happened to be walking past. I mean, I had an invitation. But you see I came to London this evening so as to run away, to, to go away.'

Mr Wilcox accepted the confession with perfect composure.

'So you'll be leaving college? Well that's kind of a shame. I liked your work.'

'*Work*. You people always call it work. I call it doodling.'

'No need to be so breathless baby. What's eating you?'

'I just want to go. Away. To Italy. To think.'

Mr Wilcox roared, throwing back his black beast's head.

'Now how about that! Going to Italy. To *think*. Really, I blame the Queen. And so young.'

Ashley also laughed: an unfortunate gesture, which seemed to trigger off a sudden crisis in the world. At once Mr Wilcox made a jump, hit the ceiling, and then bounced back, disappearing through a trap door which Ashley had previously failed to notice. Simultaneously Ashley found himself amalgamated into a strange soft polyp, consisting of the mouths, hands and bellies of all the people in the hallway. There was a roaring noise, but Ashley could still with difficulty understand what Mr Wilcox was saying, since it was bannered aloft in numinous italics, the long trails of s's and g's fluttering from the ceiling like paper chains. The polyp dissolved, releasing him. He noticed that the people in the hallway were directing towards him accusatory eyes and fingers. He wanted to speak, to confess, to be redeemed of his sin. 'Yes,' he mouthed. 'Yes. It was I who laughed. Forgive.' But nobody seemed to hear what he said and he had no energy to repeat it. Mr Wilcox, he saw, was praising the body of a whore called Maria, whom he had enjoyed behind a sarcophagus on the old Appian Way. *Like that's the real Italy. Copulation, death, birth too, if you can't avoid it. That's my scene. No before and after, no anticipation, no regret. None of your Henry James Junior, your Piranesi, your light of the campagna, your German professor's Renaissance man. Just whores and heat. Whores and heat.* Ashley created for himself the experience lauded in Mr Wilcox's gasconade. But he knew that he had no right to it. 'You see,' his father said, standing beside him, dressed most oddly in an artist's smock, 'there is a fundamental corruption at the heart. Believe you me: a fundamental corruption.' He smiled on his son a gentle Christ-like smile, and then slowly took his way towards the dance room, nodding politely to each figure as he passed. Ashley wept. He knew it was wrong to admire someone as he admired Mr Wilcox. But he could not help it. He accepted everything, even the armed policeman who advanced on all fours from behind the bowl of punch. 'I love you,' he cried, 'Christ knows I do.'

'Is there any need to blaspheme?'

His father's face was cold and angry. But somehow, perhaps because of the policeman's uniform which was far too big for him, Mr Ashley seemed lonely and fragile as he shook inside it.

'I didn't mean it. It was only a toy gun. Honestly. Ask Mr Wilcox.'

The word *Saturnia* appeared on the ceiling. Mr Ashley began to hang his head and crouch down into the uniform, until at last the empty pillar of clothing telescoped to the floor. The head of the girl who had served the punch appeared before him, supported by putti whose wings flapped in his face. She was brightly lit and smiling, and her eyes stretched open until they were wide and blank as saucers. The make-up crinkled in long dry rills across her forehead, and in each little rill tiny creatures made their home. Ashley did not actually see these 'evil weevils', as his father called them, but Mr Ashley was busy again at his elbow, explaining their presence, and describing in vivid terms how they maintained the natural symbiosis of the face.

'I'm coming back. I never wanted to leave. It was a mistake.'

But again his father moved away, still smiling politely at the figures in the hall. *A deep black pool, sulphurous, warm*. Suddenly Mr Ashley sank and bubbled under. The yellow crust of sulphur reformed itself in wrinkles across the hall. Now Mr Wilcox scampered towards it and plunged, pulling behind him a girl out of school, a little hothead with titillating preludes of priest-nurtured shame. Ashley wept again as he observed it, the limp black pool glimmering beneath its crust like water in another world, like the Styx; the new moon breaking its membrane and pouring out on the misty sky; the warmth, the sensitivity of the skin, the pedagogic explorations underwater. He wanted all of it. He wanted it so much he thought he would die. But before he could move Josephine came and stood before him, sequined from neck to knee, and with long pendants of onyx dribbling from his ears. 'Darling,' he said, and reached out a hand to Ashley's cheek. The hand was rough, dry and masculine, and black hairs protruded at the sleeve. Ashley pushed it away and the fingers began to wriggle. They had become worms. Josephine's smile was no longer lewd, but Christ-like and all-enduring. A drop of blood dribbled from his punctured brow.

'I'm coming,' said Ashley. 'Please. In a moment.'

It seemed strange and dreadful that Mr Wilcox – in whom he had placed all his trust – should now abandon him. Ashley began to call out for help. He felt himself being gripped by the shoulder, and voices pouring imprecations in his ears. He tried to hit out at the punch-serving girl, as she floated like a balloon a fraction out of reach. And then suddenly she vanished, and with her all the web of finery in which she had entangled herself. His vision cleared, his ears unstopped, and the hubbub of the party cascaded around.

'Well baby,' said Mr Wilcox, who for some reason was wearing his wife's brown hair, 'I think you had better get home to bed. If it's help you want, give me a ring in college tomorrow. Any time between two and five.'

Ashley began to feel frightened. All around him voices rose in choirs, sometimes angels descending, sometimes devils out of *Faust*. He said goodbye and staggered to the door, pushing against the rump of an elephant that pressed him to the wall.

'Mind you go straight home sweetheart,' said Mr Wilcox. 'A nice cup of Ovaltine. Goodbye to Childe Harold. And take this bird with you. She's got the itch. Hot as a tinker's monkey.'

He pushed the girl forward, panderously pinching her plump bum. Ashley felt worse than he had ever felt in his life.

He wanted to sit down, and then to dance, and then to stand quite still, and then to plunge in ice-cold water, and then to run in the garden dizzily. He wanted to do everything and nothing at once. He stared round at the dancing room, and then ran into the street.

'*Amore*,' Mr Wilcox shouted after him. '*Amore*. Which is, being interpreted, how's your father. Go to Sirrah, go to.'

The girl too was running after him in the street. He looked back and saw Mr Wilcox waving from the porch. His wife stood beside him.

'I'm staying with you,' the girl cried.

'You can't. I'm not staying anywhere.'

'It doesn't matter,' his dead mother said, 'it doesn't matter.'

He stared, and the illusion vanished.

He began to run from her down the street. The air was cold; it caught in his throat. She was following at a distance. He turned and saw her, clutching a long woollen scarf about her neck. He ran faster. The pavement seemed to be spinning sideways beneath his feet. At the corner Ashley caught sight of his father, who zoomed in silence across the street and began to run at his side, panting quietly. Mr Ashley was naked, and sported an erection, which he half-hid with the cup of one hand. Ashley screamed and sprinted on. At last his father fell back and sank in a heap. Ashley continued to run. And then suddenly he was overtaken by a galloping cow who somehow managed to grip hold of him and pull him to a stop. Her breath was sweet, moist and heavy.

'What was it?' he cried.

'It won't harm you. Hang on to me.'

She caressed his neck and began to coo. He laughed. It was a ferocious sound and reminded him of Mr Wilcox. He tried to hit her, but his arms were soft like a doll's. Now there were two women holding him. One was Mrs Wilcox, who was negotiating his release. His attention was caught by a curious howling that came from the basement of a nearby house. He took advantage of their haggling, and broke away, running across, to peer through the grill and the dusty window. A black dog lay on a concrete floor, heaving its side in convulsions. A broken chain was twisted about its neck, and from time to time a groan would circle in the creature's mouth, from which the tongue drooled, congealing in the dust. A bare lightbulb hung from the ceiling revealing other dogs, huge, black and softly panting, fastened by chains to the four dark walls. Furiously they threw themselves against these chains, rushing forward with such force that their red mouths opened like split figs, and their bodies rose in the air, often turning completely over, and landing with a soft thud on the concrete. Then they would slink back, moving their forelegs from side to side in an effort to control the springing haunches. One or two of them had the habit of sniffing at the wall before beginning to run forward again, but their activity, despite these hesitations, would rise to terrible heights. At one time it seemed as if all the dogs had leaped together and were rising in a circle above their doomed companion; for seconds they stayed there, silently pawing at the air, their chains stretched so tight that Ashley gurgled in horror, crying 'Stop it! Stop that!', until a voice from the basement swore at him and he saw only a group of black men gyrating in a dance.

After a while he found himself being led to a taxi, and then, later, descending half-comatose at the door of Mr Wilcox's house in Highgate. He had begun to tremble again, and Anne Wilcox's hands seemed to sink into him wherever they touched, as though he were made of blancmange. As they mounted the stairs, spinning mobiles swept past his head like birds of prey. He tried to fight them off with his fists, but it only caused them to clatter and shriek. He turned and made to run down the stairs. A white creature stopped him, pointing her finger to the landing door.

'Don't be a fool.' She gave him a smile, but her eyes looked cold and jellied, like old fried eggs. 'I'm with you baby.'

'No. Go away. Let me go.'

His words sounded faint and distant, as though someone else

were speaking from far down in the bottom of the house. Anne Wilcox reached out and sank her hands again into the muddy fibres of his flesh. He tried to control his horror.

'Will you give me some money?' he said. 'So that I can go? I'll pay it back.'

'Money? That's charming. You want everything baby.'

She was moving him towards the bedroom, kneading his soft interior with iron hands.

'Look. I don't want much. Twenty pounds would do. It's not much to ask. I'll pay it back.'

'Later sweetheart. What you've got to do now is lie down.'

'No. I can't. I have a train to catch.'

The door of the room was opening. He struggled free and looked around him. The room was full of water, with a bed washed up in one corner and dolphins plunging and singing in the middle. He felt that if he could get past them unnoticed he would be able to rest and recover his strength. He waded patiently across, lay down and closed his eyes. But one of the dolphins, red, wet, and somehow less healthy than the others, dropped on to the bed beside him. He picked her up and ran with her to the door. On the staircase she shivered into a thousand coloured fragments which fell through the air for several seconds with a gentle weeping sound.

IV

Ashley stood by the gate and stared at the grass that pushed from under the fence into the unused roadway. The stalks leaned outwards in the windless air, their angular poses made somehow drastic by the horizontal boarding of the fence. He felt in his pocket for a sign of what had happened. He remembered only that he had left the house at dawn, swaying on puppet-knees down the red-painted stairway and falling on a child's tricycle in the hall. All day he had been sitting in parks, mindless or half-asleep.

He found a scrap of paper, a bill, a billet doux, a doodle. Spidering ink-tracks webbed his perception. Wilful ancox, dreadful praecox, telephone, telephone. No. He steadied himself.

'Anne Wilcox. Telephone 836 8270, between 2 and 5.'

Ashley held the paper very close to his eyes and watched the letters whirl like Catherine wheels. He returned it to his pocket. 'God!' he said aloud, and leaned red-faced against the gate-post. He could not show his face again. Besides, his father, he was sure, had observed it all, following at a distance and taking notes.

How it happened he did not know, but once again he was in the garden and closing the wooden gate behind him. It was a pity. He felt certain that, had he waited a little longer in the roadway he would have thought it all out, providing himself with everything he needed, with clear explanations for the past and clear intentions for the future. For some reason the gate would not close properly and Ashley fumbled for a moment with the latch. He knew his father was watching since now the desultory and spasmodic sound of digging had stopped altogether. Ashley turned round very slowly, stepping sideways with an awkward movement and crushing the stem of a rose. And yet there was no sound, no yell of indignation or gasp of pain. Ashley watched his feet as they moved. They reached the point where Mr Ashley had been digging on the previous day. Still there was neither sound nor movement. Eventually Ashley looked up and saw his father, who watched him out of red-rimmed and expressionless eyes. The face was livid as the sun, rigid as a mask, and yet somehow stretched and papery. Ashley, surprised at himself, stopped unbidden.

'Well,' he said at last, 'here I am. In time for a dig.'

Mr Ashley continued to stare in his son's direction. Only his fingers were moving, writhing slowly against the dry handle of the fork.

'Perhaps I'll go down and get changed.'

Mr Ashley snorted, putting his whole body into the gesture, so that his shoulders rose to the level of his ears and then dropped again.

'Perhaps I won't.'

Suddenly Mr Ashley began to dig, with a quick methodical thrust of the arm and foot. He stared down at the red earth, blinking and breathing heavily. Then he pushed the fork violently into the earth and stood back.

'Agh!' he said, and stared again at his son.

'I decided,' said Ashley, 'I decided not to stay on at college.'

There was no reply.

'I thought I might try for a job.'

Ashley felt weak again. His father seemed to be changing into a bird, raising his brown wings and flapping them slowly. Soon he would be airborne, squawking over the garden.

'Don't go. Just let me explain. Nothing's happened really. It was all Mr Wilcox's fault.'

Now Mr Ashley seemed to be getting smaller; he was coughing or sneezing into his hand. And then slowly he slipped off the end of the potato patch, and began to roll judiciously towards the house. Ashley stared after him, shouting:

'I'll be down soon. I must just finish this patch.'

He fought for a moment with his weariness, and then tentatively reached for his father's fork. The dry wooden handle seemed to take all the life from his fingers. He stood for a moment and then quietly began to dig.

A Dove
Descending

In loving memory of Ian McFetridge

Like lovely bodies which never grew old
Sealed with tears in a bright mausoleum,
Settled in roses and jasmine I see them –
Desires unfulfilled which now have grown cold:
Forever denied their one joyful night,
Their morning of pleasure, filled with light.

after Cavafy

The true way is along a rope that is not spanned high in the air,
but only just above the ground. It seems intended more to cause
stumbling than to be walked along.

Kafka

I

ONE EVENING after class Zoë Kostas decided to leave home.
The matter needed thought, and she spent two hours on
the Circle Line, sometimes hurrying from the carriage at a
station, so as to walk on the platform until the next train arrived.
Once she climbed the escalator, breathed the night air by the
ticket desk, and quickly descended when a man's hard eyes
caught sight of her. Changing at King's Cross, she took the last
train north to Seven Sisters.

Most of the Greeks from the village of Ayios Yiorgos lived in
Argyll Street, from whose Victorian bay windows they watched

each other through nylon jalousies. Yannakis Kostas had settled here with his family in 1972, two years before the Turkish army had removed Ayios Yiorgos from the map of Cyprus, and four years before Yannakis had died of a heart attack, while coaxing his favourite pigeon – a short-faced tumbler called Evyenia – into the dovecote at the bottom of the garden. For three years now the house had remained as he left it, his desk undisturbed, his clothes, books and records in their former places, and the few ageing birds fed each morning on the mixture he devised. Even the blank insurance policies – from the sale of which he had made his living – remained stacked in the corner of the living room, like unchiselled tombstones in a sculptor's yard.

Neither Zoë nor her mother really believed in Yannakis's death. They had buried him, and mourned him. Priests, cousins, friends and neighbours – all had visited and wailed and wrung their hands. But Zoë and her mother had already shifted to another sphere, just beyond the reach of sympathy. Although they never spoke of it, they conspired to deny their loss. Zoë believed that nothing united them so much as Yannakis, in whose honour she referred to her mother as the Kostaina. And until recently, when for some reason the Kostaina had begun to waver in their common purpose, his presence in the house had been vigilant and reassuring.

The Kostaina was asleep in the living room, her head thrown back against a pillow. The mouth sagged open, and a little rivulet of saliva flowed on to the chin. Her nose was stern, imperative and hawkish, while Zoë's was fine and slim like her father's. The Kostaina's eyes were grey, puffy and set far apart as though they distrusted each other, unlike Zoë's which were black, close-set and spiritual. Their skin too was different – Zoë's smooth, taut and sensitive, her mother's coarse and worn. Zoë believed there was something wilful in her mother's ugliness. That's why she slept with open mouth, so that the lyre-shaped lips of Ayios Yiorgos – her one good feature – loosened into worms of flesh.

She watched the Kostaina for a while, and listened to the enamel alarm clock as it ticked on the mantelpiece. A cyclops eye opened wide in the sleeping face, and closed again.

'*Panayia!*' the Kostaina said.

His pipe had been pushed to one side on the bookcase, and the box of Beethoven symphonies lay open by the record player. For some weeks now the Kostaina had been departing from the rules. She had removed his jacket from the bentwood chair in the kitchen; she had hidden the rusty woodworking tools and the black iron *chytra* which he used for his famous rabbit stew. She had done this unobtrusively, by way of adjustment to an order which she otherwise grudgingly maintained. Zoë did not reproach her, since reproaches would be an admission that the rules could be discussed. Instead she had acquired a habit of irony, as though some outsider had stepped in with these weird instructions, which must be obeyed in silence and with winks of complicity.

Thinking of their life, a great weariness came over her and she saw this weariness pictured in the Kostaina's face, as a snore rumbled past her mother's epiglottis and broke in the mouth with a popping sound. Zoë stepped forward and turned off the light. The figure shifted in the rocking-chair, and then spoke slowly and distinctly into the darkness.

'Another adventure.'

The voice was grave but sarcastic. Censorious Greeks said that Zoë slept with men and read poetry. The Kostaina denied both stories, though there was some truth, she knew, in the second. Now she had begun to wonder about the first. Every late homecoming had therefore become an adventure – a *peripeteia* – and the word was aimed at Zoë's heart. It made her feel unclean, a disgrace to Yannakis and his family. Zoë went into the kitchen, took his brown Oxford shoes from the cupboard beneath the sink, and began to polish them furiously. After a while she felt better, and, hearing the Kostaina creaking on the stairs, she tidied the kitchen, swept it with a final glance, and went to bed.

She dreamed her habitual dream. They were flying along the paths above Kyrenia, his brown shoes kicking the dust into puffs of cloud before them, his strong arms cradling her. Their laughter echoed from the cliffs, danced over snake-filled crevices, and filled the olive grove. It was a godly laughter, beyond reproach; the white shrine of the Virgin stood undisturbed in its panoply of prayer. He had given her a caper plant, torn from the rock of St Hilarion, and she squeezed it against her palm, enjoying the prickles.

They reached the crest of a steep incline. Before them was the crescent plain of Kyrenia, bordered by a white-edged sea. Far above the north horizon stood the white ramparts of cloud, crowding each on each like the sails of a vast armada, frozen in their momentariness, remote and picture-still. Below was the town, with the new hotel where the British soldiers came, the outworks piled against the fortress and trailing their yellow fingers in the sea. Nothing moved in the streets or on the white road to Bellapais, and the olive trees stood captive, their grey-green clusters of leaf stuck on the air like cut-outs from a book. For a little moment she was safe.

Then it happened. He shuddered, pushing with huge movements of the abdomen against her. The landscape too began to move, heaving like the canvas of a stage. The fields swayed and buckled, while the sea hurried up to the land's edge and loomed there, brimful of menace. The sky was on the march, black squads of raincloud roaring past them in an armed parade. Everything writhed with his movement, and gasped with his breath.

They had set up his bed in a banana field, and the leaves slashed the air like swords. He turned his white eyes to her, but they were sightless and through them grinned the empty mask of death.

'Lord Jesus Christ, Son of God, have mercy!'

He was adrift now and alone; death, which was to have tied them for ever, death the saviour and the promised end of time, was pulling them apart. Clouds, trees, fields and buildings;

people, birds and animals – all were fleeing before this death. She reached out to him, but her hand was full of pain, which filled him as her fingers touched his chest.

'No!' he cried. 'No!'

He seemed to see her, not where she was standing, but somewhere far behind, isolated in some evil light on the higher terraces.

'Zoë! Zoë! Help me! – *Voithise me!*'

Fending the real Zoë away, he reached to the distant phantom, his wide eyes staring, poised on the last thin line of hope before the end.

Again she touched him; again the pain rushed from her hand into his tortured body; again he waved her away, rejecting her for a ghostly version of herself, which sped swiftly down the hillside with its white hands outstretched. Zoë sensed its approach, and knew that its touch would kill him finally. In an effort of will she turned to face her antagonist, to stare into its evil eyes and cancel the false promise which they offered him. But it was not her face at all, this white gleaming thing: only a ball of rags, a featureless twist of cloth. The winding sheet rushed of its own accord towards them, swaying like a human form. She put out her hands to protect him, and then, as the cloth rose up to cancel the air, she started awake. Bright sunlight danced in the bedroom, and she could hear the Kostaina crashing about the kitchen in habitual dismay.

Zoë was accustomed to the dream, to its strange light and movement, and to the sight of herself destroying him; and though it distressed her – this strengthless appeal for a mercy that she could not give – she had grown a carapace around the feeling, and harboured it undamaged. She pushed away the blankets and the pain returned. That was a novel detail – the caper plant.

She thought of her distant relatives, on whom the sun poured down its unresisted stream of light, dissolving every I in loyalty. From this pool of life Yannakis rose, miraculous as a hero's sword, affirming, refusing, and pulling from his head, she knew not how, a daughter – rational, thinking, free as he was. No doubt the caper dramatised the sleeping Zoë, incorporating some fact of her, along with all the other rumours and murmurings that hummed along the channels of her body, into the nightly tableau of his ruin. Before she discovered the little point of blood in her palm, she had deduced that a drawing pin had fallen from the board over her bed. This small triumph of reasoning set her on the path of resurrection. Just as the caper plant could be traced to the punctured hand, so did the other dream-pictures start up from her body – from rapid movements of the eye, from the popping and sizzling of synapses, deprived of current but alert none the less and eager to interpret, even where there was nothing to interpret and no meaning to be found.

It was one of her teachers who had urged her to read *The Interpretation of Dreams*. Dr Peter Leacock – whom she knew as Little Peacock, *Pagonaki*, endowing his swagger with an iridescent tail – was constantly pointing the way to sexual freedom. But she had found in Freud no authority, either for sexual freedom, or for the vision of an unconscious mind. No part of Zoë lay beyond the reach of thought. And if she dreamed from time to time, what of it?

You can interpret dreams as you can interpret anything. All religion is an interpretation of the meaningless: especially the Kostaina's religion, in which she had once imprisoned Zoë's soul. What other significance did they have – those unending services, the monotonous chanting, the Opening, the Little Entrance, the Reading, the Great Entrance, and all the men-only fidgeting at the iconostasis, that core of gilded glamour where the bearded priest sat solemn and shrouded like a waxwork dummy? What was it, the *prokimenon*, the epistle and alleluia, the *anamnesis*, *epiclesis* and Great Commemoration – this endless mind-numbing repetition of things which had been fastened in her infant soul unbidden – but the embellishment of nothing, so that 'now the celestial powers are present with us and worship invisibly'? Gilded nothing, the thought of which filled her heart with longing, and her mind with scorn.

Zoë dressed carefully, for it was a special day, the day of her departure. White shirt, tan pullover, and brown buttoned corduroys, belted at the waist – English clothes, which Argyll Street abhorred. She tied her thick black hair in a cotton scarf, and round her neck she hung the good-luck charm – a tiny silver revolver – with which a sad English boy had purchased her only kiss.

II

The birds came to her. Need, not love, compelled them. But her own love comprehended them, for always in her mind she saw his hands made gentle in the art of holding them, buried in white feathers like a child's sweet head in sleep. She approved of the birds for their monogamous habits, which meant that ten varieties could breed without crossing in a single dovecote. Zoë had joined Yannakis in his hobby, raising ring doves, barbs and spots; turbits, pouters and carriers; trumpeters and laughers, and the wonderful short-faced tumbler, which fell head over heels through the sky above the dovecote, down to its roost. To the Kostaina all these birds were *peristeria*: but to Zoë and Yannakis, who knew their English names, they were symbols of the outer world and its variety, messengers sent across the roofs and fields of England, preparing the day when they too would take wing.

Evyenia had died, but her mate, Patrick, survived. Zoë lifted the old bird gently and peered into his startled button eye, which caught the sun and shone with a pinkish glow. A white fan-tail shuffled over her feet, strutting on its self-made stage. She placed Patrick among his companions and opened the hopper for their feed: maize and barley, with a dash of bran – enough for a week. She scattered the seed into the sea of flapping supplicants and, taking a pad from her pocket, added 'bird corn' to her list.

'Goodbye,' she said, *'adio.'*

III

Her mother's face was jammed like a wedge of pudding against the kitchen window. Zoë smiled facetiously, and came inside.

'I was waiting for you.'

There was self-pity in all the Kostaina's words, and only now and then would a gleam of satisfaction light her face, when her tragedy was recognised. Zoë looked past the mournful head to the flasks of yellow wine on the sideboard – to be opened on his sixtieth birthday – and thought 'Why is my mother so old? Ten years his junior, yet so old and weary and neglectful?'

'Well, here I am.'

The sunbeams overran the sycamore, and laid a brocade of shadow on the kitchen table. The Kostaina's charcoal jumper and long skirt of black tulle created a nub of darkness wherever she stood. Zoë began to lay his place at table.

'First,' the Kostaina said, 'you are to take off those trousers.'

'There's no law against trousers.'

Law counted for nothing among her countrymen; but law, Yannakis told her, is the secret of England, and the source of its power. He had hoped for Zoë to be a barrister; but fate had willed otherwise. Little Peacock taught Social Theory and Philosophy; law was a subject of which he would not approve.

Yannakis always sang in the morning, and Zoë sang too, English hymn tunes she had learned in school. Singing was useful in several ways. It imposed order, musical logic, saying this, now this. It joined the kitchen to the outer world, where others sang for the fun of it. It imbued her actions with an air of necessity, so that it ceased to be strange that she should place the dead man's plate and cup upon the table, with a bowl of olives and a tray of fetta cheese. Her singing was also conclusive proof that they lived in England, where trousers could be worn.

'There's no law against . . .'

And another thing: singing adds to the nowness of the world. Everything shone with nowness, even the crumpled old mother, as she prepared her next rebuke.

'I know,' Zoë said, breaking off; 'there's no law against prostitution. But we Kostas have principles, and principles are against trousers. *And* against prostitution.'

The word *porneia* prompted the Kostaina's sermon. Her words peppered with impatience, she explained again the wonder of Orthodox marriage, as displayed by Zoë's brother Manolis, who five years ago had hooked a loving girl from Limassol; by Mrs Zenofidou's Leniou, now at university and engaged to a converted Englishman; and by countless other people who had held to their principles and come out dandy in the end. She castigated Zoë for her waywardness, her obsession with books and birds, her bohemian ways, her foul language and her *enfant-terrible*-ism. She dwelled on the dangers of England in general – of which she had heard the most alarming things – and of London in particular, some parts of which she had even visited herself. And she explored the possibility of a return to Cyprus, not to Ayios Yiorgos of course, but to the South, where she would build herself a bungalow and live in seclusion by the sea.

At this juncture, however, she would begin to hesitate, stunned by the inaccessibility of her dreams. Her lines became vague, irresolute, abruptly breaking off, as sometimes old monks who have chanted an identical psalm at every hour of a lifetime begin to forget the words, pausing in the middle of a verse with a vacant expression and a drop of saliva on their chin. To believe, and to doubt, thought Zoë, are equally matters of performance. She ate some olives and took the pad from her trouser pocket.

'Here is your list of things to do.'

'Are you deaf? I asked you to take off those trousers. What do
you mean, list of things to do?'

'To do when I'm gone.'

The Kostaina's eyes froze in her face, like a waxwork's. Her
gaze was fixed above her daughter's head, where a calendar
picture of St Hilarion hung on the wall, showing the jagged
fortress of Dieudamour, surrounded by a sea of mist. Slowly
her arm unfurled from the blob of darkness, and a white
trembling hand came forward like a creature from its lair.

The list consisted largely of 'don'ts': don't play the records,
don't shift the antiquities; don't leave the door unlocked; don't
let the weeds grow in the garden; don't fill the house with
wailing women and crumby priests; don't touch Zoë's books.
Three 'does' came as an afterthought: renew the insurance, tie
back the medlar, buy corn for the birds. The Kostaina studied
the list, and then slowly raised her sainted eyes to the picture of
Dieudamour.

'*Panayia!*' she said in a whisper, and dropped the paper to the
floor.

IV

Zoë's room already had an abandoned air, the books compressed
too neatly into the shelves, the bed-clothes folded for storage,
and the sash window fastened against the rain. She took down
the poems and postcards from the board, and rearranged the
drawing pins in a cross over her pillow. Then she changed the
cross to a star. Another week and the house would fill with
widows. She imagined the sound of cups and grief and gossip,
remembering the male talk of animals, politics and war, which
had hummed like a turbine in her father's presence. A wave of
nausea swept over her.

'Cancel it,' she said aloud.

She took a small duffle bag, with a change of clothes and

Cavafy's poems. Her other things withdrew from her, mute and accusing. She re-tied the scarf about her head, checked the wicked buttons on her trousers, and cast a solemn glance in the mirror.

'Idiot – *Anita!*'

Behind her mirrored face the black-shawled widows lingered, patiently killing each other as the church prescribed.

v

The Kostaina was standing on the stairs, her body shaking and clanging in its black bell of clothes.

'I suppose it's a man.'

Zoë wondered what was wrong with her, that the thought had not crossed her mind.

'Yes,' she replied. 'Aren't you ashamed of me?'

'Ashamed of you? I've been ashamed of you for months, ever since . . .'

'OK little angel.'

Zoë used her father's epithet, *ayioula*, recalling his easy ways. She took after him, and no one was to forget it. She had his eyes, his nose, his cheeks and his laughter; she had his cool enquiring mind, his quiet toleration, and his non-negotiable presence. She had loved him severely, as a man loves another man. Therefore she had room in her heart for strangers, for novelty – even for England, with its unexplored remainders, thrown from fortune's wheel. She knew about many things – Shakespeare, for instance, socialism, sexual fantasy. She went alone to the theatre and pondered those terse modern plays, in which people stood amid the ruin of dismembered sentences and watched the meaning flow unhindered away. She had friends whom her mother did not know, whose virtues and vices she could not guess at, so far were they removed from the paddock where the Kostaina's imagination trudged wearily around in its trail of dung. The Peacock for instance, vain and creepy and brilliant, and Michael, whose face it would do no harm to touch.

'Well, who is he, and what does he do?'

'What does he do with me, you mean? Nothing.'

She gave her mother a long theatrical look, denying by implication that she denied those interesting rumours.

'It all went wrong when you began to think of yourself as educated.'

'You mean when I was *sixteen*?'

Zoë still looked sixteen, although she was seven years older: for time had stood still in her body, waiting its day.

'I mean when you started those evening classes.'

'Oh those!'

'Yes those. I suppose he is one of your teachers.'

'He is,' said Zoë, imitating a defiant toss of the head. This sparked off the Kostaina's second sermon, which concerned the Island, her ancestors and the principles which bound them, generation to generation, like pearls on a never-ending string.

Zoë much preferred this speech, although its histrionic delivery marred the quieter details. Her mother was no Homer; but she did a competent job on Ayios Yiorgos, evoking the harbour, with the fishing boats bobbing quietly, the god-like breath from the sea shaking their rigging and sending up sparks of sun-filled water along the quay. Zoë recalled the Ottoman houses of stone, with their tripartite windows and outside flights of steps, and the open-fronted workshops where lined old craftsmen, who looked as though they had been chiselled from olivewood according to some immemorial formula, chiselled from olivewood the likeness of themselves. And she loved the still afternoons, under the dense incumbent light of summer, when a lavender haze hung on the bed of sea. Tiny fingers of foam fussed at the water's edge, pulling it tight and tucking it in. And out at sea the gulls perched on a foundered cargo-boat, clinging motionless to its rim with proprietorial airs, like the souls of sailors drowned.

But these images of stillness were not on her mother's agenda. She had hurried onwards to the church, to Father Fillipos who painted so well, to the miraculous icon which watered the fields, to the holy hermitage where even the Turks had prayed before those days of violence: Safiye, Banu and the other girls, who danced with them at weddings and spoke to them in Greek.

'We can start again in the South. They have made an agreement with those heathens. We have a right to property, the equal of what we lost . . .'

A menacing smile had set in the Kostaina's face, as though something in the mechanism had jammed. Zoë, however, was recalling Yannakis, and a visit to the monks of Bellapais, in their narrow-windowed outhouse: the clean damp smell of whitewash, and the great black table on which he laid out papers for the Monastikos to sign. Long tablets of sunlight were spread on the floor like slowly moving carpets, islands of experiment and play. She looked at the laughing beards, at the grooved fingers sliding on the strings of a bouzouki, at the moist brown eyes which spoke of a supreme irresponsibility, as near to renunciation as laughter to tears. And she thought how strange it would be if some other hand than his should touch her. The hands of the monks were the colour of henna, in which the Kostaina washed her hair. A tremor ran through Zoë's body, and her mother's face, with its wide mad eyes, broke across her vision like the moon.

'How could I be a good mother in this God-forsaken country? We should go home now: we've tried here, God knows we've tried; but we failed. We failed because we were far from home.'

'Home!' Zoë protested. 'The truth is we're a nation of lackeys, though we disguise it with faith and family and pious crap. We pretend we are Greeks, but we are miserable mongrels, with the blood of all the world's randy sailors in our veins. Our religion is a bundle of pagan superstitions, local gods and goblins. Not that *I* mind so much, in fact I used to be quite fond of them, especially St Mamas the Tax Evader. And all that dainty virgin-worship barely concealing the cult of Aphrodite. Our famous virtues, what do they amount to? *Philoxenia*, for instance. Of course we love strangers, provided they're not Turks, or Arabs, or anyone else who is likely to stretch our imagination. Or chastity – the springtime of the body, the divine light of Thabor! *Panayia!* Just a way of selling yourself at more than the going rate. "Cleanse us from all impurity" indeed: we live on spiritual enemas, and turn ourselves into stinking cripples . . .'

Zoë could go on in this way for some time, mentioning the calamitous events, in which the God Archbishop was deposed and the Greeks ran wild for *enosis*. She would remind her mother of what really happened in Ayios Yiorgos, to Safiye and Banu and the other Turkish girls, long before the terrible retribution. She would turn her scorn to the mainland, to the Greek Colonels who began it all, and the enfeebled culture which sustained them. In the past her erudition had given her an advantage over the Kostaina, and enabled her to restore the balance of insult. For she could run circles round her mother's meagre reasoning, and always reward her with an opposite conclusion. But now, long before she reached the socio-political sections of her discourse, she had ceased to believe in it. A troubled sadness filled her soul, a longing to be reunited with all those dead, and most of all with Yannakis. The strange power of the dead overcame her, that we cannot harm them, and therefore come before them weaponless, our words mere air. Zoë began to weep, and the Kostaina, without relinquishing her moon-like smile, added lamentations of her own, the tears flowing as though her eyes were loose stoppers in a cistern. For a few seconds the women stood motionless. Then Zoë pressed her nose into the ruined face of the Kostaina, and ran to the door.

'Who is it?' her mother called out. 'And where will you be?'

Struck by the question, Zoë awoke from her grief. The Kostaina carried on her war against the world in her own personal way, indifferent to established methods, and not for one second relinquishing the core of settled futility in which she

had made her fortress. In this she had a kind of distinction, and
to leave her without explanations, without some recognition
of her individuality, was to do a great injustice. Zoë, who suffered for all her injustices, was not prepared to commit
another.

'His name is Peter Leacock, and he teaches at Bewley.'

VI

Of the many products of Victorian philanthropy designed to
provide the working classes with an opportunity for self-
improvement, Bewley College was the most widely respected.
Housed in a gothic barn in Kentish Town, it prepared students
for external degrees and diplomas offered by a variety of
universities and polytechnics; for certificates in art, music and
architecture from the academies and institutes of the capital; for
the examinations of the legal profession, and for its own
'Diploma of Study' which, if without any positive significance
in the world of affairs, at least warned any prospective employer
that the holder had lived for three years uselessly at the
taxpayer's expense. Two cultures inhabited Bewley – that of the
full-time students, who came and went by day, and that of
the evening classes, frequented by sprightly autodidacts in
corduroys, and childless women on the edge of divorce. Zoë
belonged to the evening culture, the unelected president of
which was Peter Leacock. But it was not Dr Leacock who
attached her to Bewley; it was Michael, whose surname she did
not know, but of whom she was thinking even as she described
the Peacock to her mother. For the Kostaina's sake, Zoë
endowed the Peacock with every mental and sexual privilege,
setting him in the context of an unhappy marriage, ended on
account of Zoë, an arty entourage of friends and mistresses, a
busy involvement in radical politics of a faintly ironical kind –
every attribute, in short, that he claimed for himself. But it was

Michael's face that lodged before her mind: pale, sardonic, slightly Jewish, with wide-set, slow-moving eyes, veiled by translucent eyelashes. Michael made a point of sitting next to her in the Peacock's classes, his eyes turned downwards to a notebook in which he executed rapid sketches of eery people, his head cocked to one side as though listening to some other noise than their teacher's triumphant crowing, some secret inner voice that disdained the clumsiness of speech.

If Michael were there Zoë would go after class to the pub. This was the central fact of the evening culture, and the illustration of its root ideas. Freedom, Zoë had discovered, is collective solitude. The pub – with its sweet, damp, smoke-tinged air, as though you lived for a moment in the mouth of some living monster – was a place of fragmentation. People came here not so as to overcome their loneliness but so as to experience it to the full. The students sat in a cluster, Ellen pressing rolled cigarettes between lipsticked lips and uttering cryptic sentences about space and time, while the Peacock trumpeted the news of human liberation. Zoë would fasten her eyes on the middle distance, where groups of bearded men in youthful middle age sparred together with brief stabbing gestures. Feeling Michael's solitude, all wrapped up beside her, she began to enjoy her own. He was carefully composed as she was, parcelled against disaster, and travelling to his final home. She knew this from his way of dressing, in old black denims just a bit too small for him, and from his way of holding his hands close against his body, wrapping them beneath his arms and hugging the sides. She knew it from his down-turned eyes which even in conversation would consult the floor. She knew it from his voice, which rose to a kind of shout of exultation as the words arrived. He would finish his sentence, look up with a brief glow of triumph, and at once fall silent as though perceiving that he had overstepped the mark. With Michael, too, laughter was rare, and occurred in a kind of explosive outrush of air, used, like the ink of the squid, to renew his defences. If the worst came to the worst – and in

England, Zoë realised, it generally did – she would live with
Michael.

VII

The cool October sun came running past her on the pavement,
moving with the speed of thought over the astonished upturned
faces of the flagstones. Argyll Street was awake, the widows
alert in every bay, and in Clevedon Avenue the morning crowds
were gathering. Although she was small, and moved quickly to
avoid the eyes of strangers, Zoë was the cause of considerable
obstruction. Grey-suited office workers, preoccupied and
hurrying, prevented themselves by last-moment efforts from
walking into her. Pullovered arms, leather jackets and tee-
shirted torsos all swished against her and staggered momen-
tarily in their mad parade. She did not look at them: not looking
at men was her main outdoor occupation. Her eyes were
directed sometimes to the dusty sun-paled sky, sometimes to the
ebb and flow of shoes surrounding her. She darted among their
supposititious pathways like a sensitive insect, scurrying on
business of its own. Only when she made it into the bus, and sat
upstairs with her duffle bag beside her, could she look around as
others did.

The map which adults draw lies across the landscape of a
child like a geometer's grid, insensitive to real distinctions, and
sundering things which are in reality finely joined. The child
lives in a world whose titles have yet to be discovered, and
things acquire their names less by fiat than by revelation: the
dip, the dump, the damsons, Willie's yard. So it was with Zoë,
who felt no obligation to those who had mapped out this world,
and styled it after monarchs, battles and heroes from which her
race had reaped no benefit. She had presumptuously re-titled
all the districts through which she daily passed. Some of her
names could be explained in mental footnotes; others remained

mysterious even to herself: Macedonia, Mickey Mouse, Happy Grass, Byzantium; Alexandria, where levantine figures gestured from strangely empty shops and offices; the Fly-pond, where a slur of muddy water lingered all summer between grey concrete blocks.

They were speeding through her favourite district, the Solitudes – *i monaxies* – where isolated people were framed in rented windows, and Edwardian houses, divided into tiny units, stood alone amid rubbish-filled gardens. The sun had finally won its battle with the clouds, and now looked down with interest on the world, pointing rudely into swaddled bedrooms, and laughing at the old woman in a lemon nightdress, who painted her face beside a window full of green and yellow chinaware. Then she saw a man in a white shirt leaning from the second floor, so fat that he seemed like bed-clothes hung out to air and swollen in the breeze. A tessellated crown of yellow brick was stitched to the wall above him, and in the shadow-haunted morning light the little scene was framed and iconised. 'O heavenly king, O comforter, the spirit of truth, who are everywhere and fill all things, the treasury of blessings and giver of life, come and abide in us.' The ritual words returned in every plenitude. She needed them far more than she had ever needed God – who in any case did not exist, as she had discovered. The words kept vigil in her soul, setting bounds to the invading chaos.

The life to which the bus was carrying her would not be easy. Nothing was easy for a Greek. When Yannakis Kostas had begun to ply his trade in London, he discovered that the sophisticated policies handled by London brokers were beyond his competence. He settled down to insuring the cars and houses of his fellow immigrants. From such a trade there was little to be earned, and after a while it was the pigeons that kept him principally occupied and from which, by skilful breeding, he could make a pound or two on the side. His son had been scarcely more successful. For although, like Zoë, Manolis thought and spoke in English, had English manners, English

ambitions and an English sense of humour, he had been
hampered by his wife's glutinous attachment, by the need to
build, in the midst of freedom, the little island prison where,
behind gauze curtains in modernist rooms, amid awkward
furniture of slabs and pillows and tubes, love is manufactured,
clinging to the legs of chairs and tables, coiling everywhere like
a malignant plant, impeding, stifling and at last destroying for
the sake of those unborn. Manolis had therefore taken a regular
job that would send him home, suit uncrumpled, face set rigid
in a smile, at five. This job, the precise nature of which Zoë
could never recall, though it had been many times explained to
her, was regarded by everyone except Manolis and his sister as a
pledge of security – though what security for self in all that
sacrifice it was hard to know. The fact is that mortgages,
children and yearly trips to Limassol had caused Manolis to
become steadily poorer, steadily more devoted to his puddingey
wife, steadily more quiet, dependent and depressed.

Only Zoë had succeeded, not by becoming rich or even
comfortable, but by finding a job, when the time came and her
mother's pathos compelled her, which left her mistress of
herself, poised on the edge of a life into which she might leap at
any moment – or not, as she chose. Zoë was a representative,
paid by commission and working her own hours. She was
retained by a sweatshop, where Cypriot girls sewed and clipped
and stitched and twined, making dresses and costumes for the
fringes of the market. The owner and manager was Mr
Tzouliadis, a Greek from the mainland, whose grey sagging
face swayed on his neck like a pumpkin on a pole, and whose
generally sepulchral appearance so disturbed the assorted cou-
turiers and fetishists who patronised the factory, that he em-
ployed Zoë to deal with them, if possible on territory into which
he had no cause to venture.

On the whole Zoë enjoyed her dealings with the customers,
and especially with her main theatrical client, a tense hollow-
eyed lesbian called Bill, who had prehensile fingers and short
boyish hair. Bill called her 'darling', 'delicious', 'petal' and

'love'; she praised Zoë's way of dressing, saying it made her look simultaneously provocative and untouchable. What had been instinct then became conscious choice and Zoë, when not impeded by the Kostaina, dressed in no other way.

It was not only Bill whom Zoë liked. For Anna, the principal seamstress, she felt a kind of protective love. Anna was from Famagusta, and, alone among the girls in the sweatshop, she was not planning marriage, being three months pregnant by a man who was married already. She mutely awaited the day of discovery, when her parents would disown her and Mr Tzouliadis, anxious for his reputation, would send her away.

Anna was tall for a girl, with blue-black hair, high cheek-bones and a long, marble-white face like a statue. Her brown almond eyes seemed mute and suffering; but if you met them, a defiant glow quickly kindled in their depths, breaking the stillness of her antique features. Some would have called Anna forbidding; but to Zoë she was beautiful, and when she moved about the shop, high-breasted, long-limbed, in full-length dresses which she made from off-cuts in a faintly pre-Raphaelite taste, she reminded Zoë of a spirit drifting through the trees in summer.

Zoë had never spoken to Anna of the things that preoccupied her – of philosophy and poetry, of England and its strange inhabitants, of the cold light of irreligion that bathes the objects of this Northern world, cancelling their inner luminosity, and laying a mask of solitude over every human face. But she was sure that Anna instinctively comprehended such matters, and that she lived, like Zoë, outside the society which had given birth to her. Anna, she believed, was pure and original. What she retained of Cyprus were only those faint echoes of pageantry and dance, that breeze-fed longing for departure which stings the eyes and braces the heart for solitude. Zoë was even a bit in love with Anna – not, of course, as Bill would be, but with a kind of aching tenderness all the same, which often, in the quiet cupboard where Anna worked alone and where Zoë came to visit her, spilled over into fingertip touches and (to their joint surprise) a brush one morning from her lips on Anna's brow.

If Zoë loved Anna it was because she would journey forever through this alien country utterly alone, utterly contained, utterly without comfort save for the words which Zoë offered her. And from Anna Zoë learned of that other love: how it comes in its fullness only once, like a flash of light showing the vastness of invisible things, which were thereafter always present, always huge and alarming and unforgettable, though shrouded in darkness. Living in that darkness, Anna could never belong elsewhere – her desires were not of this world, and her slow quiet face stared at the world's accidental glories across a vast distance of solitude. Such, at least, was Zoë's view of her.

Zoë thought of Anna as the bus sped down the hill towards the industrial area which she knew as the Jaws and which formed the last stretch of the journey before her stop. They would live together at the Solitudes, and the more Zoë thought of this plan, the more obvious and right did it seem to her. Already she had made an inventory of kitchen equipment, with unbreakable cups and a plastic chair for the baby. And a precise image had settled in her mind of their bay-windowed sitting room, large, irregular and English, with heavy Edwardian armchairs, Toulouse-Lautrec posters, an old-fashioned fireplace burning illegally on Sundays, and a view over ragged gardens towards the mist-shrouded city.

She peered from the window into each successive dwelling, adding details to her inner picture, while hopes settled in her mind. Then, looking round to make sure that no one was listening, she sang 'Onward Christian Soldiers', in Sir Arthur Sullivan's version, giving up at the line 'See, His banners go!'

VIII

The sweatshop existed in a space of its own, surrounded by betting-booths and pawnbrokers, amid slummy terraces, which protruded long gardens like junky tongues. People dressed provisionally here, in clothes that did not belong to them, and they loitered in groups, with an air of waiting for orders. Gestures seemed to hang in the air, awaiting completion; nothing was firm, nothing defined; everything festered with promiscuous impulse. Life itself seemed perverted, running like a river underground through dark, hidden passageways, and noticeable only as a brief, faint sigh, erupting from the churchyard and the corner-shops. It was in these spots that she paused for breath, listening to the tumult in far-off places, and fixing her mind on her goal.

Out of this nameless region, at a place where the street ran out into dingy alleyways, there rose an iron staircase, which hugged a wall for twenty steps, and then ended in a metal door. Behind the door was another world: a world of light and noise and industry; a world where people of her kind shouted to each other in the language of her childhood, moving as though on air in a parody of girlishness. Only Anna stood outside this life: Anna and her boss. And to get to Anna, she must pass by Mr Tzouliadis.

In the art of reducing Zoë to helpless exasperation, Mr Tzouliadis had no rivals. The very sight of his pumpkin head, with its smoothly plastered, greying hair, its vague, character-less eyes and protruding ears, reminded her that time was running out, that everything depended now on her being as soon as possible in some other place, that not a moment could be wasted; while his deep, hesitant voice, as it stumbled over pedantries like a cart-horse over stones, seemed to have been created expressly for the purpose of announcing, in a tone of pained revelation, that women differ from men, that war is an evil, that science has made many discoveries, that not all people are to be trusted, and that two plus two makes four. And yet he was a good, kind, simple man, an excellent husband and father, and a dependable colleague, who had gone out of his way to offer to the daughter of his late insurance-broker a job suited to her eccentric temperament. Indeed, the most exasperating feature of Mr Tzouliadis was his ability to induce a state of acute guilt in his victim who, trapped in unjustifiable rage, could only nod pleasantly, offering concessions, promises and favours, in the hope that they would not be taken up.

He stood by the iron door with an eager expression on his face that seemed to indicate some advance knowledge of Zoë's arrival.

'Oh,' she said, looking past him, '*kalimera.*'

His thoughts tended to dwell at this time of day on the mysteries of the universe; stepping confidingly into Zoë's path he began to discourse about the galaxies, their astonishing size, weight and remoteness.

'What a small thing is man in so much matter, Zoë. So isolated, so helpless. What is the point of his toing and froing, always working, always running, always . . .'

Zoë made an impatient gesture.

'Getting and spending,' she said in English. 'We lay waste our days.'

'What's that? A quotation?'

Mr Tzouliadis collected quotations, which he wrote down in a notebook – a process so efficient that he never referred to them again.

'No,' said Zoë, 'just something that occurred to me. I must see Anna.'

Putting out one hand to detain her, Mr Tzouliadis surveyed her with a gaze that was in all probability quite innocent, but which caused Zoë, as it roamed across her laced and buttoned person, to retreat within her clothes until a little film of air lay round her body, producing a faint tingling sensation. He began to lecture on stress – a peculiarly English disease, unknown, he argued, in the Mediterranean, where people divide the day into natural sections, giving leisure equal rights with work. Zoë let her thoughts start off in every direction, exploring the plans which she had not made. Into the Solitudes she would bring her father's dear possessions, setting them side by side in their old relations. She would have her books there and maybe, if there was a garden, one or two of the pigeons. When the baby came they could take it in turns to work; or she could buy a Singer by instalments, one with electric action, and Anna would work from home. She wished she were a man, so as to shove Mr Tzouliadis away.

He considered the question of stress from every angle, citing an article written by some expert in the *Guardian*, and another in a Greek magazine; then suddenly and without warning he mentioned Yannakis. She started and looked at him. With his lined, grubby skin, his fat lips and bulging eyes, he seemed like a blind man's model of a face – a face guessed at by exploring fingers. The nose was a hillock, pinched at the sides, but globular in front as though it had been pulled from some plastic material. The cheeks were ridged, gritty, lined by bluish channels where the uncropped stubble gathered. The ears had been stuck on at different heights, with special care to exaggerate the hairless, knobbly spaces behind them, while the bulbous eyes seemed to reach forward like antennae, feeling what the artist could not see.

'I don't know what you're talking about.'

Her words were dead and distant. Mr Tzouliadis too seemed dead, a statue through which some alien voice was sounding. Ignoring her, he began to meditate on the need to harmonise their cultures – the English, so nervous, active, rootless and full of experimentation, and the Greek, so decent, loyal, religious and wrapped in blessed indolence. He had put considerable thought into how they might be reconciled, in some single personality, whole, outgoing, harmonious. And, he submitted, it could be done, provided the personality were feminine: Zoë, for instance. Men, her father included, labour under an incurable disadvantage; their whole identity must be expressed in work, and even when a man lived among other exiles, other creatures who dreamed, in their vacant moments, of irrecoverable home, he must enter the world around him and take hold of it or, failing that, must die. Contracts, duties, profits, the frenzied race against the other who will get there first in any case

– all this compelled you into the flux of competition, forcing you
to be an Englishman, though you could never be better than a
second-class Englishman.

'I might have stayed in Greece. I could have been a shepherd,
for instance. Even a monk.'

She heard herself laugh; cold and spectral. Locked again in
his death, she must suffocate in used-up air. A panic seized her:
there in the dark his form lay still and decomposing. The walls
pressed close against her, and she gasped from empty lungs.

'What's the matter?'

Mr Tzouliadis's voice rang out in alarm. But she was past
him, leaning on the bales of printed cloth outside his office.

'I must see Anna.'

'You are all tensed up, like an English girl.'

'Maybe. Maybe that's the trouble.'

She looked at his spongy form, and felt a rush of distaste. For
a long moment Zoë observed Mr Tzouliadis, whose eyes she
had always avoided. This man had known Yannakis, and was
still alive. She could make nothing of the fact, and turned
suddenly away from it. The sigh with which she left was all her
thought: a cloud of darkness from a vast abyss. She paused in the
doorway; the alphabet of blackness swam into words, drifted
unreadably and decomposed again. Bad dreams, calling to her
with a voice that would never be answered.

IX

They were playing the radio, and the air vibrated to a bass
guitar, above which yells of sexual ecstasy danced like flames.
The sound came from the nearest trestle, where a roll of cloth,
printed with a design of flying doves rocked through the air into
jaws that hemmed and panelled it. It was warm in the sweatshop, with a faintly acrid smell. Strip-lights glowed like wands
beneath the girders, and brightly coloured off-cuts patched the

floor. Zoë hesitated for a moment; then suddenly her feet were light with purpose, and her small brown hand reached outwards with the swiftness of a bird. It had no doubts, this hand, that it was Zoë's: and the silence as the radio ceased its screaming was filled with Zoë's will.

The girls looked up. Zoë was a Greek, and had no excuse to be so weird and arrogant. They took it in turns to brave her short-fused temper, to batter down her pride, and then (since they were not vindictive and lived as a herd) to include her in their small hilarities. Today it was the fat Melissa who waddled over to the radio. A pool of pink lipstick lived in the centre of her face, flowing freely in its search for pantomime smiles.

'Zoë mou,' she said, and wagged an admonitory finger. Clumps of red hair sprouted on the backs of Melissa's hands, which were like the hands of a man. Bright-eyed Aliki blew a sarcastic kiss from pretty lips, while the Karavakou twins – who continued to coax their flock of doves into metal jaws – looked up with their bold mice faces and said 'her again!' in unison.

Melissa asked, 'Why are you so angry, Zoë?'

And in truth she was angry, but for what she did not know. Or rather she knew a little: she knew that Mr Tzouliadis had affronted her; she knew that this music, which divided the soul like a metal blade, had exposed a seam of pain; she knew that the danger of her life, to which she could give no precise name, but which often rose up to surround her in these busy corners of normality, had somehow made itself felt. But it didn't add up; the true object of her anger remained out of reach and indefinable.

'You get brain damage from that stuff,' she said at last apologetically.

'Only if you've got a brain.'

The speaker was Lisa, an ugly girl, boss-eyed from lace-work, at which she was particularly skilled, and with a tongue sharp as a needle. Picking up a tousled skein of orange cloth from Lisa's table, Zoë blew her nose in it, just to make clear that habits which were Cavafy's were good enough for her.

'Filthy bitch,' said Lisa.

Zoë stuffed the cloth into her trouser pocket.

'*I* get brain damage from it,' she said. 'I've got to preserve my brain. I need it for survival.'

Melissa agreed about Zoë's brain and said how sorry she was. On the other hand, the problem was not incurable. With a man between her legs a girl forgets about the top part of her anatomy. Zoë should try it.

Zoë hoped she would not blush, but the blood rushed to her face regardless, like a wild thing released from its cage. Soon the girls were laughing so much that Mr Tzouliadis came and stood in the doorway, staring beadily in both directions like a stuffed octoroon Turkey.

'Go away!' shouted Zoë, stamping her foot. With a baffled look he staggered backwards through the partition.

'Look at you,' said Lisa, when her boss had gone. 'You've gone jealous all over your body!'

And she hunched her little shoulders in a giggle.

Melissa stepped forward to squeeze Zoë's elbow. Her body exuded a soft vanilla smell.

'It takes all sorts,' she said. 'You like Mozart. We like the Rolling Stones. You've got a brain, Lisa's got a tongue, Aliki's got a face. And I've got a bum like a stuffed hippopotamus.'

Zoë raised her eyes from the floor. Rolls of cloth were stacked against the windows, whose small leaded panes, smeared with dust, trembled sightly from the hum of mass-production. Through the glass she glimpsed a row of yellow chimney pots, wedged in the white sky like teeth in custard.

'So there you are darling. Just calm down.'

'I *am* calm,' said Zoë.

'Who are you kidding? Sit and listen to the music. Have some coffee. We've got some *loukoumia*, with dates and almonds. Aliki's granny sent it.'

Zoë's eyes sought the next partition, beyond which Anna waited. She rehearsed again the image of their future dwelling-place, with its great bay window, its kitchen, and the view

across the garden down to the city. With a flick of the arm she
escaped from Melissa's fingers.

'You know I don't eat that Greek stuff. Turkish to be
precise.'

'Suit yourself. Cut off your nose, darling, if it feels better
that way.'

Melissa might have elaborated on the darker side of Zoë's
nature – a favourite topic, and one in which all the girls could
join – had not Lisa chosen the moment to propound something
entirely unexpected. Laying her hands on the table, and poking
her crumpled face over the backbone of the sewing machine,
she said, in the tone of one betraying a secret,

'Zoë's going to live with an Englishman.'

At this piece of hilarious news, the twins chorused 'an
Englishman', and Aliki clapped her hands. Zoë turned on Lisa.

'Who told you that?'

'A little bird,' said Lisa, through a mouthful of giggles.

'An old crow, you mean.'

'Is that a way to speak of your mother?'

'Whom did she speak to?'

'Everyone,' said Lisa. 'Me and Melissa and the boss,
and . . .'

'*Mr Tzouliadis?*'

'Of course. He needs to know. Reputation of the firm;
influence on workmates; distress of clients. He will have to cut
your salary.'

Zoë's blushes were insubstantial flowers; but the growth
which they adorned was rooted deep in her body. Through
shame the community reclaimed her, its ever-vigilant eye
turned suddenly in her direction. So it was for all the girls,
whose knees trembled, whose hands shot involuntarily upwards
to shield their faces, whose voices were damp and half-ex-
tinguished with the force of this great emotion, as it swung them
from their small ambitions and pledged them to the tribe. It was
not the act which gave rise to shame, but the thought of someone
knowing it. For Zoë, therefore, shame was the highest

form of enslavement, a negation of her bid for life. She ran down the aisle between the trestles, swinging her duffle bag high in the air over the periscoped heads of her tormentors. She caught her thigh against a metal ruler, and seeing the v-shaped tear in her trousers, and the arrow of olive flesh beneath it, she began to cry.

'No harm meant,' said Melissa, with a faint suggestion of concern.

The door of the partition resisted her.

'Anna? Are you there?'

The sun shone on the dirty workshop windows, a watery yellow which alighted on a slice of wall and trembled there like a visiting insect.

'I don't care,' Zoë said, to no one in particular.

X

A key turned in the lock, and the door moved inwards haltingly. Zoë stepped through the musty cupboard. Anna's back was turned in taut refusal, as she swept her long green skirt across the floor and swirled into the bucket chair behind the sewing machine. Her fingers settled at last unpeacefully on a sheet of pale blue cotton.

'Something's wrong,' said Zoë.

'Yes. You have been crying. And your trousers are torn.'

Zoë sat on the edge of the bench and, taking a needle from the pin-cushion which stood beside the sewing machine, began to probe the rent in her armour.

'I was being silly. That awful music – like a spray of acid. I meant something's wrong with you.'

'Nothing's wrong with *me*.'

The long lashes came down firmly over Anna's pale brown eyes.

'My mother rang, and of course she has been telling you dreadful things.'

Anna's fingers bunched the pale blue cloth into little hillocks. Then suddenly she lifted it to her face, gripped a loose thread with her teeth and worried it. Her face was locked in the present moment, like the face of an animal; the pieces that lay beneath it on bench and floor were like the remains of victims, scattered about her lair. The off-cuts were of pink, blue, lamé and lichen green; Zoë recognised the designs for *Perverts' Panto* which Bill needed for November. She felt the distance between Bill's world and Anna's world, and a rush of warm protective feeling for the Cypriot girl ran through her body and into her finger tips. She reached out to touch the hair, which was the hair of an animal, without meaning to its owner, but to Zoë full of light. How good it would be to look after her. Anna had said her father was a surgeon and her mother a nurse, but Zoë knew that Anna's parents were disreputable, the one a drunkard, the other (who met the Kostaina in St Nikodemos's church, where they stood side by side in the choir) a kitchen maid in a Greek taverna. Zoë would take Anna into realms she had never dreamed of – realms of light and exploration; she would show her England.

Anna looked up with a fierce expression and drew her head away.

'You told your mother about me.'

Zoë let her hand fall. It was true. In the course of their squabbling, and because it had been necessary to prove a point, she had mentioned Anna's case. What had she not said and invented in those dreadful battles?

'It was stupid of me,' she said. 'I lost control. But I made her promise never to tell.'

'She's no better at keeping a promise than you are. In fact, she has told my mother.'

'When?'

'This morning.'

'I think I understand,' said Zoë. 'She wanted to find

another of our crowd whose daughter has disgraced her.'

Anne turned back to her work, and shrugged her thin shoulders. There was something hard and defensive in her manner that Zoë did not like. She did not believe Anna's friendship could be ended by so small a mistake.

'Forgive me Anna. Please. Listen, I am going to rent a couple of rooms, and you can have one of them. I'll look after you . . .'

'You? I thought you were going to live with an Englishman?'

Zoë raised her hands to her face.

'Oh God! I said that only to annoy the Kostaina.'

'Well, you certainly succeeded. She's not having *you* back in the house.'

Anna gave a small triumphant smile.

'Good,' said Zoë; but a chill ran through her, to know that sentence had been publicly passed.

'What do you think of my idea, of renting somewhere?'

'In some house where no one speaks Greek, and curious men come knocking at all hours of the day?'

'But I shall be there.'

'Of course you'll be there, filling the place with intellectual music, unreadable books, arty posters, and those weird friends of yours – like that filthy lesbian, who can't see a piece of cloth without thinking how it would turn out as knickers. If only she'd keep her fingers out of my hair, at least. No thanks!'

Zoë sat for a moment with downcast eyes.

'I thought we were friends,' she said at last. 'I thought you wanted my help.'

'I did. But that time is over. Now it's you who want *my* help.'

Zoë looked curiously at Anna who, for some stubborn cause that Zoë could not fathom, was discarding her only chance. She began to describe how it would be at the Solitudes, where they could live as they liked. She would teach Anna English, introduce her to English people – Michael, for instance; she would take her to the theatre, and to the museums and galleries on Saturdays. And she would buy a Singer, on the never-never, so that Anna could work from home. Zoë would cook: calamari and octopus, which you could buy for next to nothing in places where the kipper-eating natives lived.

Zoë told the story with a child's belief in it. She remembered their mornings, when she and Manolis would climb into the big bed with its lace-fringed counterpane, he on his mother's side, she on her father's. And clinging to their slumbering parents, they would peep across at each other, choking back their giggles, rising and ducking like buoys on the waves that dappled the morning sea and cast their gay reflections on the ceiling. And on that ceiling they would paint in words their paradisal landscape – fruit-filled gardens, houses brimming with children, animals running, leaping and tumbling, fairies, dragons, saints and witches, and in the midst of this Yannakis and his bride, enthroned within the temple of their marriage, the beginning and end of all the Kostas possibilities. As they threw drunken words like coloured ribbons across their bothered parents, a feeling of safety stole over them. And the wilder their fancies, the more deeply protected did they feel, as though the real world too obeyed them. Zoë recalled that sensation, as she rounded off her narrative with the idea that Anna might not have to work at all, that she, Zoë, would get another job, give up those stupid classes from which she didn't learn much anyway, and work enough for two.

Anna's beauty was the beauty of dreams, the beauty of Aretousa in the tale of Erotokritos. On her breast she wore a lizard brooch of moonstone set in silver: her lover's only gift besides the baby. And it reminded Zoë of those long hours in the garden, teasing pale grey lizards on the grey-stone walls. They slithered nervously from stone to stone, froze into lichens, and disappeared at last like water down some dark crevasse. Yannakis told her to respect them, for they cleared the air of insects, and also, he said – though she never quite believed him – carried messages to the dead, who picknicked in darkness below the garden, patiently waiting for the words to come.

Anna's silence, her solitary ways, the soft light that flaked along her cheek-bones, the magic of her pregnancy – all these spontaneously confirmed in Zoë's mind the girl's release from calculation. Zoë expected her to melt at last, and to raise those big veiled eyes in a look of gratitude, as a wave of resignation passed below the grey-green muslin robes like the rustle of a creature that finally overcomes its shyness and slides from its hiding place. To her astonishment, however, Anna sat coldly through the narrative, and then, with another shrug, reached out again for her work.

Anna pushed the blue cotton into the jaws of the sewing machine, and set the needle going. The bonnet of hair fell across her face, and the delicate thin shoulders, hunched against the world, were those of a distrustful child. When she looked up at last, it was with a hard, self-centred glance, so that Zoë stepped back a pace from the bench on which her hand had been resting.

Anna said, 'You go round looking for perfection, when nothing even half bit good is allowed to happen in this world. It's so exhausting!'

'Everything is allowed to happen,' said Zoë urgently. 'Don't you see?'

'No, I don't see. You think I am allowed to live with someone half-crazy, and bring up a baby in a rooming house full of drunks and drop-outs and Englishmen? And if such things are allowed, they oughtn't to be.'

'What will you do, then?'

'I'm sorry, Zoë. I didn't mean it. Only – I've just had enough.'

'Enough of what?'

'Enough of unrealities.'

'I see,' said Zoë, who didn't. How dingy and close had Anna's cell become: all dust and dreariness and the sickly smell of repetition. Nothing of world entered here, save only a few thin rays from the partitioned window, which honed a blade of light against the whitewashed wall, competing faintly with the neon brightness. All of a sudden her image of Anna slipped away, and nothing stood between the girls save fear, and the calculation born of fear, ruthless as war.

'Tell me your plans.'

'Well,' said Anna, with a sly smile. 'I'm not going to live with an Englishman. In fact, I shall live with your mother.'

'The Kostaina? Impossible!'

'Not impossible at all. It's natural for two disgraced women to live together.'

'But this is ridiculous! You'll go mad!'

'I am mad. So's she. It's the perfect solution. We'll close ranks together – her and me. So she said. She was really kind. Also she said you're a whore, and that you corrupted me.'

'Panayia!'

The blood rushed to Zoë's face, and she put out a hand to steady herself. How quickly the Kostaina had acted, to impose her full measure of shame. Zoë envisaged Anna, occupying her room with the immovable selfishness of a breeding beast. The Kostaina would take the moral credit that was to have been Zoë's, and fill the house with a routine of sacrifice. She recognised a terrible truth. Her intention in leaving home had been provisional; she had counted on the possibility of return, and all her courage, in setting forth that morning, had been the mere bravado of a prodigal child. She must leave her father's possessions, his clothes and antiquities, his books and his birds, in the hands of other women, women who refused to be free. She sat down on the empty bench behind her.

'You can't do it!' she cried. 'You can't live there.'

'I don't see why not. *You* lived there.'

'I had to. You don't understand.'

'Don't worry Zoë. I won't touch your things. I'll just curl up in a corner and give birth.'

Anna gave an embittered smile, and looked away.

XI

As she tripped through the sweatshop Zoë thought of Anna's smile. It was a thin line drawn across her world, like a crossing-out of cancelled words, making them legible for the first time. The girls were talking of sex – and yet they were virgins, dancing on this vast desire like the flies which hug the crest of moving waters and are never wet. Gay peals of laughter mingled with the radio. When Zoë came into view the laughter did not cease but turned in her direction, became languid and expectant, gently annulling her movement, until she looked up timidly with a shamed paltry smile.

'Sorry for my temper.'

Melissa left her trestle and gave Zoë a masculine hug.

'We never believed it. Zoë make it with an Englishman! You'd have to switch the sun off first!'

'She will,' said Lisa. 'She'll find some wet artistic type in jeans and fall flat on top of him – mop him up like a sponge.'

'She will, she will!' chorused the Karavakou twins, and Melissa hit them with a roll of cloth. Laughter splashed about like threads of a cataract. Zoë thought of Michael, and said,

'Lisa's right. That's what I'll do.'

As she walked with regal posture through the door, she felt sick inside and trembling. Mr Tzouliadis was waiting for her, with an expression of theatrical amazement.

'Get away,' she said. 'I'm going.'

He nodded sagely; Zoë paused on the iron stairway, holding the outside door ajar, and looking down into the street. A man in red trousers was pacing back and forth, as though impatiently waiting for someone. The chill smell of masonry was suddenly extinguished, as she raised her hands to her face and breathed the iron scent of railings. She looked back at Mr Tzouliadis.

'You had better find another representative. I'm quitting.'

Again he nodded.

'You owe me some money. I'll come back to collect it.'

Something pitying in his expression caused Zoë to run down into the street.

XII

Bridges, some steel, some brick, some stone with balustrades and raised abutments, connected the towpaths over the canal. Along one side the crumbling warehouses stretched their rusting cranes above the water; lights shone here and there in the austere windows, where the newer, smaller industries had taken root in the dereliction. Between them were non-conformist churches, empty now and boarded, with schematic facades of gothic sandstone. A row of terraced houses stood propped against each other, bewildered and unvisited like childless old people who wait for death. Rubble-filled wastelands divided the buildings, their marshy clumps of brown willow-herb resting the eyes from the igneous glitter of cast-off metal and broken glass.

The canal, after rainless weeks, was low, black and rimed with duckweed. The few trees on the towpath were parched, their papery leaves brown and wrinkled. Zoë looked up at the Edwardian clocktower of the town hall, with its classical clockface framed by pilasters, and a voluted copper dome, smeared with verdigris, sitting like a helmet on its top. The Peacock described it as a phallic symbol, and would point to it from the lecture room at Bewley whenever he needed, as he frequently needed, to refer to sex. To Zoë it symbolised a society that had once believed in itself and in its right to rule over people like Yannakis. It stood there, a memory of England amid the ruin of England, signalling its hopeful message of reprieve. We do not go unnoticed into the dark, it declared, and our lives are righteous and full of dignity. And beneath was the milling crowd of satirists and drop-outs, the Peacocks who scoffed and the Michaels who kept silent counsel. To neither did its message make sense.

A shabby middle-aged man passed the bench where she sat, a raggle-taggle dog stringing along at his heels. The man wore an old black jacket from a uniform too small for him, which he had tied with string across his paunch. On his head was a toy policeman's helmet, held by an elastic chin-strap. He limped on stout legs towards the water, looked down at it, and shook his head reprovingly – man, so social in his loneliness, so keenly aware, as he drifts into the endless space of solitude, of uniforms and offices and rules.

She thought again of Michael, who had gone open-eyed into loneliness, leaving every deity behind. All other men alarmed her, especially the Peacock, with his ironical manner and his air of knowing her desires. Yet the Peacock could tell her where Michael lived, and in a peculiar way she needed him. Queer though it was, she needed the unprincipled permission that he extended to the world, and which included even her. Especially did she need him now – hearing in her mind the gates clang shut behind her and knowing that the piety and prudence of home, which even in their fiercest quarrels had surrounded them, were locked away for ever. Someone must tell her that she *could* do what Lisa so horridly said that she would do. She sat by the stagnant water, studying the shadows that fell on it from figures that she dared not see. And her thoughts took the form of so many crimes, from which only the Peacock could absolve her. Thinking of him, she shuddered and closed her eyes.

Dr Leacock worked in many fields – sociology, philosophy, literary theory, politics – and advanced the same idea through all of them. Modern Man, he argued, was trapped and denatured by the discourse of power. To every question Dr Leacock brought the incandescent light of disobedience, seeking authority everywhere, so as to declare his rebellion against it. In the course of time, therefore, Bewley College, which existed more to massage the attitudes than to improve the learning of its students, and which had long thought of itself as part of Her Majesty's permanent opposition, had entrusted the thirty-year-old Peter Leacock with its most popular evening courses, in social philosophy, literature, political theory and the performing arts. To these courses came people like Zoë, people who had lost their way, and had caught – in a novel perhaps, a political movement, a love affair, or a spurt of oriental religion – some distant glimpse of a certainty of which they felt themselves deprived.

Dr Leacock made no distinction among those who might be prompted to admire him, and was therefore a man of egalitarian convictions. He treated every student as a victim, and offered to each the path of liberation that passed through himself. He would bless them with a look of intense personal concern, coaxing the dreary narrative of their disappointments, searching their features with his eager forget-me-not-eyes, and uttering soft words of encouragement. Then, at a certain point, he would switch on his megawatt smile, throw back the hair from his handsome forehead, and lean forward across his desk. His voice would resume its special quality of seductive vigour, as he explained the student's misfortunes in terms of the conspiracy of power which ruled over England. And as he unfolded the tale of general misery, touching on matters as far afield as the laws of association and the style of Kingsley Amis, his patients would experience a warm feeling of relief. Their sufferings expanded under his gaze to fill the whole tragic space allotted them. Listening they thrilled to the vision of struggle, and were joined with all the other victims in a sacred communion of revolt. The men were inspired to admiration, and the women frequently to love.

With Zoë the technique had not worked. Visibly moved by her looks – and Zoë appeared in Bewley like a golden pheasant in a chicken run – impressed too by her air of propriety, he muffed his lines. She had never gone further by way of confession than to express her dissatisfaction with the Orthodox Church, a form of bondage which – not belonging to the 'system' of England – he was not in the habit of condemning. In fact the Peacock favoured everything alien, everything offensive to the way of life surrounding him, and therefore quickly passed over Zoë's grievance, in search of some more seething cause. She offered none, and it was quickly settled between them that his advances were unavailing. Thereafter Zoë assumed the habit of calling on the Peacock, wary always of his eyes and hands, yet pleased to be treated as an equal – or as near an equal as his nature recognised. His failure to tame her caused him to be especially brilliant in her presence. He would look at her from his bright blue eyes, the hair falling in blond ridges over his head like a regiment of napkins, and he would blaze out his peculiar smile, parading his thoughts through the room as though she herself had summoned them. In his office she ceased to be a student and became instead a partner in the most elaborate intellectual game. No one else besides Yannakis had credited her with a mind, and she could listen to the Peacock's scintillating banter, as he debunked one by one the myths and meanings of the world around them, with a sense of wandering outside the cage of her life, into forbidden areas where no Kostas had ever been before.

At the same time there was something unreal in the experience, as though she wandered also outside her body. The walls of his office were pasted with ladies: ladies by Vermeer and Rembrandt, ladies by Gainsborough, Boucher and Ingres, ladies by Bonnard and Dégas, and ladies from the centre page of *Playboy*. Sometimes, sitting there, overlooked by so much greedy incarnation, she would feel like a spirit, returned to the curious changed world of living things. A queer mournful light then played around her, a light of disbelief, such as shines in tragedy. It was as though she stood on some bleak promontory of feeling, utterly alone, before a sea of turmoil. Sometimes, when the feeling came over her, he would laughingly snap his fingers before her face, saying 'Wake up Zoë!' and doing the little dance of self-congratulation which was his habit. She would indeed wake up, and long to be elsewhere, away from the contamination of his presence. And yet the next day she would return, not knowing what compelled her, and unable to look him in the face.

Once, in the pub, the Peacock had taken Zoë's hand, catching it suddenly in mid-air, as though trapping a bird. His grip was soft but strong, and she fluttered helplessly inside it. Eventually she withdrew her life from the captured extremity, and existed for the five minutes of her imprisonment without a hand. She neither looked at the Peacock nor spoke to him, until he had relinquished her fingers.

'OK,' he said, 'you win. I'll buy a round to celebrate.'

And all the students drank at his expense. How gross and sycophantic they looked, as they downed their pints of beer, their lips moustachioed with froth like disfigured posters. All except Michael, who refused the Peacock's offer, and stared at the floor. Yet she had not blushed. For even on this occasion there had been something that did not displease her in the Peacock's attentions: a sense of his bafflement, perhaps, and something else – a feeling of power, of being above and beyond this world which ached so much to include her.

Sometimes, emerging from the Peacock's office, after one of those impromptu sermons which passed for tutorials, Zoë thought that deep down she was a conservative – not sexually only, but morally, socially, even politically. Of course, she would not admit to such a failing in Bewley, where it would lead to immediate ostracism. Nevertheless, while she enjoyed the Peacock's wit and erudition; while she agreed with his vision of England, as built upon the alienation of the many and the power of the few, she had no faith in alternatives. The task is to find one's place in the world that is, and then to live in freedom: so she had been taught by Yannakis, and so she would always believe. The force which animated the Peacock, as he shook the pillars of society and fulminated against the ways of power – this constant sparking of negative energy – was the exhilaration of the short circuit, which casts a deceptive light, but which gives power to nothing, and vanishes, leaving a whiff of sulphur.

The Peacock was not only the absolver of crimes; he was also their cause and object. Once his image had settled in her mind, it began to seem as though there were no step she could take from this place that would not be the first of many errors. How careful he was, when Zoë said or did something in his presence, to operate on it until, by some chance working of her panic, she would throw up the word or gesture he was seeking and show herself to be, like him, an animal. She would be mad to see him.

A small dumpy man in black was watching her, looking as though he had been carved from a fat black radish. A surging blue mass of verminous pigeons had gathered around her, clawing one another, outlining Zoë's legs as though to conjure into the space they occupied some more beneficent existence. She looked down at them with loathing, recalling the runculations of the dovecote, and feeling disbelief that a single species could produce Evyenia and these. The cold beads of their eyes reflected nothing – no love or interest had found itself in them, no dream had shone back from their depths. Zoë kicked them aside, saw the black radish wince in disapproval, and then glanced at the sky. A rook paddled past, and the last swallows, which had been skimming low on the ground with beaks twittering after the fainting insects, rose in the air, staggered, and settled softly on the wires above the towpath. A breeze struck up and then died again. The sun moved on, and the shadow of a warehouse touched her face: time to go. She jumped to her feet, untied her scarf, bunched her hair, and tied it again. Lifting the duffle bag she went with rapid steps to the lane which led to Bewley College. As she turned behind the houses, she looked back at the staring radish, and quickly put out her tongue.

XIII

Bewley's day-time culture was androgynous. The boys wore long dyed hair, lipstick and ear-rings; the girls jeans and denim jackets, their hair cropped to combat length, their unsmiling faces tense with military resolve. They provisioned themselves from the Paki shops in Spicetown, as Zoë called the nexus of streets north of the college building; you would find them leaning against the glazed walls at every hour of the day, pushing parathas into their mouths with saffron-coloured fingers. They did not speak, for they belonged to a new race which had dispensed with words, and which gleaned its sparse information from images alone. In the evenings they listened to music so loud that words could not compete with it, and if they moved occasionally under the rhythm's impulse, it was only so as to emphasise the solitude which surrounded them, like a negative electric field. Only on Demo Days did they exercise their lungs, gathering spontaneously into surprisingly ordered lines, and goose-stepping up and down to the promptings of a bearded officer with a megaphone, who would direct their shouting against the target of the day.

It was the first week of term, and the day's demo had been large and well attended, scattering its hate-filled leaflets through all the surrounding streets. She heard the distant shouting – 'Out! Out! Out!' – as the cohorts wound their slow way towards the place of battle. And on the steps of the college, looking after them with an air of ironical approval, stood the Peacock, his buttocks neatly cupped in jeans and wearing a scant summer tee-shirt which showed his chest – hard, lustrous and curved like a shield – to all who cared to notice it.

'Zoë!' he cried, and his face shone down at her.

'Can I see you for a moment?'

He observed her with that ecumenical calm, that imperturbable acceptance of every cranky emotion – even of decency and shame – which comes from believing nothing.

'Of course you can. That's why I'm here.'

She hurried past him into the corridor. This was a mistake; but she needed the sanctuary of his office, the contours of which no longer threatened her.

'I guess you're in trouble,' the Peacock said, as he closed the door. He gestured, as he always did, to the long couch spread with durries and carpet cushions. And she sat, as she always did, on the hard chaste chair against the wall.

'Do I look like someone in trouble?'

She fixed herself in her accustomed posture, dropped the duffle bag on the floor beside her, and placed one hand on the half-mended tear in her trousers. She stared at the objects on the Peacock's desk – an exercise which had a calming effect, since it translated him from the realm of necessity into the fast-flowing tide of accident. Books, papers, string and letters; trays, knives, scissors and elastic bands; cigarette packets, paperweights, lumps of ethnic wood and arty fibreglass; suggestive postcards, soiled handkerchiefs and a coronation mug; tapes, films, paper-clips, and a broken-heeled woman's shoe in red morocco – all fought for space, clinging, struggling, clambering each over each as though magnetised by the desktop. Whenever he sat down the Peacock cleared with a sweep of his strong hand a new space before him; the objects arched and bristled into their new positions, clinging with the same angry tenaciousness as to the positions they had lost. Strangely nothing ever fell from the desk, which was always acquiring things, never losing them. When the ritual hand-sweep was over, Zoë allowed herself to glance at the Peacock's face, which was smiling volubly. Quickly she turned away.

Through the window she could see the courtyard of Bewley College, where a tall plane-tree grew, its dry leaves tinged with yellow. At the far end a row of Victorian houses extended their backs towards her, and here and there a line of washing waved in the breeze. The Peacock took a cigarette and an old tin lighter from the desk before him. As he bent his head, Zoë turned from the window, and she felt a strange sensation at the sight of his sinewy neck. He lit the cigarette with a vast orange flame, and shot a smoke-veiled look at her. A faint smell of paraffin filled the office.

'Of course,' he said, 'you always do.'

'So then, there's nothing special today.'

She sat in the glare of his covetous glance, impregnable as stone, and his eyes, after briefly trying their rights over every inch of her body, drifted lazily away.

'Well, baby, you haven't come here to talk about the weather.'

'No,' she said truthfully, 'I like coming here. Except when you call me baby.'

'Good. That you like coming, I mean.'

The Peacock took the cigarette from his mouth and leaned back in his chair.

'You're beautiful, Zoë. Did you know that? The most beautiful woman I know.'

'So you tell me. But it's not the greatest of my disadvantages.'

He laughed, a long happy horsey sound.

'Well, Zoë, I have a disinterested scientific curiosity in the disadvantaged. That's why I work in this place. So why don't you tell me about your other problems.'

'What, *all* of them?'

'All that you wish. Except that damned Orthodox Church, which bores me rigid.'

'It bores me rigid too.'

'So then, what's up? Except that you've forgotten how to breathe?'

Zoë took a deep breath, and smiled wanly.

'You see, it's crazy, but I want your help.'

'Why's that crazy?'

'Because I can't give anything in return.'

'My God, Zoë, you are about as encouraging as the Ten Commandments.'

'That suits me fine.'

'OK, you don't need to tell me I repel you. I guess you think of me as an animal. An ape, perhaps, or an ox; a pig even.'

'I'm no zoologist.'

He laughed again, and stubbed out the cigarette, which lay in the ashtray like a broken column.

'And you look at me from Byzantine eyes, fresh but faraway, like a miraculous icon, which moves when you pray to it. All buttoned up and jerky and full of zigzags like an old mosaic.'

'Thanks.'

'Aren't you flattered?'

'Not much. Anyway, that's all irrelevant.'

The Peacock nodded sagely, and then clapped his hands together behind his head, which he rested on them as he rocked back and forth.

'OK, you win. Back to business. So you've run away from home.'

'How did you know?'

'I wasn't born yesterday. Tell me about it.'

'There's nothing to tell. I just thought, maybe you could give me the addresses of some of the students – Enid, for instance, or Jimmy. One of them might have a room.'

'If that's all it is, you've got the solution right here. There's a spare room in my place. I intended it for the kid, but his bitch of a mother won't allow him to visit.'

He spoke in cheerful tones, as though summarising the life of someone he had never met.

'I couldn't,' she replied in alarm.

'Of course you couldn't,' he pursued; 'ridiculous idea, but try anything once. So let's consider the students. By the way Zoë, do you believe in God? No, you don't.'

'I believe in – in the transcendental.'

And a vision came to her of something large, white and unpolluted: something infinitely beyond the shabby world of fact. Even as she pondered the image, however, it fluttered and folded, adopted human form, and fell like a winding sheet through interstellar spaces. She started up in surprise.

'A poor second best,' said the Peacock, whose head was buried in a drawer. 'Too far away to be reached and not sufficiently like us to take an interest. Sometimes I believe in God, formed in man's image, only awfully old and worn out, lacking the will to take charge of things, now that we've buggered them up. In the end,' he said, surfacing with a file, 'God is the self. So let's consider the students, since that's all we've got. Enid for instance.'

Enid was an exceedingly thin girl, probably anorexic, with mousey hair and sharp angular features, who drifted quietly in and out of the class with a look of startled apprehension, as though she were not quite certain that she was real. Her skin was the colour of stewed onions, and her greenish clothes — always too big for her, and perhaps handed out as a kit by some organisation that had temporary charge over her life — seemed like a form of camouflage. When she spoke, which was rarely, it was in a squeaky voice, full of halts and hesitations, as though some hidden accomplice pinched and prompted her. Taking a sheet of paper from his file, the Peacock recited the basic facts of Enid Winterstone, born August 1947, educated Haringey High School, occupation artist, also part-time sales assistant.

'Enid,' he said, 'goes faintly after life, like a cage in search of a bird.'

He mimicked her tone of voice, her mispronunciations ('pair too' and 'freedge' for Pareto and Frege), her frightened glances, the murine scrapings of a creature which startles at the scent of human flesh. According to the Peacock, Enid nibbled green leaves and biscuits in a rented kitchen, and dreamed of carcasses and the drip of blood. A tyrannical mother visited, large, angry and respectable, and against this mother there was only one defence — the boyfriend, whom Enid had pieced together from tough American novels, soap operas and glum modernist plays, before discovering him in the local health-food restaurant, brooding over a tofu sandwich. Henry did something bohemian and distinguished, like proof-reading or cartoon graphics. He was large, with a winter coat of rabbit-skin worn to the hide. He had the special smell — cornflakes, tobacco, motor oil, with an after-scent of armpits — which women of a certain kind take for the smell of wisdom. His slow unfocused eyes created in Enid the impression of a man who looks through every fact to its hidden core of meaning, and, since he responded to her rare bursts of discourse with judicious silences, she had decided that he alone, of all the many who would otherwise have courted her, could see into the depths of her soul. Magnificent though he was, however, Henry had one serious defect – which was that, after an initial show of interest, he visited only rarely, was inexplicably absent from his telephone during the evenings, and unobtainable during the day. Confined to her kitchen, Enid expressed her grief in art, returning in the afternoons from the shop to stand before a square of varnished hardboard, which she slopped and dolloped and pollocked with raw acrylic colours until the inner turmoil had subsided, and the new creation could be imprisoned in its frame of steel. Then, dry and doomed, Enid would ferret around the kitchen, obedient to her small routines, putting on and off her woolly clothes, and meditating on death. Sometimes, in her solitude, she imagined the high towers and pinnacles of the city, beneath which she scraped among sewers and wires; then she would venture out, to the arts centre, to the health-food restaurant, to Bewley College, in the hope of meeting Henry or another like him, only to discover that no orders had been given for her rescue, and that she was better off at home. Day after day the nightmare continued, to be out-kafkaed now and then by some special gesture of fruitless defiance, such as the fifty-page letter to her mother, who had spirited Henry away.

The proprieties of Bewley College were inscrutable. For all Zoë knew, tutors were advised by the high command to dissect the students for each others' instruction; maybe this was an essential part of the Bewley therapy. She had discovered too that the English were in the habit of story-telling, setting their acquaintances in impromptu novels, and maintaining the peculiar distance which comes from being not quite convinced that the other person is real. Mr Tzouliadis, who had been the cause in Zoë of so much innocent torment, had never aroused contempt – he was part of her, just as Anna was and Melissa and the Kostaina, and their battles and exasperations took place against a background of tenderness, of tribal immersion, which no Englishman could ever understand. Henceforth, the Peacock was reminding her, such battles would be comfortless and real.

Prickling with embarrassment, Zoë sat without a murmur through the Peacock's narrative, which was in any case embellished with frequent marginalia of a well-meaning kind, as though he wished also to give vent to a frustrated charitable concern. If he described Enid, he implied, it was not because there was anything special about her case – on the contrary, any of the students would have offered the same moral opportunity. His purpose was to draw a picture of Zoë's future solitude, and to offer himself as the cure. All this went rapidly through Zoë's mind as she listened, thinking the Peacock to be quite the most disagreeable and most brilliant person she had ever met.

'Oh yes,' he was saying, 'she made at last the definitive modern gesture, turned to her mother and said excuse me, but I reject your definition of me. And now she floats like a drowned baby down the tide of herself. Look,' he added cheerfully, and pointed through the window.

In one of the distant backyards a woman in a yellow shift was gesticulating, her lips apart in what may have been a scream – though no sound reached across the courtyard and the face hung open like the jaws of a dummy. A man in shirt and braces suddenly bowled his body from the back door of the house; a hand shot out from it, slapping the woman's mouth. The two fought each other to the ground, disappeared, and then rose again, clutching urgently and running indoors as though impatient to be alone.

'Strange things happen everywhere,' said the Peacock in a relaxed voice, 'things you couldn't necessarily deal with; things you would have to try not to see.'

'I can manage,' she said.

'Oh yes, better than Enid, certainly.'

Zoë caught her breath indignantly.

'Dr Leacock, I don't think . . .'

'Peter.'

'I don't think you have the right to make fun of Enid.'

He roared with laughter.

'Listen Zoë, only a genius could make Enid amusing.'

'It's true you're not a genius.'

'Ouch!'

'I mean, Dr Leacock . . .'

'Peter.'

'I mean . . .'

Defeated, she turned to him. His brilliant smile was shining into her eyes. Then, without warning, he switched it off and leaned across the desk. Something strange and new came into his expression: a kind of vulnerability, as though he appealed to her for help.

'You don't need to tell me that we're not suited, Zoë. I haven't knocked around the world for as long as this without learning a thing or two about the matter which is of the most pressing interest to me, namely the effect I have on women. I can read the signs well enough, and though I suspect my mind appeals to you for its radicalism, it isn't to be honest a patch on your mind, and the radicalism is partly a bluff since it is so much easier to make an effect by denying things than by affirming them. There, I've never thought of that before!' he added, breaking off and staring before him with a startled look.

'In a very short time,' he continued, 'you will see how inadequate I am even in those areas which have gained your attention – which is why you should consider my offer very carefully. I am not a rapist, not even a seducer; I am offering you a bed – not my bed, but a bed, and a room all to yourself – in full consciousness of the fact that you won't like me for longer than it'll take to find a place of your own. Why not accept?'

'Thanks. It wouldn't be right. I'll try the students. Not Enid perhaps; but just give me Ellen's number; and Michael's.'

As the blood rose to her face, his supplicating look intensified.

'I'm offering you what you really need, Zoë: an arrangement that is thoroughly non-committal, temporary, free of obligations. I understand you. I admire your old-fashioned chastity, I really do. Just think: the amount of energy released between the sexes when they come together is proportional to the distance between them when they are held apart. What insipid encounters we liberated people have, and how we long for such as you – I exaggerate – how we admire such as you, who rescue sex from nature and turn it into art – the female transfigured into the feminine. Ah!'

He caught sight of something through the window, and the queer, soft expression gradually receded from his features.

'I thought they were at it again! Filthy buggers, pardon my French. Michael, you say, with that face sunless as a mushroom farm, Michael Ashley?'

He met her gaze, and something he read in it – something defiant and committed, like the glint of an animal defending its lair – caused him to hesitate.

'It is conceivable that Ellen has a telephone, unlikely that Michael even has an address. Ah, you see,' he went on, shaking the papers, 'I am right: a number for Ellen, but nothing for Michael, except "obtainable during the day, in case of emergencies, at 14 Capey St." Well Zoë, are you an emergency? Capey Street is right across the canal, you could walk there, no need even to call an ambulance.'

He switched on his smile, and leaned back contentedly.

'I'll try Ellen,' she said.

'Suit yourself: there's the number, right before you. And if you run out of luck, you know where to turn.'

'Thanks.'

'Thanks for zilch.'

A wave of desolation swept across her. She was utterly alone, a leaf on the autumn wind, a dove whose cote has been rifled and thrown to the flames. Her trim had been kept this long, but must soon disintegrate as weariness conquered and she fluttered to the ground. She thought sadly of Anna, whose distrust was Zoë's doing, of the Kostaina who had calculated so coolly behind the veils of rage. And she thought of Yannakis, whose dear face came to her in dreams and shone with undiminished vigour from the wall of his possessions. A strange rustling transpierced these things, as though the people in her little world floated beside her, carried by a tireless wind. 'Holy God,' they whispered, 'holy and strong, holy and immortal, have mercy on us.' Eternity in person managed the breeze that carried them, buoyed them up to realms of breathlessness, and then suddenly ceased and betrayed them, so that one by one the souls plummeted to destruction. Perhaps some unhoped-for providence could be summoned by prayer; but she doubted it. The Peacock, as he gently swayed behind his desk, his eyelids drooping over electric eyes, was like a watching satyr. He was one of the *kallikantzari*, whom the priests hunt with incense, and whose mesmerising antics lure the pure souls from their azure fields, and bring them fretting to earth.

She started to her feet. She must move out of his reach, so as to fall, when she fell, in some cleft that he could not see. She remembered a flamingo, flown in from the Caspian sea, which had tumbled from the skies above the village. It lay dead in a bed of rockroses, its eye half-closed, its long neck bruised and broken; and around it the smell of myrrh. It was Yannakis, with his bird-catching eye, who had seen the creature fall; together they buried it beneath a carob tree, where the seed-pods clinked in the sultry breeze, an endless tinkling farewell.

'I'll see you this evening, Zoë.'

'Maybe.'

'What do you mean, maybe? You're starting us off, remember? And Bonini's coming: all the way from Florence, to tell us about the semiotics of the unconscious.'

'It's too far ahead; I can't tell.'

He shook his head slowly.

'I don't make you out, Zoë, just don't make you out.'

'I think you make me out very well.'

'You won't stay for lunch?'

'Thanks. No.'

'I'll come out with you.'

'There's no need, Dr Leacock.'

'Peter.'

'There's no need, Peter.'

'At last!'

And with a robust laugh he stood to open the door. She scraped past him as best she could, but not before a part of him had rubbed against her arm, making a patch of heat which seemed afterwards to grow and spread until it invaded the whole of her body.

XIV

The house was modern, spruced with pebble-dash, a porch of tiles shielding the door. The bell sounded on two tones, trance-like and far away. Shadows began to move in the mottled glass panels, like shoals of fish beneath a ruffled sea. Zoë was running now, her last resources gathered. With the map, she had bought a copy of the *Evening Standard*, but a roof was not enough. She must put down her burden in some pace of gentleness before strength gave out. She had briefly thought of Bill, who coddled her and called her 'love'; but Bill's love would be a bath of vinegar. Michael was her fate, and all other paths led downwards.

The door opened slowly; it was held on a chain, and when human flesh appeared, it was no more than a slice of face – an eye in middle age, a wisp of greying hair, a woman's mouth enlarged by crimson lipstick and split like a rotting fruit.

'Yes,' it said.

'Does Michael live here?'

'No Michael here.'

'Michael Ashley – tall, with dark hair, an artist.'

Zoë felt a surge of panic.

'One of those?' said the woman in disgust. 'Try the shed at the back: there's one works there. Only he's not called Michael. Something fancy like Jeremy. Doesn't like to be disturbed.'

Having cancelled all she could of Zoë's interest, the woman closed the door.

'Thank you,' Zoë said.

The slice of face quickly reappeared.

'For what?'

'For letting him work in your shed.'

'I don't. It belongs to the council. Ought to have been demolished.'

The woman was right. The shed, standing in the middle of a concrete yard, was a disgrace to its surroundings. Its roof of felt was patched with corrugated iron, and the boards had fallen away in shards, being nailed back criss-cross over the cavities, and covered by plastic sacking. A bank of windows was let into one side, its symmetry spoiled by the dirty white cloth which served as a curtain. Zoë had inherited from Yannakis his love of snug, right-angled things, and when she found her nest it would be boarded and skirted and book-cased into a temple of order. This shed was not her home, and she studied it with the profound disappointment of one who allows herself only now and then to hope. The yard by contrast was well cared-for, fringed by a herbaceous border, with cornflowers, Michaelmas daisies, and other finer things. At the far end was a wooden fence, frilled by the tops of buddleias, growing in the escarpment of a railway line. The shed stood in these neat surroundings sour and sad and somehow vagrant, like a tramp stinking in a polished doorway.

The door was fastened by a latch, and she heard a gentle tapping behind it, like an animal preparing its winter nest. She hesitated, and then played a five-finger exercise on the slats. The tapping abruptly stopped, and a long listening silence ensued, before it began again with a faster and more urgent rhythm, as though some work must be completed before discovery. She knocked more loudly, and once again the tapping ceased.

'Jeremy,' she said.

'Who?'

She stood back in alarm, for it seemed like Michael's voice, defensive and accusing. How could he possibly understand her motive in coming here? How could she appear before him, except as an aggressor, an intruder, a canceller of privacy? Now it was her turn to remain silent. There was a sudden scuffle, and the door flew open; she jumped back from the iron latch.

Michael stood on the threshold, his brown eyes looking to either side of her, as though something far larger and more threatening lurked in her shadow.

'Oh. I thought you were that woman.'

Zoë blushed.

'No. I am this woman.'

Michael uttered a get-me-out-of-this giggle, which he instantly repressed.

'Yes. That's obvious.'

He made no move to invite her in, but simply stood in the doorway, staring beyond her, holding a box-handled chisel in the pale fingers of his left hand. He swallowed, and a kind of tremor in his cheeks suggested some repeated fear which her presence had awoken.

'I'm sorry,' Zoë said at last. 'Maybe I'm intruding.'

'It's just that nobody's allowed in here except me.'

He spoke as if reporting some regulation which he was powerless to alter. Michael's personality, she supposed, was entirely circumscribed by interdictions.

'And Jeremy,' she said.

'I am Jeremy.'

'Then I've made a mistake.'

'No. Not that one, at least. Jeremy's my *nom de guerre*.'

'Maybe you feel like a walk?'

'How did you find my address?' he asked, ignoring her question.

'The Peacock gave it to me.'

'Who? Oh, you mean Dr Leacock. How did he have it?'

His haunted look intensified, and he frowned, as though endeavouring to solve some enigma on which his life depended. Suddenly, however, a change came over him, and he looked more directly at Zoë, attempting a wan, forgiving smile.

'It's not your fault,' he said.

'What's not my fault?'

'The address. He shouldn't have given it. I mean, I shouldn't have given it.'

Zoë sighed, and looked pityingly at Michael. Something in his puzzled eyes detained her, and for all his rudeness she felt she would injure him more by going, than by waiting patiently for the wound she had jarred to close. Suddenly he stepped back.

'You're to come in,' he barked, as though revised instructions had just reached him by secret telegraph.

'Are you sure? I won't stay long. I only wanted . . .'

With an impatient gesture he stood back to let her pass. She did not look at him, was indeed incapable for a moment of looking at anything, since the room, the pale window, the peculiar pale forms which hovered everywhere just out of reach, the white mass of plaster in the centre, his white face and hands, the white sheet which was draped across the back of the shed, all coalesced into a twisted knot of whiteness, a thing of dreams and danger, which hovered before her eyes and blinded her. Then she noticed a chair, and walked quickly towards it, sitting heavily and with half-shut eyes.

Michael closed the door and remained beside it, so that she felt his eyes turned down to her.

'You can sit down if you like,' he shouted.

'I am sitting down.'

There was a silence, during which a train passed with a slight commotion, and a voice singing in a nearby house was faintly audible. Zoë looked up to find herself surrounded by figures in wood, plaster and stone, which peered down on her from lop-sided faces distorted by suffering. Their bodies, mounted on meticulous classical pedestals, were wrapped with strange muscles, which seemed to bind their limbs together and prevent every movement. Their legs were twisted like corkscrews, their bandaged chests had collapsed inwards, and they wrung their vast hands, not for comfort's sake, but in a vain attempt to free the self-trapped fingers. Their faces were masculine, hard, with tight, thin lips and bone-like noses. The eyes sloped sideways to meet the upward-slanting mouths, and seemed to be fleeing from the pressure of peaked Neanderthal skulls, whose shape and size suggested a capacity for one single but all-encompassing thought. Only the ears seemed to break free from the terrible tension, standing like sentinels to either side, guarding this private drama from the world.

Michael quickly snatched a sheet from the work-bench beneath the shrouded window, covering one of the figures so that she could see only the wood-shavings surrounding it, and the mallet which lay against its pedestal.

'Don't bother with them,' he cried, 'they are only sketches.'

And indeed each figure did seem to display, as she studied it, an unfinished quality, as though the idea advanced always to a certain point, and then held back in horror from its final crystallisation. But why had he worked so hard on the pedestals, each with its beautiful crisp mouldings, its little frieze of masks and cherubs, its carved date in Roman numerals, and its bold central design of dancing satyrs? Nothing about the work more affected her than the contrast between this selfless Renaissance gaiety, and the tortured selfhood that had been locked on top of it. The figures might have been chiselled out in days, while each pedestal seemed to represent months of arduous finishing.

'Is there something wrong?' he asked. His voice was quieter now, with a suggestion of real concern – though the concern was perhaps more for himself, than for her who had caused it.

'No, nothing serious. I lent you a book – you remember? Ritsos.'

'So you did. Ritsos. Socialist drivel.'

'Everything modern is socialist.'

'Then everything modern is drivel.'

Zoë felt foolish; her lips began to tremble slightly so that she could not answer him. Jerking into movement, Michael began to tidy the tools and papers which lay scattered on the bench.

'Here's the book,' he said, coming across to her.

He bent down slowly and placed it at her feet, as though this space had been reserved for her and hers.

'I'm sorry, Michael.'

'It's alright. I don't mind. You could have some coffee,' he added, as though to compensate for what she could not have. She shook her head. English coffee disgusted her.

'You are wondering why I came,' she said at last.

'You came for Ritsos.'

'Why I *really* came.'

Michael looked at her with sudden interest.

'You mean that, up to now, this visit has been entirely imaginary?'

'Yes, if you like. I came in a dream.'

He sat on the edge of the bench, his hands gripping the rim, his black denim trousers screwed up around the knees like the springs of a jack-in-the-box.

'I don't mind you being here,' he said. 'I don't mind it at all. I don't mind you looking at these things either. Isn't that strange?'

Zoë, who did not find it strange, nevertheless nodded and cast her eyes once more over the grim totems which surrounded her – a gaggle of lunatics whose great ears took in from every sound some new despair and suffering. She must not threaten them: that was their meaning.

The edge of anxiety had gone from Michael's face, and the yellow sun, diffused by the makeshift curtain, brought colour to his features. There was even a smile of sorts in his pale brown eyes, a hesitant invitation. She felt that, with care, she could advance to the very brink of his loneliness and shine her thoughts across it, like an archaeologist pointing his torch into a musty tomb. What she would discover there she did not know: but it would be beautiful and secret, and accessible only to her.

'I didn't know you were a sculptor.'

'Oh well, I'm not really. I paint as well. I'd paint you, if you'd let me. I often think of your face. It's a kind of classic really, an archetype: close-set eyes, long slender nose, olive complexion, a look of continual astonishment. Like a saint. You need a gold lustrous background, from another world. You ought to be peering at us, from outside space and time.'

It was the Peacock's view of her; but now, far from recoiling, she eagerly endorsed it, wished even to incarnate its meaning in her self.

'That's not the way I *look*; it's the way I feel. The way I am.'

'Well then; there you are.'

Michael seemed pleased, as though a disputed point had been settled in his favour.

'But maybe, if you painted me, I'd end up looking like these,' she said, pointing to the figures nearby.

'You don't like them?'

'Oh, I wouldn't say that. No. They are powerful, disturbing. But I don't know much about art. You should tell me what they mean.'

'They don't mean. They are.'

His tone was defensive.

'Well, what are they?'

'Ancestors, fathers, those who went before.'

'I see.'

She tried to understand them in this light: the tight wedge-shaped skulls suggested ancestors so distant as to be barely human, standing fearful in a primeval night. But the eyes and hands were recent, compromised, steeped in the guilt of modern life. Zoë held the two ideas together in her mind, trying to form some fruitful union. She was not sure that she succeeded. All she knew was that a terrible wrong had been done to those figures – a wrong lasting centuries, millennia even. Now nothing remained in them but fear, guilt and the desire – thwarted in their very limbs – to relapse into primal nothingness. It was a desire which matched nothing in her. Whence had it come, and by what strange alchemy had it formed itself as art? If it *were* art, though of that too she could not be certain. Michael had put her in mind of the frescos of her childhood, with their cool incurious stares from the world of exaltation and forgiveness – that, to her, was art, the constant cheerful message of the soul's survival, the overcoming, here and now, of time. From these ancestors all cheer had been expelled, and the line which led from them was twined in time, a never-ending line of death. What little hope there was in Michael's work was contained in the pedestals, with their ironic finesse, and their quiet hymn to pleasure. She asked him about them.

'Do you like them?'

She got up, and ran her finger along a moulded lip of stone.

'Yes,' she said, and then started. It was not stone at all, but some kind of plastic; the delicate lines were not carved but embossed.

'Isn't it fun? I get it by the yard from the timber merchant, and then make it up at the corners with polyfilla.'

Zoë felt a pang of disappointment.

'I think I preferred the way they looked before.'

'Before what?'

'Before you told me you didn't make them.'

'But I did make them. With prefab and polyfilla.'

He had raised his voice again, and she turned to find him standing behind her, swift of movement as a cat. He began to explain the figures, in short exclamatory phrases which he relayed from the high command.

'These are first attempts, you understand. The real thing is there, behind its sheet. You can't see it yet. Nobody has ever seen even the sketches before.'

Zoë sat, a warm glow of relief spreading through her,

cancelling the grief over Anna, washing away the Peacock's contamination. She looked up at Michael, and studied his face, as it grew in animation. His eyes were now fixed on her, the black points in the centre of the pupils like targets offered to her gaze. His brow had widened, his temples trembled slightly, and little by little his voice quietened, liberated itself from the weight of orders, and ran free and confiding, with an almost child-like eagerness. The figures, he explained, march through our dreams. They are prisoners of our anger, the whipping boys through whom we appease our fear. And each generation adds another wound to them, as child turns on father, and blames him for the tragedy of life.

'It's scary,' said Zoë, though she wasn't scared.

Michael described some figures by Rodin, Moore and Giacometti which had inspired him, and she listened in silence, impressed by his erudition, and wondering how to match it. So here I am, she thought, part of England; and mentally she shook her fist in triumph at the Kostaina.

'Maybe I am boring you?' he asked, and as he did so he gently touched her elbow. She could find nothing wrong in Michael's gesture: it was neither painful, nor frightening, nor outrageous, but simply a recognition of her life.

'No,' she said. She talked about the art of her own country, the art of icons, which were not ideas but people, who stepped into the day-to-day of Cyprus with the same concerns as the worshippers who prayed to them. She told him of the Panayia Galatoussa, who increases the flow of milk, even the milk of goats and cows; of St George of the Black Hill, whose talent is broody hens, and of St John the Baptist of Silikou, who cures malarial children when they are rolled before him in the ruined aisle. Nor are these mediators helpful only; the icons are as temperamental as the people who believe in them, and will not accept mistreatment. The Virgin of Yiolou will often refuse to be taken into the fields to perform her rain-making function; the Eleousa of Salamiou once raised an army of avenging snakes; the Virgin of Lagoudera killed an impious Turk with hailstones, while that of Lophos, being touched by an impertinent restorer, struck the man dead in indignation.

The stories were the best she could offer him, and all she really knew of art. Recounting them, she felt warm and cheerful. She observed the community from which she was forever locked out with amused and patient affection. Michael nodded and she rather liked his expression of gentle cupidity. As she rose he laid a hand on her shoulder. She glanced at him, and gave a barely perceptible shake of the head – a brief rigidity of the neck which could mean, 'no', 'some other time' or 'not just yet'. It was a gesture she had never made before, and which came to her instinctively from that abundant repertoire provided to Mediterranean women by the gods. In her too the pulse of ancestry commanded. But it was a pulse of life, and for a moment she felt it cut across her plans and calculations, disclosing a path down from the high paved road of reason, to a tree-shrouded altar, bathed in an enchanted light.

'Why *did* you come, Zoë?'

'Perhaps we should go for a walk.'

'Don't you like it here?'

She sat down again, and stared at the white sheet which concealed the final martyrdom of Michael's race. It did not surprise her when Michael suddenly knelt beside her, on a worn Turkish kelim which lay amid woodshavings and plaster-dust. It did not surprise her that he too should rehearse, in half-swallowed phrases, the familiar tale of her beauty and her otherness. It did not surprise her that she liked what she heard, that the episode – far from being the usual fruitless cul-de-sac of revulsion – was natural, healing, a stage on the way to something vast and warm and consoling. She was not a spectator, but a participant. Michael's life and hers had intersected, but with infinite gentleness, like two rivers flowing together and becoming one.

Michael was telling her the strangest story, and this story, he implied, was the real meaning of the chalk-white figures that surrounded them. It began and ended in grief – the grief of a son, alone with an obsessive father, and subjected to the harrowing inquisition of a mind in torment. Michael described the occasions of humiliation: the moments when, with a mad glint of triumph in its eyes, the little gnome would jump from its perch among the shelves and wardrobes and cling to him with bony claws, crowing its accusations in a voice which scraped and grated like a hinge. He told the story with compassion, not neglecting the gnome's own humiliations, as it attempted in vain to find a place in the world, losing first the wife who had promised security, and then the job as insurance agent behind which stood its only avenue to promotion.

Zoë started, but said nothing, since it was fore-ordained.

Condemned to meniality, as assistant clerk to the local bus company, the gnome had only two resources: the elaborate pantomime of the garden, in which it sowed and reaped unceasingly, and Michael's moral education, which required a concentration, an intelligence and a moral stature – the gnome assured him – so rare as to be found only here and there, glowing like a nugget in the silt and slime of society, sinking to the bottom, but only so as to shine with a light all the more wonderful for the surrounding darkness. It was this virtue which justified the gnome, as it dug its claws into Michael's shoulders, and pulled from his eyes and mouth the long confessional scrolls of moral failure. It accepted only one penance – the penance of the garden, in which digging, hoeing, clipping, shifting and watering would occur to the accompaniment of the gnome's squeaky singing. Here too, however, the outcome was uncertain, Michael being frequently kept in suspense as the gnome deliberated whether to pronounce a sermon, and, if so, whether to conclude it on a note of accusation or forgiveness. Much depended on the condition of nature. Was the gnome able to read, in the signs provided – in the seeds and tubers, in the roots and loam, in the worms, centipedes, woodlice and dung-beetles – the confirming signature of pardon? Or had the order of things been thrown into too great a disarray by the son's transgression, so that the gnome, disturbing its surface with his trowel, saw only grief and anarchy below? Then would vengeance be at hand. The son must be unpacked like a broken watch, his cogs and springs spread out for divine inspection, and every fault laid bare.

Finally Michael had shot the gnome. The episode was primeval, and, like a religious ceremony, existed in many versions. Sometimes the gun held only paper bullets; at other times darts tipped with silver; there was even a version in full battle dress, in which the offending crown was pierced by dum-dum bullets and the fragments of the gnome's horny skull embedded in the ceiling.

Zoë shuddered, and studied the bent form beside her. Michael held his hands, the fingers long, white, meticulously separated like a pianist's, on the trousers over his knees. His long soft hair fell on his face, concealing it, and his words came painfully, breathlessly, as though he had been saving them for a long time. He was indeed a penitent, and something cramped and self-accusing in his posture recalled the figures of the damned, chased into the pendentives of the church at Ayios Yiorgos by the huge avenging archangel which threw its white robes across the dome. Perhaps he was asking her to save him, to lift him above the region of his crime, to hold him to the breast he had never known, and whose milk would re-create him out of ashes. Zoë reached out a hand to him, and with a sudden hunger he seized it and covered it with kisses. She shuddered again, and then stood up, tugging him so that he stood beside her. His eyes were red with unlicensed tears, his lips pale and taut. How strange and monstrous he was, and how strange and monstrous that she should like him so.

'I wonder why I told you that,' he said at last.

'Maybe because you needed to tell someone.'

'Not anyone.'

'Why me?'

'I suppose because you came here to find me; and because – because I let you in. It's never happened before; not properly.'

'What strange credentials I have,' said Zoë.

'Not so strange. But why did you come, Zoë?'

She went to the bench, lifted the dusty curtain, and stared out over the concrete yard, with its herbaceous border. Someone cared about the yard, for there were difficult plants – lavender, cat's-paw and tuberoses – planted neatly in the sunnier places, and a cut-back rose, flowerless now, and studded with golden hips, which climbed onto the wooden fence and nodded at the next-door garden. Two tubs of blue anemones stood symmetrically, with candid imperturbable faces, on the centre-line, and the concrete had a brushed, dry, dead appearance, like a canvas awaiting paint.

'Whose is the garden?'

'It comes with the shed.'

'But you don't look after it,' said Zoë, who saw a woman's handiwork before her.

'No, not me. A friend.'

'Ah,' said Zoë, 'that woman.'

'No. Not that woman. Another one. Nobody important.'

Michael's manner was confused.

'And this other woman – she's not allowed in the shed?'

Zoë dropped the curtain and looked at the bench. A row of boxwood chisels, their blades crisply ground at the tips and glistening, lay in a rack beneath the window. Beside them was a leather-covered tape-measure, a stick of charcoal, and an iron pot of fish glue, whose rim and sides were stuck with frozen lava. The sun lay across the objects in perforated shafts of orange light, creating a unity among them, like a still life. She was on the verge of understanding something – a secret lay revealed beneath her, if only she could see its pattern.

Michael did not answer.

'Why did you come, Zoë?'

'Because . . .'

She glanced again at Michael's bench, and all at once she saw its meaning. These objects had souls. Yannakis believed that disorder comes because people barge into the world, heedless that its moral space is already occupied. Zoë admired the theory, not for its truth, but for the way her father's gentleness was preserved in it and authorised. She had applied it to Yannakis's possessions, and now to the things on Michael's bench. An enormous transition was accomplished; for the first time, she had moved on from her father. The effect of this was grief – grief so strong she could hardly contain it.

'Because you are the only one.'

'The only one?'

'The only one I can tell.'

Large tears had begun to make their way down her cheeks, and she made no attempt to hide them. They welled into her eyes like spring water – another of those gestures which came silent and unbidden from the ancient dead.

'Tell me, then.'

Michael stepped forward, hesitated, and then took her in his arms.

'My father died,' she said simply.

'I'm sorry.'

'He died three years ago.'

'Then it's not so bad.'

'Not so bad?'

'Not so bad as if it had been today.'

'But it *was* today.'

Michael held Zoë away and looked curiously at her. There was alarm in his features, but he did not speak.

'I mean it was today, just now, just this moment, that I knew it really happened. I have wandered in a half-light, neither believing nor disbelieving, looking for the person who . . . the person who . . . oh, I don't know.'

This speech surprised Zoë very much. Not even when Michael opened his heart to her – if 'heart' were the right name for the organ which prompted his confessions – did Zoë imagine she might offer a reciprocal confidence. She was equally surprised to find that she did not regret her words. It did not matter even that Michael found them alarming, though she would rather he did not. She detached herself and sat down, her hands folded in her lap, watching him through her tears. How frozen everything had been until now, and how perfect he seemed in his awkwardness, like a mountain creature, startled in its lair.

She found herself recounting her father's life, which, she now saw, was only a wrinkle of transience on the skin of things. She remembered a thousand details: how she would wait for his homecoming in the garden, her mind awash with the sea-cry of cicadas; how they wandered together in the Troodos mountains, visiting the hesychasts in their crumbling cells, eating in dusty olive groves by the wayside, overlooking white abysses and deep blue lozenges of sea. She described the monks at Bellapais, and Yannakis dancing with them to the sound of a *laoutaris*. Beneath his immovable trilby the face was always firm, bold and prominent, with an expression of humorous regret. She described sybaritic pilgrimages to Ayios Neophytus, and how he loved and kissed the icons in church after church. He was not a Christian, but a pagan; if a single God existed, he thought, Islam would be true – from which he drew the logical conclusion that the God of religion does not exist. Yet always the icons would spring awake, as their dreaming lips touched his. Everything he touched acquired a soul. She spoke of the dark events, which she hardly understood, except as the work of some vast conspiracy. They had saved themselves, washed up like castaways on a cold Northern shore. But Yannakis never recovered – every effort of life, even the pigeons, had been hesitant and crowned with failure. He too had been an insurance broker, and he too had played a losing hand. There followed the unreal stillness of heart disease, the vivid body motionless with terror, sensing the ferment of decay. She described his death, falling to earth with the fluttering Evyenia in his hands, and then the nights drenched in loneliness, and full of dreams. Through her disbelief she had kept her countenance; it helped too that the Kostaina had shared her illusion, and fought from this common premise with the ferocity of one who defends a lie. And now those years of preparation were rewarded; she had left home for ever, she was no longer trapped in his tomb, no longer bound to him, no longer the Kostaina's daughter, no longer a Greek. She had come through a dismal antechamber of the world, where the dead and the unborn lie marble-still and silent. And now she would touch the living, and their eyes would blaze with purpose.

'What are you then?' Michael barked.

'I don't know. Something free; something transcendental.'

He faced her with alarm, as though terrified of some huge responsibility.

'You needn't worry, Michael. I'm only telling you this. I'm not asking for anything.' And into her voice came all the gentleness she knew.

'Oh it's interesting. I mean, I collect dead cultures. Some people collect eggs, when the life has been blown out of them.'

'The shell I left behind would crumble in your hands.'

'Possibly.'

He looked at her, and seemed to recover his equilibrium.

'Can I kiss you?'

'You can.'

His awkwardness vanished. Placing his mouth on her lips, he expertly drew the life into them, until her body was in deepest need. When she withdrew, it was with a jump.

'You don't know me, Michael.'

'I am beginning to know you. You came here to be known. I discovered you,' he went on, his voice rising again. 'Don't deny it. I let you into my shed, my life.'

'And now?'

An enigmatic expression crossed his face.

'Maybe we'll live together. Maybe that's it.'

He spoke as though rehearsing plans which did not concern her. And he rubbed his hands together anxiously, trying to free himself from unseen chains.

Zoë looked at him, and her eyes said 'I love you. You are the only being I can love absolutely, with my complete self, with body, mind and heart. You are my mate, my husband, my guardian. I am yours and you are mine as two fires that meet and penetrate. The bond that joins us is free and also necessary; we exist in it for the first time fully, the first time in reality. This is *eros*, holy and happy as the gods themselves.' All this and more her eyes were saying, as they blazed at him. But he did not notice.

'No, no,' he went on. 'We can't live together.'

His face looked pinched and calculating. He reminded Zoë of a hunted animal, skilled in the practice of survival. She watched him as he muttered to himself, performing some feat of mental arithmetic.

'No, not yet, we can't. Only – only I can find you a room. I know a room.'

'A room?'

A moment earlier she had wanted nothing else.

'Where I live there's a room. How much can you afford?'

She shrugged her shoulders.

'I don't know. How much is needed?'

'Will you let me into this room?'

'Maybe.'

'I've offended you.'

He shouted the words, as though in triumph.

'Not at all.'

Not being offended had for years been Zoë's speciality: not being offended by the Kostaina, who abused her as a whore; by Mr Tzouliadis, who offered her charity; by the Peacock who paraded his sex. She dutifully added Michael to the list. In this new world, she thought, love is almost certainly an error.

Michael had lapsed into his old posture, with downturned eyelids and solemn lips, hugging his armpits.

'It'll be OK,' he said.

'What will be OK?'

'Me and you.'

'You and me.'

'You and me,' he repeated.

'That's good to know.'

'You must let me kiss you again.'

'Must?'

He took a step towards her.

'No,' she said, 'stay there.'

He nodded thoughtfully, as though he had expected this, as though all hope, all risk, all adventure, were deepest error.

'Dr Leacock said I could live with him.'

She pronounced the words slowly, with a shudder.

'Live with *him*? You can't.'

'I know.'

'Well then. I said I'd find you a room.'

'It's not a room I want.'

Michael looked up in surprise.

'What do you want Zoë?'

'What does a woman want?'

'The unobtainable.'

Zoë sighed.

'Listen Michael. I've never had this kind of conversation before. Never with anyone ever. It's scary. I don't know the rules. Why don't you help me?'

His eyes widened in astonishment.

'Help you? How?'

'If I knew I wouldn't be asking. God, you are so exasperating!'

'Yes, yes,' he said enthusiastically. 'That's exactly it!'

'I thought you wanted me.'

'I do. Yes, I do. I've always wanted you, I think.'

'You don't sound very convinced.'

'I'm convinced alright; just not convincing. It's my way. Can't you see?'

He appealed to her with beseeching eyes, solemn and theatrical.

'If you really want me, it's simple,' she said.

'Nothing is simple.'

He began to pace around the shed, rubbing his hands

together, and casting strange defiant looks at the sculptures. And then, as if his behaviour up to this point had not been strange enough, Michael, with a queer sideways look from the window – perhaps to verify that his action was being recorded in the book of credits, or at any rate was not being ignored by those from whom his instructions came – suddenly threw himself before her on his knees, which struck the concrete floor through the thin carpet with an unpleasant clicking sound like dice. He pressed his lips to her thigh and wept with such passion that Zoë could feel the hot tears pouring through the rent in her trousers onto her skin. Because there was no other response that seemed remotely appropriate, she gently stirred his soft hair with her fingers. After a while he rose to his feet. His eyes were red but not swollen, as though the tears had merely flown over them, from some other source.

'I'm sorry,' he said.

'Please don't be.'

'I'll work it out,' he went on. 'It'll be OK. All shall be well, all manner of things shall be well. I'll see you this evening. Don't worry about it.'

He grasped her by the shoulders. But his expert kisses were in such contrast to the hesitations which led to them, that Zoë could not trust them: they were not the gleaming face of a soul, but something darker and sadder and drearier.

'You are confusing me,' she said, recoiling.

'No,' he replied, with a nervous giggle, 'it is you who are confusing me. I'll see you this evening. It'll be OK. It's sure to be OK. God!'

XV

She ran beside the canal, her thoughts blanked out as though by a giant hand. People collided with her, and her fear augmented. Danger had once been known and circumscribed; she had weapons then, bright as daggers and broad as shields. But now danger was unbounded, and she confronted it unarmed.

Her feet clattered on the iron bridge, from which she entered a street of half-demolished houses. In one of the windows an old woman's face was hung like an extinct lantern, yellow, dusty and crusted with grief. Zoë pitched her way through rubble, across the empty lots where the council planned to build their sterile towers, and so to abolish misery for ever. Débris lay in the street: nesting baths and toilet bowls, obscene headless trunks of plastic dolls, treadless tyres, punctured cans and oil drums, rusty spring beds, death-stained mattresses, and shattered blocks of concrete with their jutting fingers of rust, like snakes that have died in agony.

'She will fall on him, mop him up like a sponge.'

But Michael was mercury, and could never be absorbed.

Zoë was drawn to these unfrequented streets, for they were England – not the proud imperium where ghostly heroes wave from abandoned spires, but the camping site of future nomads. And she sniffed with a peculiar abandon the malignant wind that scattered about these places – a wind of darkness, which seemed to blow from every quarter of the compass, without rain or mist or dust, hurrying into those vacant lots like the unshriven spirits of the dead, taking no space, acquiring no rest, and rushing onwards unconsolably.

The afternoon sun was haunted and blanched by cloud, and the leaves of a few sparse fruit-trees, planted in the demolished street, were shaking fitfully as though conjuring a storm – only without violence, and in an air so dry and thin and exhausted that nothing could really be carried by it. Zoë sped onwards, electric, foreboding, the scarf slipping from her hair, and the strap of the duffle bag gnawing at her shoulders.

She stood in a phone booth, watching the sun spear itself on St Botolph's spire. After a few minutes, she rang Bill at the theatre.

'I've run away,' Zoë said. I should be announcing the resurrection, I should be crying for joy.

'That's grand, darling. Come and see me.'

There was a commotion outside: birds, flapping around a piece of bread. And somewhere a siren, howling down disorder.

'I'm going to live with a man.'

There was no time to explain, no time to find other words. There the image was. A man, indefinite article, *enas andras* – one single man.

'Men are no use my sweet, unless they are old, rich, and well-connected. Besides, they smell. Come and see me all the same. The costumes are delicious – I collected them today. Not tonight petal, I'm busy. Tomorrow. That Anna's a genius, whatever you say. Lots of love, darling, and for God's sake don't get attached to him.'

'Bill . . .'

'Yes love?'

'I'll come to the theatre tomorrow.'

'That's my girl. Ten thirty, after the show. 'Bye darling.'

'Goodbye,' she said, *'adio'*.

XVI

The class had begun. Five blunt heads watched from the graffiti-studded benches as the Peacock strutted on the dais, his head high, his voice triumphantly crowing. The air was thick with smoke, and it was almost impossible to read the 'No Smoking' sign which had been pinned to the blackboard.

Mr Cobb the radical grocer sat motionless behind his pipe, his khaki overalls draped like a cloak over sloping shoulders. Ellen was rolling cigarettes for the evening, running her tongue along the gummed edge of the paper with a lingering suggestive glance, and leaning in the direction of Edgar, the half-drugged pianist who sometimes dropped in on his way to

work at the nearby Lamb and Garter. The delicate white-haired
Mrs Winthropp smiled quietly as Zoë entered, with the air of
one who is about to offer a secret, while Jimmy, the librarian,
stared straight ahead, his pale bespectacled face rocking above
his Adam's apple, like a ball in a fountain. The fifth student was
George the philosopher, who lived alone in a garret, and whose
conversation consisted of long mysterious quotations from
Heidegger, booming through a forest of beard, while his small
gold-tinged eyes danced ecstatically. She had no idea whether
Michael's absence were a good sign or a bad sign; but it was
definitely a sign.

'OK Zoë,' said the Peacock, beaming at her, 'are you ready?'

'Ready for what?'

'For your apotheosis.'

She pushed into the second row, in the place which she used
to prefer because someone had scratched 'Leacock is an arsehole'
in the varnish. Now, however, she took off her pullover and
laid it over the offensive sentence. A queer sensation came over
her, as she tried to meet the Peacock's smile: a mixture of grief
and resignation. She took out her papers from the duffle bag,
with the neat bird-like gestures of a creature seeking to protect
itself. There was nothing: only an empty notebook, the Cavafy,
and the poems of Yannis Ritsos, which Michael had stained
with red circles of wine. She remembered one of the poems, of
homecoming to a ruined house, where clay statues stood in a
garden, their glass eyes fallen into rotting water. How strange
and bleak and comfortless those statues were, perforated, many-
eyed and blind – *diatrita, polyommata, tyfla*. She thought of
Yannakis, and of the impassable space that divided him from
now.

'You know, Zoë,' the Peacock continued. 'Your presenta-
tion. Descartes – you remember? "I think".'

Michael's absence was like a frame bordering everything.
Each sight and sound was pictured in this frame and somehow
discredited, passing through it like a procession of ghosts.

'I think,' she said. 'It thinks.'

She sat down. The red evening sky through the metal-framed window; the jagged crenellations of Spicetown; the seagulls circling and crying in the dusty air: all archetypes of absence, which she contemplated through the window with a sphinx-like stare.

'Good,' said the Peacock, 'if a trifle cryptic. Any comments?'

There was a murmuring and shifting of cloth, a popping of lips as pipes and cigarettes were pulled from them. George said that the thing which thinks posits itself as *Dasein* for whom (or which) being is essentially problematised. Edgar said he liked Zoë's speech and had nothing to add to it. Mrs Winthropp said thought is a web, Ellen said 'yeah' and Mr Cobb took his pipe from his mouth, made as if to speak, pursed his lips, shook his head and fell meaningfully silent. As they struck their attitudes the door opened and Zoë looked up with a start. It was Enid, who shot ferret-eyed looks to left and right, and scampered to the back of the class.

The Peacock strutted on the dais, illustrating his thoughts with slow magniloquent gestures. He seemed to mock the world and her, moving in a sphere untouched by love or suffering. And as he levered reality to one side with his strong-armed paradoxes – showing that nothing is certain, and that in every utterance sounds the hollow voice of power – he became a great force of destruction, superb and irresistible. Beliefs came before him like Cypriot wedding cakes, spindly and trembling on their sugar columns. And with a look from his smiling eyes he shattered them to dust.

The door opened. She did not dare to look at him, whom she had touched. To meet in this place was madness. He must see that: he must recognise at once, as he comes through the door, the impossibility of the thing. And if it is not Michael – which it isn't, she sees – that is to the good. He is too fine to enter here; he is waiting outside, his hands pressed to his sides, his eyes turned inwards to another world. The man who has entered is tall, with a shaven head, heavy jowls, horn-rimmed glasses, and the grim expression of the existentialist. The Peacock is introducing him

— not Bonini, who has been summoned to an international conference, but Bonini's confidant and disciple Caravisco, who has come on the master's behalf. He wears a theatrical outfit of carefully tailored oddments, something that Bill might have commissioned: burgundy-coloured velvet jacket, speckled red bow-tie, green-striped shirt, and flared trousers of creamy chamois. He raises his hands in the air before him, and his crimsoned fingers, stretched and spatulate, flutter for a moment before settling on his cheeks, forming a box from which his clown eyes stare like headlights. On his index finger grows a large emerald, like a shining wart, and in one ear a silver fly is perching, drinking from the poison which boils in his brain. Suddenly he lowers his hands, and takes from his pocket a bundle of cards, which he shuffles with studied inattention while his eyes settle on Zoë, gradually freezing to a look of desire. He rotates the turret of his head, raises it, lowers it, and aims again at Zoë. Without lifting his eyes from her he signals to a technician who has entered at the rear of the lecture room. The lights are dimmed, a white screen descends over the blackboard, and suddenly an array of figures and diagrams is projected before them. Caravisco speaks with an American accent, constantly adjusting the position of his head, turning it with strong prehensile fingers, the tips of which seem to sink into his brain as into a sponge, and then releasing it, so that it swings back fixedly to Zoë.

'Here you see the sequence A1, A2, A3 by which Bonini designates the passions, A1 being a passion, A2 another passion, A3 another and so on; below you see another letter which is the letter Q. Beneath A1 there is a Q, beneath A2 also, and beneath A3, and so on. In other words Q does not change, does not vary; it is a constant. It is also a quantity, hence "Q" for quantity; but sometimes a quality also, hence "Q" for quality. This constant Q is there behind every passion, in every passion. And here we have another sequence L1, L2, L3 and at the end a question-mark, which I have written a little to one side, since the question must be raised only later, only by a delayed response, an *aphasia.* Each A relates by Q to its own L, and therefore L1, L2, L3 must also occur in sequence, the same sequence as the original passions, A1, A2, A3, and so on. We call L the legality, or law, of A, each passion having its own legality, its own transformation into law. Hence we can arrange the laws of the passions in a sequence which, however, I have also suggested we must question, the question too being a "Q" which stands between each A and its L, which interrupts, so to speak, intercepts, the passage from A to L. And so now, using this scheme, what did Freud wish to tell us about the work of mourning?"

Mr Cobb let out three puffs of smoke, a serene expression on his face, as though at last encountering the benefits of education. Ellen held an unfinished cigarette poised before her mouth, which had fallen open as she stared at Caravisco's head. Jimmy's Adam's apple bobbed up and down, while Mrs Winthropp, who had laid aside her needlework, was trying to catch Zoë's eye. But Zoë could not move. In this harlequin costume, this spongey, hairless head, this alphabet soup of words, she saw the great soulless one, the doorman of the future, who stared into her with the cathode light of pure desire. And somewhere outside the classroom, not wishing to enter because this charade displeased him, and because he was too fine to hang out his soul in tatters, was Michael, waiting for her, his nervous hands stirring the air, his eyes haunted with absence, regretting his final words, recalling the chrism of a kiss.

O heavenly king, O comforter, the spirit of truth, who art everywhere and fillest all things, the treasury of blessings and giver of life, come and abide in us, cleanse us from all impurity, and of thy goodness save our souls.

Caravisco paused and glanced at his cards.

'Here I must end,' he said, and stepped from the dais in Zoë's direction.

She must go to him now, while the gift could be made. 'O heavenly king, O comforter . . .' Words, mere words; and Caravisco's outlined eyes owl-like and targeted.

She was on her feet and running. The brass handle of the door slipped in her hand. And the sweet sticky scent of the pursuer surrounded her. Her hair filled with his breath. Then she fell, limp and relinquished, travelling onwards into the dark.

XVII

She was in the Peacock's office, lying on the couch and covered with a woven durry. A camel-hair cushion, dry and itchy, was propped beneath her neck.

'OK now, girl?'

The Peacock was pouring whisky into bottle-green glasses and looking down on her with a vagrant concern.

'You're in trouble, Zoë.'

She waved the drink away; he held it out of reach then offered it again. She took the glass and placed it on the floor.

'It was that dreadful zombie, Caravaggio.'

'Caravisco. Well, you certainly sussed him out. The problem is, Zoë,' – he adopted a benign expression – 'that all intellectual paths have been trampled from time immemorial. That is why they seem so hard and lifeless, and why people like Caravisco have to run out into the pastures of absurdity. Sometimes it makes sense, not to make sense.'

'That didn't worry me.'

'What worried you?'

'Oh, his eyes. His head. His fingers.'

The Peacock studied her for a moment with interest. Then, with a brilliant smile, he said, 'Here's a letter for you. It was left this afternoon.'

'A letter?'

The envelope was typed: 'To Zoë, pupil of Dr Leacock, by hand.' So this is how it ends. Strange that Michael should know how to use a typewriter.

'You know, Zoë, I'm serious about that room. You won't be in my way, and you can sort things out tomorrow – find the place which suits you. Meanwhile, liberty hall, every vice permitted, even virtue. See you in a minute.'

He rose to his full height, swallowed his whisky, shot her a compassionate look, and went to the door.

'My bag,' she said. 'It's in the lecture room. I'll need it.'

'It's there by the window. In case you want to run away.'

Zoë gave him a grateful look.

'Thanks Peter,' she said.

'Don't mention it; or rather do mention it, if it helps my case.'

The air in the street was cool. The last violet flower of daylight dwindled over the city, moulting its lustrous petals on to the iridescent rooftops. Light from the lecture room shone across the pavement, and she stood in its arc, the letter shaking in her hands.

'Dear Zoë,' she read. 'It wasn't possible. She turned up. Not that woman, but the other one. I've put you back in the icon, and your eyes shine on me from untouchable gold. M.'

Zoë stood for half an hour, until Peter Leacock took her home.

XVIII

Three years later, on a dull November day, Zoë entered the Three Crowns, on the edge of that web of Edwardian streets which she used to call the Solitudes. It was not her habit to enter pubs unescorted; though for the first time in several weeks she could afford to, having just collected from Mr Tzouliadis the fifteen pounds which had been owing to her for three years. She had stepped off the street in order to avoid Peter Leacock, Little Peacock as she used to call him, who was swaggering towards her, his latest girlfriend – a cropped-haired eighteen-year-old, with painted circus eyes and a ring through her nose – skipping at his heels.

In the warm interior of the pub, men were playing snooker, chaffing blue chalk against the tips, and dropping down to sight. Their eyes slid back along the cues like shining curtain rings. They elbowed space away, making room for their purpose, and cornering the world. She remembered the pub next to Bewley College, where only Peter would claim more than his own body-space. Here self-assertion was the norm, and the sound of the men as they raised their voices in affable disagreement was like the noise of water pouring life into life.

Michael Ashley was seated at one of the tables, eating, as was his habit, a three-course lunch. His dark suit and bombay shirt, his stiff collar and dashing scarlet tie, his neatly brushed hair and preoccupied look as he read the *Times* law reports, marking a passage with an expensive-looking biro, seemed like a disguise. But his character too had changed. Catching sight of Zoë, he greeted her boisterously, affecting innocence. His eyes were still handsome, but no trace remained of their poetry; while his hands, on one of which a crop of gold had grown, were relaxed, competent, gripping even in stillness the ladder to success.

He beckoned her forward, and she sat down opposite him at the table.

'How extraordinary! What are you doing with yourself?'

There was no trace of his former bark.

'What are *you* doing?'

She pointed to the suit and tie.

'I always dress like this. It's my uniform. I'm respectable now; pure as you.'

She said nothing.

'I work in the solicitor's office next door. Baines and Burbage Ltd. You must have seen it. *You* haven't changed though.'

He pinched her woollen sleeve, and she quickly withdrew her arm.

'Same old jumper; same old trousers; same little chain round your neck, same little revolver.'

After a pause she asked,

'What about the sculpture?'

'Rubbish!'

A small flicker of regret seemed to pass across his features, and he stared down at the table. 'Pretentious rubbish.'

'The shed?'

'They demolished it. Quite right too.'

'That woman?'

He raised his eyes and scanned her face. Zoë had acquired the ability to meet such looks, even though she blushed a little.

'Rubbish too,' he said. 'And the other one. I've come out of that. It was all provisional, like those ghastly lectures at Bewley College. What's the matter?'

'Nothing.'

'I shouldn't have said that. Shows you still mean something to me.'

She made an impatient gesture.

'I heard you were living with Peter Leacock.'

'Really?'

Michael's face was strange to her, sealed, impersonal.

'I mustn't stay,' she said, rising to her feet.

'I'm always here at this time.' His face was suddenly overcast and sad. 'Maybe we could have lunch?'

'Maybe.'

XIX

It had begun to rain, a grey English drizzle, which smeared the streets like tears. Zoë thought of her mother, who lay dying in Argyll Street. Anna and the child had gone to live with an Englishman, and the Kostaina was alone.

'Time to go home,' she thought.

And she walked up the hill, through the place she used to call the Solitudes, grieving for Yannakis.

Last
Impressions

'OF COURSE I loved you,' Peter Barton said to his wife, whose frail body lay where he had propped it on her side of the bed. 'I treated you badly, I admit. But it was beyond my control. This place changed us; it changes every one. Even the strongest ties are corroded, you know that; and ours were not so strong.'

He stood with his back to her at the window, drinking from the glass in his hand. The night wind breathed through the imperfect sashes into his hair, which was thin now and wispy.

'I'll say it to Alice when she comes, and to Dr Jenkins too, why not. He has been a friend, he ought to know. "You must take account of this place," I'll say; "you must remember the flimsiness of human arrangements when the winter comes, and you are together day after day with a person whom you once chose as your lifelong companion. I am an active man"' – and here Peter Barton raised his voice in emphasis – '"an adventurer. I wanted to be the leader. I wanted the settlement to depend completely on me. I was galvanised by this ambition. When we first came here I would run out of the house in the morning full of joy, throwing up fistfuls of pebbles at the gannets. To me they were birds of paradise, and their voices were the voices of angels. But to her their cries were foreign and repulsive; so were the skies in which they hovered and the cliffs where they bred. She disliked the smell of usefulness which I collected from the docks and farms. She disliked the smell of action, of the old giving way to the new and the new to its newer substitute. The sacks of seed and cement, the barrels of oil, the bundles of twine and packthread, the objects like kettles and clothes pegs, ugly in isolation, but beautiful as they piled them on the shore in heaps, so clean and perfect and identical. She never knew why I liked myself then. For her," I'll say, "it was just another triumph of the commonplace, another reason for losing herself in books, for weighing silently the words which she would not speak." Oh yes Margaret,' he added, lowering his voice again, 'you have been a close friend of words. You turned them over in your mind, sorting the good from the bad, preserving those which touched you and copying them into notebooks. You handled words carefully, secretly, anxious that I shouldn't touch them with my fat merchant's hands. Words passed through you, from book to book, without so much as disturbing the air. And then, when Alice grew up and away, the silence took on another quality. It was as though you had finally taken wing: as though only your body remained, and I alone had the responsibility of maintaining it. My energies declined, I was not what I had been. I couldn't believe in myself. Everything became wrapped in silence, and I began to be afraid. I hesitated to put down my fork at dinner, lest the noise remind me of silence. I began to seem unreal . . .'

Out on the hill he could discern a flashlight, as it played over the backs of sheep in a pen. Soon the night wind would bring cloud from the sea, and Dr Jenkins would have to swing southwards over the valley, avoiding the air-current above Frobel's Creek. Peter Barton listened for a moment, fancying he heard already the sound of the helicopter. Then he glanced round at his wife, who lay still on the pillow, her grey hair fallen on to her forehead, her lips pale and motionless, her hands hidden beneath the counterpane. It seemed to him that she could not take long to die, that already her body was becoming light and insubstantial, with the dry transparency of a chrysalis from which the moth has flown.

He drank again from the glass. The whisky, fiery at first, died quickly inside him, leaving a taste of ashes. He watched her for a moment, and in his thoughts he begged her to speak.

To know that she had attempted to say something, had felt some obligation to acknowledge him, to respond to him, to console him, even to accuse him – to know this would be a gain over adversity. She did not move. He wondered why the wind, which troubled the tassels of her dressing-gown, did not lift her hair. She seemed to be made of some fibrous stuff that resisted every motion.

'Of course I loved you,' he began again. 'I was proud of you. I shall show them how much I appreciated you. Your writing, your music, your observations of this place – they are part of me. Even if I did not seem to understand you, I needed you. I was incomplete without you, for all that you despised my operatic character.' Peter Barton paused to contemplate with a small thrill of pleasure the word which had occurred to him: it seemed to give dignity to his helplessness. 'Operatic': it would appeal to her, this word which had no connection with the settlement or the rites of daily survival, a word to be used in cities and country houses, so as to convey the luxury of full redundant choice. It seemed to measure their difference, and also strangely to demonstrate his rough self-sufficiency.

'When you're in hospital you'll see how well I can behave. I know you don't expect me to give up drinking. You don't think I'm capable of that. But I shall show that I am. Capable of that, and of many things. I shall be over every week. I shall bring you the best of everything, operatic basketfuls of delicacies – turtle jelly, gull's eggs, pigeon pasties, refined literature, gentle gossip. Every sort of reassurance, a kind of moral Fortnum's. I shall show you how much I need you to be well, how much I believe in you. Alice too will be kind to us, I know. You should have called, she'll say, you should have given me the chance to look after her. She's a capable girl, Jenkins said so himself, and of course he doesn't credit her story about the breakdown. She's on her way home already; he's bringing her over. We'll look after you, you'll see.'

The wind rose and rattled the panes of the window. Peter Barton looked up and saw the lights of the settlement begin to flicker as the trees on the hill swayed in darkness. He thought that one of the lights also moved: perhaps it was the helicopter, hovering over the strip by Weber's farm. He felt vexation that help should come so soon, just as he was beginning to speak to her. He looked towards the bed. Only her eyes revealed the ounce of life in her. They were clouded with tears of pain. It had been eery at first, finding her motionless beside him. Margaret was a creature of routine; in the mornings she would be sitting at her desk in the conservatory. He would expect to wake alone, muddled perhaps by a hangover, but already busy with his solitary speculations. Finding her he felt a kind of bitterness; she had removed the moment which was his, the moment that he devoted to his projects. Angrily he gripped her arm: the flesh was cold and malleable, like meat. He was certain at once that she would die. He did not believe her to be capable of half-measures. She had set her heart on dying, and the thought of this, and of all her other obstinacies, filled him at first with a pitying disgust.

The bottle stood on the floor of the landing, beside the linen press that she had brought from home. He went out to fill his glass, and then leaned over the banister, staring down into the hall. The light shone in the porch, as a signal to Alice that she should bring Dr Jenkins in. Peter Barton did not believe that his daughter had suffered a breakdown in London. He did not believe that the look of pain and bitterness with which she had left were really meant for him or Margaret. Her letters home had been regular, solemn, dutiful. But he knew from her stories — a collection of which had been published by an Edinburgh firm — how strongly the settlement had affected her. One of the strangest told of Mrs Swale, a drunken store-keeper of an outlying hamlet, whose son had joined the paratroopers. It told of isolation, of a love between mother and son that gradually turned to suspicion, to loathing, and finally to an obsessive need to negate each other's existence. To the son the settlement represented all that was hateful in his mother — her pinched isolation, her rough survivor's attitudes, her drunkenness, melancholy, and the far-fetched belief that, belonging to such a place, she was somehow doing good. Peter Barton had been impressed by the death of Mrs Swale. One day she received a packet from Northern Ireland, its brown paper cover torn here and there to reveal a gold tinsel wrapping. It was a birthday present. She hesitated to open it, fearing it as a sign of her son's estrangement. Then, after a few drinks, she understood his purpose, and furiously, almost joyfully, tore open the packet where she was sitting on the steps of her shop. The explosion blew her face away, and sent her right arm flying on to the roof of the neighbouring farm. There it remained for some hours, its chewed-up end leaking blood over the tiles, and its open palm turned helplessly towards the heavens. Peter Barton wondered at his daughter's imagination.

'It's quite untrue about the breakdown,' he shouted. 'Dr Jenkins had been worried; he told her to see a specialist in London. But apparently it was nothing – an imbalance of hormones. They put it right immediately. She had been going without sleep too, writing every night. It's all over now. They think her book might get a prize.' He lowered his voice and looked back into the bedroom. The bare whitewash of the walls, and the two black-framed engravings had the air of a hospital. Margaret was invisible, and only the mahogany corner of the antique bed testified to her enduring influence.

'I'll tell her how proud I am,' he said. 'Apparently she writes to Dr Jenkins. He sends her clippings from the newspaper, and little items of gossip. I suppose he told her about Mrs Swale – only that wouldn't have been her real name.'

A noise interrupted him, like a beating of wings, and he listened. The wind soughed as it bent the branches of the maple tree. A sheep bleated somewhere on the hillside; a dog howled and then was silent. Peter Barton filled his glass, and thought of the calamity that had overtaken him. His eyes filled for a moment with tears. Everything depended upon whether Margaret would speak. He went back to the bedroom, and it seemed strange to him that she had taken her hands from beneath the counterpane and exposed them to view. They were very white and bony. The wind dropped, and through the stillness came the threshing of the helicopter, like a slow tearing of heavy cloth. They had not heard the sound for a year, and suddenly he was apprehensive. When he spoke of Dr Jenkins, it was on the strength of a friendship that had been extinguished one summer evening for a reason that had something to do with Margaret, something to do with a remark the doctor had made. Peter Barton remembered throwing down his cards and beginning to shout. He often shouted, but not usually in anger. The episode was vaguely sketched in his memory. Perhaps it had happened to someone else; perhaps it was an incident from one of Alice's stories. He inclined to the second explanation. He should assume that Jenkins was still their friend. The doctor's manner over the telephone had suggested the deepest sympathy for the fortunes of the Barton household. Peter Barton liked the word 'household', and it lingered in his mind. He thought of another that seemed to match it: 'affliction'. The words were dignified and biblical. He laid claim to them, and to the experience which they contained. He had a right to his tears. He drank from the glass and turned to her. His wife's eyes were closed now, although she was not sleeping; her features had tightened at the sound of the helicopter, and she seemed to be shrinking from an experience that she could not bear.

'No doubt Jenkins will reproach me. He will say that I drink too much, that I neglect you, that I have allowed us both to decay. He will have his theories and his maxims. And I won't reply – what could I say? Since we sold up I have been drawn like you into solitude. Drawn like a ship into a whirlpool. And you have been angry with me, I know. You expected more – or less. At any rate, you expected peace. You have always had the purer heart.'

Peter Barton wondered how they would carry Margaret, when they lifted her from the bed. He imagined that she was past walking now, and when he thought of her carefully handled like an armful of eggs, the tears rose to his eyes and brimmed over. Her death was the one thing that he had not arranged, and it seemed a great injustice that he should have no time to prepare himself.

The helicopter sound died away, and now voices were shouting over the landing strip. Margaret did not stir, but he sensed her listening. He took a book from the mantelpiece, but the words squirmed before his eyes and he could make no sense of them. The book fell from his hand on to the floor. There was a slight movement from the bed. He turned to find her looking at him with eyes that saw a stranger where he stood. He crossed to her and fell on his knees beside the bed, surprised how quickly he moved. He had not expected to be able to take her hand before she hid it again beneath the sheet. He pressed it in both of his, and looked down at his fingers, which were marbled with engine oil from the Landrover that had broken down that morning. He knew that his roughness was hurting her, and he pressed harder against the imprisoned hand, which lay crumpled and unresisting in his. Voices were downstairs, and Peter Barton began to mutter tearfully, as though in answer to them. It seemed to him that he had been in conflict all his life with her, and that Alice, the doctor, nature herself, had conspired to take Mrs Barton's part. He was overwhelmed by the extent of his misfortune, and saw himself wandering through a desert future, to which she banished him without a word.

Then a terrible blow struck him. It was as though a kick had splintered his side, and sent him reeling into orbit, beyond the reach of his earthly life. Pain invaded him; he opened his mouth, but began at once to choke on the airless vacuum in which he swirled. His limbs flailed, helpless and unresisted, and a swell of darkness shut out the last gleams of meaning which signalled to him from the receding world. Now there was only pain. He had been transubstantiated into pain. His organs tore away from each other in the effort to release themselves from pain. Everywhere within him he felt the rushing and exploding of violated flesh. His lips formed the word 'help', but no sound would issue. His lungs pumped and pumped, but air would not enter them. With a last terrible gasp his life gathered itself and rushed into his mouth. His head seemed to hit against the inside of a sphere. He was being pushed up and out of the darkness. Again and again he struck against the shell that contained him. And then at last he was free, floating in a world of light and air.

On the next bed lay Mrs Swale. They had patched her up quite nicely, and the nurse, whom he recognised after a while as Alice, smiled at the armless, faceless creature as though Mrs Swale's survival were some kind of personal triumph. In the centre of Mrs Swale's head was a small round hole, with a little worm of lip-tissue coiled around it. From this hole a thin sound emerged: a plaintive highland song that he had once taught Alice, with a refrain of 'All alone and alone-ee'. He used to sing it during their early days at the settlement, and Alice had always joined in the refrain with the quizzical expression that she wore when some new feature of their altered circumstances caused her to question life's validity. He noticed now that whenever Mrs Swale reached the refrain, Alice reassumed that old expression, and seemed to glance sideways, catching his eye. He smiled at her.

When the song was finished, Mrs Swale began her auto-biography. It was a compact affair: one husband, one son, one home, one death, one pleasure, one pain. He enjoyed the unity of Mrs Swale's existence, its immunity from outside influence. He approved too the sense of achievement and propriety with which she described the small details of her house, shop, garden and bicycle. She compared her experiences on the settlement favourably with her mother's life as a railway clerk. Not for anything would Mrs Swale have been a railway clerk. It appeared that her son had known Alice; for a while they had been engaged to be married, but Alice had doubted that her father would permit the match. Peter nodded as he listened. It really would not have been suitable, and Dr Jenkins had advised him of the dangers for Alice during her time of nervousness.

But that was all over, and it was a pleasure to see what a good nurse she made, how clean and competent her gestures had become. He began to confide to Mrs Swale his ambitions for Alice. He feared, however, that he might be tiring the patient. Mrs Swale reassured him by humming restfully as she listened. He smiled again at Alice, who renewed her quizzical look. He wished that all his life had been as simple as this.

The scene was switched off, and Peter Barton opened his eyes on the room where he had fallen. The pain had gone, and a numbness covered his body. He found that he could not move, and although words formed in his mouth, he could not speak them. Margaret stood over him, leaning on the doctor's arm. She reached out to him, but the doctor seemed to intercept her hand. They were looking at each other. And then they began to speak. Peter did not hear the words, but he saw their lips moving, Margaret's lips and the doctor's lips, lips which had surely once been joined in passion. As the hands reached under him and lifted him onto the stretcher he thought of his own body in the mortuary, lying next to Mrs Swale's shattered arm. He knew that they would pity him, that he would mean something, now that he had no words.

They buried Peter Barton on a cold autumn day, in the patch of consecrated ground that crested the North cliff. Margaret was ill and stood between her daughter and Dr Jenkins, supported on their arms. Alice's eyes were hollow, black and staring; her blotched face seemed creased in anger as she stared away from the hole into which her father's corpse descended. Mrs Barton gripped the doctor's elbow and the handful of mourners stepped rapidly backwards as she lurched towards the grave to cast her posy of autumn wildflowers. The flowers hit the ground and broke asunder, scattering on the coffin-lid and along the sticky rim of the grave.

'Easy now,' said Dr Jenkins.

Two gannets soared above them, and their staccato cries punctured the vicar's murmuring. Out at sea a tanker passed towards the dull horizon, its grey form moving in the grey of water like the shadow of a bird.

'Easy now,' the doctor repeated, and Alice looked at him long and quizzically, and then detached herself from her mother's arm. She seemed to sniff the air for a moment. And then, turning on her heel, she began to walk rapidly down the hillside, to the airstrip by Weber's farm.

The
Journey's End

I HAD NOT meant to catch that particular train. Whether it
was an effect of working late, or a consequence of the glass of
wine I had drunk on the platform, where (it being Friday) the
Western Region Brass Band was playing music of a vaguely
patriotic kind, I found myself on what must have been the
wrong platform; for, no sooner had I entered one of the
carriages that were standing there than it began to move out of
the station – a fact which considerably surprised me since I had
allowed, as was my habit, exactly four minutes before the
scheduled time of departure. My surprise was yet greater to
discover that the train was empty – or almost empty, though a
figure flitted out of sight beyond the partition. On one of the
seats, however, a little heap of luggage had been left, and for
some reason (a fact which also surprised me, for I am not of a
curious disposition, and recoil from any intrusion into matters
that do not concern me) I went up to it, with the firm intention
of discovering its owner.

The two briefcases were unlabelled, and I was about to move
on towards the seat in the far corner of the carriage which I had
mentally designated as mine, when I was struck by a curious
detail. An envelope jutted from one of the cases, the cut-off
fragments of an address legible along its protruding margin:
'ck; ns; don; re;' – 'John Rettick, 4 Clanrairde Gardens,
Huntingdon, Cambridgeshire', as I instantly completed it, for
this was my own address, and I was already sure (from the shape
and texture of the envelope, and from the sloping female hand)
that the letter was the one I had read that morning, the contents
of which had given me such cause for alarm.

I sat down opposite the two briefcases, and placed my own rather shabbier bag on the seat beside me. The train was moving fast now; and for some reason I delayed reaching across to the letter, and stared for a while from the window. The low-lying houses were giving way to a junky landscape of crumbling factories and half-demolished streets, misted over with grimy air like a sink full of yesterday's washing-up. This dismal scene was soon replaced by a muddy estuary, with banks of silt like pillows of wet satin on which a milky haze of light slid restlessly. Wreaths of dark rain-cloud hung in the sky, and in one of them a circle of paler grey, like a child's face, seemed to beg some inscrutable favour. Then came more streets of slate-grey roofs and inky crevices, the cold thin light becoming ever fainter, with pools of uncertain blue among the houses where the lights went on and off like darting fishes. At one point we sped past allotments, each with some tiny distinguishing feature – a shed, a chicken coop, a greenhouse, a clump of little trees – and all crumbling into darkness.

I saw no human figure, only a hand, bunching the nylon curtains in an upper window. I had never passed this way before. But the knowledge that I had caught the wrong train caused no concern; on the contrary, I settled into my place with a kind of grateful apathy, as though the business of living – which for some time now had been wearisome to me – had for a blissful hour or two been taken from my hands. Only the presence of the letter disturbed me, since it was a message from the world I had left behind. I would have to read it, and to live again those feelings of grief and jealousy which had been brought by that morning's post. Until then, however, I could sit alone in the carriage, feeling the soft ebb of emotion as the suburbs gave way at last to open country, and the trees and hedgerows, dusted with the last pale glints of daylight, sent through the window their never-ending promises of home. I sank back against the headrest, watched a grey spire as it journeyed peacefully along the black horizon, smiled to myself, and then closed my eyes.

Perhaps I slept; or perhaps the relief that I felt in those moments had placed me in a kind of trance. For when I opened my eyes again it was quite dark beyond the window, the lights had come on in the carriage and a man in uniform was sitting across from me, squeezed into the space between the gangway and the briefcases (which, I took special care to notice, he had not disturbed). He was looking at me with an official expression and – though his hands were clenched on the table before him, and his hips were set awkwardly to one side in order to avoid the luggage that occupied most of the seat – he clearly intended to impress me with his presence, and to take advantage of the uniform, in the collar of which his firm, middle-aged face had been set like a lamp in a socket.

At once I began to apologise.

'I'm afraid I don't have a ticket,' I said. 'Or rather, that's the funny thing, I do have a ticket, but for the wrong train. I have no idea how I managed to end up on this one, but there it is. Of course, I'll pay whatever is necessary; though, come to think of it, I may have only a few pounds left, perhaps not enough to take me to the next station, the name of which I do not in fact know, although no doubt you will be so kind as to inform me . . .'

The man watched me steadily, with the air of someone who has heard many such tales, and who is not in the habit of believing them. Except for a small tic in the corner of his right eye – a gesture which might have been part of his official duties, so detached did it seem from any outward provocation – his face was as plain and changeless as a notice board. Clearly he had been a long time in the service of the Railways, for his uniform was shiny with use, and the braid had come unstitched at the shoulders, where it had been roughly repaired with yellow cotton.

I reached into my jacket for money and, finding none, began to search through my pockets one by one. It seemed politic to explain my circumstances more fully to the official and, as I dredged up the few coins that remained from a day of average dissipation, I recounted the story of my mistake, beginning with the patriotic music, and expressing (in terms which were, perhaps, a trifle exaggerated) my warm appreciation of the Western Region for putting itself out to entertain its customers in so public-spirited a way. I emphasised the similarity – the near indiscernibility – of modern railway trains (a fact which, as a lover of the older models, I had often regretted), and mentioned the strange darkness which (I only then recalled) had hung about the platform as I boarded. I even entertained the idea of referring to the glass of wine, but thought better of it, deterred in part by the impassive rectitude of his expression, and in part by the thought (which I noticed even then was far from characteristic of me) that, as a minor railway official, with few occasions for luxury, and forced, indeed, to maintain a regime of official dignity on a budget which barely covered his day-to-day expenses, and which could not be stretched even to the cost of a decent second-hand uniform (although, on reflection, his uniform almost certainly *was* second-hand, and had about it more the character of a Central European municipal band than a branch of British Railways) he would not welcome any suggestion that I lived more easily than he. Instead, focusing on the fan of wrinkles which radiated from the bridge of his nose, I mused aloud on the curious darkness of the platform, and was struck by a remarkable circumstance. It had been broad daylight when I bought my ticket, just ten minutes before my train was due to depart. Yet the platform had been dark, and the dusk outside the window had been rapidly replaced by a dark winter's night heavy with foreboding and wholly out of character with the summer day which had ended for me in that superfluous, but agreeable, glass of wine.

It seemed to me very important to find the causes of this transformation and, as I related it, encountering no response from the Inspector (as I assumed he must be) other than the monotonous ticking of flesh around his stagnant yellow eye, I began to speak more excitedly, became a trifle flustered, even indignant after a fashion, although not so indignant as to raise my voice except by a barely discernible fraction – which was more in order to emphasise my right to an explanation than to accuse anyone in particular of putting me in the way of needing one.

'I am not saying that you personally know anything about it,' I hastened to assure him. 'I am sure that the explanation, which doubtless exists in some wholly persuasive version to be released to the public at the appropriate moment in the appropriate style, is not made available to officers of your rank (not that your rank is inferior, you understand, but that your duties lie in quite another sphere). Nevertheless you will certainly be able to advise me what I should do by way of lodging a complaint and perhaps petitioning, in due course, for the money that I shall have to waste in buying a ticket for this unwanted journey. Indeed, I do not even know that I can afford it.'

Without warning he unfolded his hands and laid them flat on the table. It was a gesture that my father had been in the habit of using when – as frequently happened – he announced to the family that he was leaving for good and that nothing more could be expected from him.

'We should like you to get off at the next station,' he said.

His voice was low, even and expressionless, and he looked slightly to one side of me, as though to imply that he took no responsibility for the words he uttered.

'Of course,' I replied, subsiding obediently, 'that's what I intended.'

'Arrangements have been made to receive you,' he continued. 'You are to proceed immediately to the ticket office, where you will be met.'

'You mean I am being arrested?'

He turned his eyes upon me slowly, and with an expression of vague distaste.

'You misunderstand me, as they all do. I merely said that arrangements have been made for your reception. You will find them adequate – perfectly adequate.'

And he folded his hands again, slotting the fingers together, and placing his wrists upon the table.

'Am I to assume that – on account of what is, after all, a minor misdemeanour, and indeed something more in the nature of a mistake than a deliberate violation of your most sensible regulations – I am to be subject to some kind of interrogation, to be compelled not merely to descend from the train (something I was quite prepared to do in any case, and which is indeed only right and proper in the circumstances) but to appear instantly before some committee of enquiry, if that is what it is, in order that my really quite innocent behaviour should be subject to examination?'

'We are not in the habit of passing judgement,' he retorted, 'and you are quite at liberty, should you prefer, to stay on the train until its destination.'

Who did he mean by 'we', and why did he refer to a habit of judgement? Who was he, to lay down liberties and concessions in this legalistic manner? And what was the significance of the choice he offered me? These and many other questions passed rapidly before my mind as I studied his expression; but I found, in his glancing, enigmatic look, no hint of an answer to them, and contented myself at last with a simpler and, as I imagined, less dangerous enquiry.

'And where is the final destination of this train?'

'That has not been decided,' was his calm reply.

'What do you mean?' I asked in alarm. 'Surely a train must have a fixed destination? It would be most irregular to invite passengers to travel to a place that has not been disclosed.'

And a chilling image came to my mind, of those transports shuffling through the night of Europe.

'Irregular, yes; and extremely rare. It happens to each of our passengers only once.'

'In which case, you can hardly regard me as a miscreant,' I said, trying to disguise the note of urgency in my voice. 'Your failure to specify a destination surely releases me from any obligation to pay you for taking me there.'

'That is correct. You have no such obligation.'

'Then what is the purpose of the reception committee that you have promised?'

'Oh, "committee" is the wrong word. For each of our passengers we make different arrangements. Some indeed are met by a committee – but they are the exceptions. More often it is a matter of two or three interested people, perhaps only one, or even none at all – a notice board, for instance, on which a message has been pinned.'

'And in my case?' I asked in astonishment.

'That is not for me to decide. I am here merely to invite you to descend, should you be so inclined, at the next station. Now, if you will excuse me . . .'

Already he had risen to his feet, and was smoothing with weary hands the shining thighs of his trousers. I made to speak, thought better of it, and turned my attention instead to the letter, which lay just within reach across the table. All of a sudden I was impatient for him to leave, so that I could lay hold of the letter unobserved and satisfy my curiosity. Indeed, so eager did I instantly become that I experienced growing irritation with the man, as he stood in the gangway, making vague and insubstantial gestures, his right eye twitching spasmodically and his feet – encased, I noticed, in dirty shoes a size too large for them – shuffling without the slightest sign of progress on the rubber mat. I cleared my throat, shot a penetrating look in his direction, and eventually surprised myself by banging my fist on the table while muttering obscure imprecations beneath my breath.

He looked at me once more, a faint tinge of melancholy in his eye.

'Yes,' he said, 'they all do that.'

With which he at last went on his way. The door of the partition shut behind him; unable to contain my eagerness I gave a sharp tug at the exposed corner of the letter. It came away in my hand, while the briefcase, under the force of my over-violent gesture, fell beneath the table onto the shuddering floor of the carriage and burst open, releasing over my feet a cascade of letters, each written in the same familiar female hand. The one that I clutched was addressed to Alfred Black, The Ferns, Copleston, Wiltshire, and a wave of disappointment, verging almost on grief, overcame me. Notwithstanding the fact that the letter belonged to a stranger, however, and with only a nominal feeling of compunction, I pulled the paper from its envelope and began anxiously to scan the lines. My hands trembled, and a rush of jealousy stopped my breath.

Dear Alfred, [I read] *How nice to receive your letter, and to know that you are so happy in your work. It won't be long before we are together. I have arranged everything with Dad, and we can be married on Easter Saturday. I wanted to come over to tell you last Wednesday, it was such a glorious day, the first touch of spring and such a blue sky, with the birds singing for all they're worth, and I began to think how really it's not so far and Dad can drive me to the station in Oxford. Besides I had found the most wonderful little blackbird's egg that must have fallen from the nest into some soft grass, all blue and smooth like finest porcelain, and it seemed the perfect present for you, a pledge of the future. Except of course you would have been that taken aback seeing me in the midst of those so very important things you do, writing those so very important articles and making those so very important phone calls to those so very important people, and I thought, why brave his irritation, when there will be so many occasions to get on his nerves after Easter? Which led to me sitting down again with that impossibly difficult book you gave me to read about St Augustine, so as to get used to another way that I was doomed to discontent you.*

By the way, Dad says how I showed the greatest perspicacity (his word) in (a) not marrying Henry (as though I could even have looked at Henry after you came on the scene), (b) not having an affair with John (who is not the marrying type), (c) not setting my sights on a country house or a large industrial fortune (which is, of course, where his sights were set), (d) not marrying you at once, but waiting till Easter Saturday. Sometimes I think I won't be able to wait that long; but then I remember your way of looking at me with that grin on your face, wagging your bony finger and saying 'Patience little girl!', and I feel ashamed for my weakness and for not being responsible as you want me to be. Then I think how right it is to make everyone accept our marriage, despite you being so much older than me and despite all those things that Dad calls complications and I call excitement. Then I feel a calm strength inside me, and know that I shall always, always love you whatever happens and from the bottom of my heart, and that these little delays serve only to strengthen the bond between us. So put that in your smoke and pipe it –

Your loving Elizabeth.

P.S. I do love you so much.

I sifted through the letters, each written in the same commonplace style, a narrative of love, marriage and bereavement, seen through the eyes of Elizabeth Parker – the Elizabeth who had not married Alfred Black at all, nor ever heard of him, but who had attached herself to me (who am not the marrying type), suffered torments of jealousy, and finally consoled herself, as she had written to me that morning, in the arms of a younger and more satisfying man.

A stupor of remorse came over me. In all those quarrels, in all that savagery between us, it had never occurred to me that Elizabeth was capable of happiness. I had always imagined – for it flattered my vanity – that her passions were too complex and intellectual to be easily requited. She asked of me, I said to myself, more than I could give, more than could decently be asked for. I recalled our evenings, at the theatre, at the opera, at dinner parties, as she, hungry for stimulation, goaded me constantly towards opinions that I did not have, and could not even conceive with the clarity she demanded. I visualised her pale anxious face, her sensuous mouth, her impatient breathing, her manner of holding forth, slightly closing her big beautiful eyes as she began to talk, as though recreating an image of her interlocutor across the barrier of a stupid question.

I recalled the way in which she threw back the hair from her forehead, and her habit of rolling round her tongue in irony, faintly smacking it against her palate. And even these distressing characteristics appeared to me as further signs of Elizabeth's innocence, techniques whereby, worn out as she was with the effort of loving me, she tried to make it known that she was still hoping for my unconditional affection, that she had not despaired of my heart, even though I made no lasting sign to her, my confidences being but the quick white foam on waves of selfishness.

Setting Elizabeth in the world of Alfred Black I rediscovered her — not her soul only, but her body too: her creamy skin, brown eyes, eggshell brow and petal-soft ears — those things which might have been, which had been mine and which were signs that she could be loved and treasured.

I sat limp and exhausted against the window, the letters scattered over my feet. It was pitch dark outside, not a light glimmered in the countryside, and darkness settled too in my thoughts. Then again in that darkness came a lighter circle, a faint twilight of the spirit — the face of a child as it babbled on the moist verge of language, wanting to be heard. It was Elizabeth's child, Alfred's child, the child which (as I learned from the letters) had inexplicably died.

The train began to shudder and the lights dimmed in the carriage. We were slowing down, and a squeal of brakes jarred against my eardrums. I cast about me for a fellow passenger in whom I could confide. Rising to my feet I set off down the corridor, consumed by an anxious desire for human company. Carriage after carriage was empty, and in each of them the same dead light, which seemed to emanate from nowhere and to cast no shadow.

I searched the whole length of the train, and found not a soul. Even the Inspector had vanished and although, at one point, I came across a glass, half-full of liquid, and resting on one of the tables, there was no sign of the person who had been drinking from it. Besides, I noticed, the glass was mine, one of a set of

Edwardian rummers with wheat-patterned engravings, which Elizabeth had given me for Christmas three years before.

The train had slowed almost to a standstill when I came across a door, set into the space between two neighbouring compartments, but suggesting a private room, an office perhaps, reserved for some administrative purpose. I beat upon this door, shouting for attention, and behaving in my despair quite shamefully. My protests and lamentations met with no response, which hardly surprised me, and I was on the point of turning away when, accidentally touching a handle which for some reason had escaped my notice, I found that the door was not locked at all, and that by pressing against it I could gain access to that secret space which offered a last flimsy hope of consolation.

Sitting at a desk, writing in a large leather-bound ledger (the very ledger that I had bought last year in the intention – as yet unfulfilled – of keeping a diary) was the Inspector, who looked up wearily as I entered and laid down his pen. The room was warm, cosy, with an armchair, a shelf of old books, and a portrait of a man in uniform – some Railway dignitary perhaps – framed upon the wall above the Inspector.

'I wonder why you people make such a fuss,' he said, with a sigh; 'you make it impossible for us to carry out our duties and in no way improve your position. The train cannot enter the station while you are endeavouring – fruitlessly, I may add – to draw me into conversation. And who knows what might happen during these precious minutes that we are obliged to wait?'

So saying he pressed a button, which must have sent a sign to the driver, for the train came to a sudden halt, with a jar that sent me flying against the panels of the partition. The Inspector remained entirely motionless, as though he were not, as I was, a prisoner of the train's movement. He closed the ledger and placed it in one of the drawers of his desk.

'Now, if you'll kindly return to your seat, we can continue into the station.'

'But first you must answer some questions. For how can I

know whether to descend or not, in my present state of ignorance? For instance, what is the name of this station we are about to reach?'

'The name? That is not decided in advance. At this point names are no longer arbitrary. But who knows what will seem appropriate in retrospect?'

This response struck me as so bizarre that for a moment I was speechless, staring at the Inspector as he seemed to listen for a distant sound.

Suddenly he said, 'ah!', and for the first time a ghost of some emotion passed across his features. 'The other train is leaving.'

'What other train?'

'Please return to your seat,' he said, 'or we shall miss every connection.'

There was a roar and a clatter, as a train without lights, more sensed than seen in the darkness, hurtled past the window.

'Tell me at least one thing,' I persisted. 'Why must I return to my seat before the train can enter the station?'

'The seat was assigned to you, and the driver must ensure that your carriage stands by the platform. Lest you should decide,' the Inspector continued wearily, 'to get off.'

'Is the platform so small?'

'It is as large as is necessary. But, you understand, there are difficulties of adjustment. Not every passenger is given the opportunity to descend. Moreover the train is sometimes less full than today.'

'*Less* full?'

'I must ask you to return to your seat. This delay is intolerable.'

As though to emphasise the passage of time, the Inspector took a match from his pocket and began to apply it to his teeth, which were ill-cared-for and yellow with grime.

'Well,' I said sarcastically, 'if the train is so full, you must be very busy.'

'Please don't be concerned for my sake,' he replied, with a

note of annoyance. 'I have only you to look after. We are never assigned to more than one passenger.'

With that he got up from his seat, with a rapidity that greatly surprised me, for his movements until then had been awkward and fatigued. He pushed me backwards with one hand, seized the door with the other and shut it quickly in my face. A key turned in the lock. There was nothing to do but to return to my carriage.

No sooner had I regained my seat than the train jerked forward, moved a few hundred yards, and then stopped again. From the window I saw an empty platform, illuminated by a single old-fashioned gas lamp. Quite suddenly my mind was made up. I must get off. There was not a moment to lose. I seized my bag, rushed to the nearest door and, even as I opened it, felt the train begin to move – not slowly, but rapidly and with an almost wilful determination. I fell on to the platform.

Looking round, I saw to my amazement that the carriage was full of people, crowding into the windows, their eyes wide with astonishment as they caught sight of me crouching on the tarmac. I watched the train recede, its orange lights snaking through the darkness until, quite suddenly, it vanished, as though snatched by a giant hand.

There was only one building on the platform: a small shack with a sloping roof and vaguely gothic windows. Even in the last century this would not have been an important stop; nor was there a sign to show its name. Yet it had not been entirely abandoned, for a light was shining from the open door of the shack. I breathed deeply and anxiously the chill night air: an air of winter, lifeless and depleted, which scoured my lungs. Who was here to receive me? Who was to conduct my trial – for that it was a question of a trial I did not doubt?

There was no one. The shack was bare, save for a notice board, above which a single unshaded bulb was shining. A message had been pinned to the board, and I once more recognised her writing – though hasty this time and infirm, as though shaken by some great anxiety.

'*Dearest,*' it said, '*I waited for you. But your train was delayed and mine was leaving. Your E.*'

Somewhere in the distance sounded the mocking hoot of an owl. It was the end of my journey.

The Seminar:
A Story

'I F YOU were to look for Czechoslovakia on the map it would suffice to place your finger precisely in the middle of Europe; it is there.' Thus wrote Karel Čapek, as the allied powers prepared to offer this little country, so rich in industry, religion, science and culture, so conscious of itself as the place where the tremors of European history begin (the epicentre alike of Empire, Reformation, Counter-Reformation and national revival), so proud of its new-found independence, its makeshift unity, and its ancient languages, in which consonants grind like the gears of some wonderful engine, milling sense into sound – to offer all this to Adolf Hitler. Some years after Čapek's died of a broken heart, the Czechs and Slovaks were given to the laughing Stalin, and the cry was raised again: we are the heart of Europe; if you betray us, you betray yourselves! In 1948, when the communists seized power, in 1950, when the purges began, in 1968, as the tanks invaded, and in 1977, when the dissidents issued their Charter; again and again came the cry: do not forget us, for we are you! And again and again the Czechs and Slovaks were forgotten. For European time moves always forward and who had time for a place where time stood still?

The stillness of Czechoslovakia, however, had a special quality. It was not the stillness of peace, nor the repose of age, nor the motionless collapse of sheer exhaustion. It was a sense of stagnant impermanence – of temporary arrangements which had never achieved the status of finality, but which instead had been left in place, slowly decaying until relieved by the next repair. Such was the impression that greeted the visitor, as he bumped in the bus towards the metropolis, beside crumbling buildings propped by rusting scaffolding, past improvised workers' flats of greenish cement, pressed together like blocks of dirty ice-cream, beneath decaying metal slogans in plain red lettering, and by grey concrete shops, where nothing could be seen in the windows save a few bleached tins, a red poster of Lenin, or yellow slabs of some waxy substance that might have been soap or butter, plasticine or cheese.

It is not in a bus, however, that you are to visit this vanished world. An angel will take charge of you, a messenger from other spheres. For this little corner of Bohemia is full of symbols, and angels make frequent didactic use of it. If, in the angelic orders, the great messages are debated, and their earthly illustrations compared, Bohemia will certainly be known there, as the place where one particular truth finds its sublunar parable: the truth about truth itself.

It is in the suburbs that your angel sets you down. Everything here seems dumped and abandoned: scraps of park, broken pavements, shattered piping, spoiled masonry, and the un-finished towers in which the proletariat – invention and victim of the philosophy that worships it – endures the chill of socialist equality. Here stands a tower of ashen blocks, roughly glued with rococo dollops of concrete. The building has been left unrendered, and stands twelve stories high in a sea of dried mud. Its girders, pipework and wiring; its stairwells, gas mains, and even the mechanism of its lifts (which have already ceased to function), are all exposed to view. People are living here; drably coloured washing hangs lifeless on the balconies, and children in moonsuits play in the caterpillar ruts and along the pitted walkways. A young woman stands on a balcony, her hands on her hips. Her face is broad, slavonic, with wide-set eyes, high cheeks, accented eyebrows, and fair flowing hair. A refined melancholy in her posture attracts your gaze; you wonder what accident of fortune could have brought so lovely a creature into so dreary a nest. And then her eyes meet yours with that peculiar beseeching light, that hatred mixed with mute apology, which lies in the eye and the soul of the informer. You

will see this look again, many times; for one adult in every five
has been recruited. Falsehood is the lifeblood of this society. It
flows over all things, through every institution and every heart.
People add their power to it, sometimes willingly, more often
not; sometimes from anger or resentment, more often from
love: to secure education for a child, medicine for a parent or
food and clothing for a crippled spouse.

And whence did this blight of treason come? Perhaps the
answer lies in the words of Karel Čapek. For Czechoslovakia is
the centre of Europe only if the boundary of Europe lies along
the Urals, and therefore only if the hordes which time and again
have swept the valleys of Lithuania, the pastures of the
Ukraine, and the plains of Poland; which have threatened the
crowns of Norway and Sweden, chewed off the tails of Finland
and Romania, and stood for centuries at the gates of Hungary
and Moravia, awaiting the collapse of Habsburg power – only
if these hordes, which once enticed the awakening peoples of
Central Europe, from the Balkans to the Baltic, with the vision
of a pan-Slavic unity, are fellow Europeans, whose imperial
ambitions offer no challenge to the religion, law, and custom of
our continent. Perhaps that is it: the Russian soul, against which
Palacký and Masaryk sounded their solemn warnings; the
Russian soul, with its ear cocked to the infinite, hearing
nothing, and believing in the Nothing that it hears; the soul of
Dostoevsky, crying 'if I must choose between Christ and truth,
then it is Christ that I shall choose'; and the soul of his
successors, who exchanged Christ for another god, and one of
their own devising.

It is a possible theory, and suitably Slavonic in its exorbi-
tance. No god however, not even the god of Marx and Lenin, is
honoured in this world of slogans. The lies are everywhere,
shameless, blatant, intended for disbelief. They spread in
hitched parabolas beneath the eaves, hang from the parapets of
bridges and walkways, and wrap themselves around the plinths
of concrete monuments on which square-jawed workers thrust
their way into the future with muscular outstretched arms.

Sometimes the script is white on a red background, sometimes red on white; always the letters are plain, straight, like ranks of unblinking soldiers. The people pass them without noticing – indeed, they seem to notice nothing at all, their heads fixed and expressionless like the grills of motor-cars, as they walk with the same unhurried and somehow obstinate pace, grasping shopping bags of frayed plastic like children gripping toys, and coming to rest at last in silent queues. Above them, around them, and to every side the banners wave: 'Long Live our Friendship with the Soviet Union!'; 'The Programme of the Party is the Programme of the People!'; 'Forward with the Party to a Socialist Future!' . . . Progress, peace, work, nation: potent words; but they seem to be intended in some special sense – and none more so than the little word *mír*, which in Russian means village, peace and even world itself, and which in Czech means only peace. *'Boj za mír!'* Fight for peace! Struggle for peace! Forward to peace! – and behind the word 'peace' there creeps another message, a message of war and suffering, and of battles that must still be fought. These slogans, written in the language of aspiration, are really threats, like the *Arbeit macht frei* above the gate of Auschwitz.

The angel sets you down again in Smíchov. A long cobbled street dips into a valley and then rises again to a little summit. Here stands a battered oval church, like a snuffbox, its twin towers topped with rust-red onion domes. The street is lined by maple trees, their leaves golden with the approach of autumn; the sun, as it slants through them onto the street, darts and twinkles like a girl teasing a sleeping lover with a straw. Behind the trees stand large square *Jugendstil* houses, once proud and prosperous in their *embonpoint*. Long wafers of stucco have now slid away from them, revealing flesh-pink brick and iron girders. Some of the walls are inscribed with verses in a *staročeské* hand; others bear large flat women in burnt sienna and eau-de-nil, whose long robes wrap themselves about the doors and windows in dreaming arabesques, and whose broad faces blankly stare from beneath the eaves. Nothing moves save the faintly rustling maple trees. The houses seem empty, shedding autumnal stucco, and on the rise the little church stands bolted and barred, as though its work is finished and nothing remains for it but to await the end of time. Here, in this still backwater, stands the grave of Europe – rococo and *Jugendstil* faces thinly plastered over rough cores of brick, a theatrical mock-up, where throngs of people once bounced their voices off resounding curves and cheered each other on in make-believe. Here, frozen in its final posture, the old order lies beneath a dancing sun. Sometimes, however, that old order is visited again, for there is a crypt beneath the little church, and someone has a key to it, someone with nothing but his life to lose.

The angel takes you to the hilltop and downwards into Prague. The road is wide now, and little stubby cars slip sideways over the tram-rails. The wheel of a tram sends out a metallic squeal, and its clanging bell disappears into the throng of traffic. The castle of Hradčaný appears, its white walls wrapping the green-capped top-knots of St Vitus like a crown. Domes and campaniles crowd into the bowl of the Little Town, and behind them, in every shade of gold and crimson brown, an orchard stretches on the hillside, towards the twin-towered monastery of Strahov. Each building embraces its neighbour, gable touching gable, curlicue wrapped in curlicue, roof sloping into roof. Cornices and string courses shoot sideways, rush together like laughing streams, and lose themselves in foreign window-sills. Turrets and pediments poke above the clutter, and here and there the plastered wall of a palace abruptly severs the street. The cone-capped towers of gates and bridges, the spikes of onion-domes, the gesticulating statues on the parapets, barely arrested in the architectural whirlwind, like flimsy pinnacles on a surging sea of stucco – this gaiety of form and detail throws into relief the slow figures beneath it, and the anxious unseeing eyes, which pass each other without a smile. But now you are crossing the river: the green and foam-flecked Vltava, where a few men fish from stationary boats, and fat white seagulls bob beneath the bridges. The crowds are thinner along the waterfront, and hug the perimeter of a large grim square, where two armed men guard a metal hoarding: 'With the people of the Soviet Union, towards a peaceful world!' Nearby stands another figure, as stiff, lonely and conspicuous as the uniformed guards. He seems helplessly to smile on passers-by, raises his eyes to other faces, intercepts those blank unseeing glances, and preserves, in his wrinkled but still youthful features, a memory of life and conversation. He is tall, slightly bent, dressed in jeans and donkey jacket, but with a tie of sorts and an unkempt Habsburg beard. His hands are large, with long elegant fingers, and in one of them he holds a book – old, thick, and bound in leather. He seems like a visitor from another world, a world where people speak and grieve and hope, a world where thinking, doing, living all have a purpose, a world in which, as a Czech philosopher once expressed it, borrowing words from Plato, the work of the *polis* is to care for the soul. His casual clothes and beard are signs of rebellion: but his gentle face hints at a deeper separation from the grim reality than sanity strictly requires. Perhaps he is a poet or a dreamer. Perhaps he is slightly mad. Or perhaps he is a character from an opera, the hero of some *Tales of Hoffman*, cast in the crazy realm of communist stagnation.

This character – Jan Zelený we shall call him – stays in your memory. In him you see a tragi-comedy – a play of false emotions, which drift on the air of the city searching for the human forms that will incarnate them. This tragi-comedy can be breathed in the smell of Prague – the smell of coal, on which whiffs of electric ozone and the sad salt odour of boiling cabbage trace their lingering afterthoughts. It lurks in passageways and in those long tunnels of wooden scaffolding, old in places and water-logged, which protect the passer-by from falling stucco. It snakes down on you from the slogans, stares at you from the busts of Marx and Lenin, and dances around the dull red stars which crown the buildings and decorate the grey facades. It glares severely from the symbols of progress – combine harvesters and hydroelectric dams – which are impressed on the paper currency; and it speaks to you from the window of the 'Agitation Centre' where, behind glass that has never been cleaned, in a window that has never been dusted, a sloping board of posters proclaims the socialist cause: Nazi-faced American GIs thrust their bayonets into Vietnamese babies, fat capitalists with bulging cigars crush the heads of helpless workers, and huge missiles, decorated with the stars and stripes, fly in regimented flocks over the cowering cities of Europe. Why did the angel set you down in such a place? What meaning in those dusty photographs, those potentates in grey alpaca, who sign with fat old hands the bits of paper that lie on modernist desks before them, while Marx and Lenin stare into the future from across their porcine bodies? You cannot tell. Notices have been pinned to the screen of cork behind the window: more slogans, written in a shaky hand, composed in the same impersonal syntax, and with the same impenetrable vagueness. Strange that some frail old person has taken the trouble to copy those empty words, to etch them round with exclamation marks, and to place them in this dusty shrine. *O sancta simplicitas!* Yet communism too has its pathos – the pathos of an 'agitation' that has ceased to move, that has dwindled at last into a palsied tremor. If the Agitation Centre has a meaning, it is that things here cannot change, that you are not to hope or plan or strive, that everything has been fixed eternally, and that nothing remains for each successive generation but to append its signature to the fixed and senseless decree.

The angel leads you past houses shored up with rusty scaffolding, over holes and ruts and broken paving stones. Often the path is blocked by tin barricades: sometimes arrows direct you into a courtyard or through an alleyway; sometimes the barriers are mute, resistant; and once, skirting the flank of a ruined palace, traipsing among the hunched unpeaceful figures as they follow the makeshift signs, you see again that wistful slavonic face, though younger now, fresher, more innocent. The girl's hair is dark and abundant; but her eyes are a faraway green; she carries a string bag, with books, papers and apples bulging through the mesh. Perhaps she is a student; yet there is something self-assured in her manner, as though she were already alert to the world, and aware of its complexity. She too is part of the drama, and the quick appraising glint of curiosity that briefly shines in her eye suggests a leading role. But where does she lead? You cannot say. Markéta – for so we shall call her – hurries on, but not before she has read your expression, slightly smiled with a soft *sfumato*, and expertly lowered her eyes. The angel grips your hand, and pulls you in the opposite direction.

You pass a corner where five roads meet. Here, beneath the window that once was haunted by his phthisic face, a bronze bust of Kafka is fixed to the wall. Unpublished now in his homeland, unmentionable in the official press, the hollow-eyed magus stares on the world that he foretold with tight-lipped irony. Beneath him someone has chalked 'Death to Communism', and 'Prague, the City of Josef K.' The orange stucco has been many times repainted, and the chalk marks are fresh: such cat-and-mouse games are all that remains of politics.

Nearby, across the Old Town Square, is the Tyn church, sheathed in scaffolding behind a ruined medieval school. The rusty iron crutches, reaching to the very peaks of the witch-cap towers, are dissolving faster than the building which supports them. Yet the church is beautiful, despite its iron chains – a fettered Gretchen in her prison cell. Prague too is beautiful – seductive and ungraspable as a woman, said Miloš Marten when, in 1917, he saw the city emerging unscathed from an unwilling war. The 'dirty, mournful, tragic Prague' wrote Miloš Jíranek (*O krasné Praze*, 1908) 'which, on certain evenings, in the golden light of the setting sun, attains to a fairy-tale, flaxen-haired beauty'. Always compared to a woman – mother, lover, virgin, whore – like one of those 'white camellias' which Max Švabinský painted at the turn of the century, a woman for all purposes, perpetually young like Eva Makropoulos and yet withered inside, coldly plotting her revenge on the world of human feeling. Before her, paying perpetual court, is a folly-ridden dance of intellectuals. An image comes to mind of a hall of mirrors, each mounted in a magnificent frame, but each with some distorting blemish: and through this hall a teeming crowd of poets, artists, musicians and writers presses onwards, turning and returning in a circle, and glimpsing in the mirrors their own reassembled faces, behind which stand the light-filled windows that open on to Prague. Towers, spires and parapets constantly rearrange themselves in those distorting lenses, always magical, always deceptive, and the faces frayed, bloated, temporary, like the faces of drowned men briefly floating at the surface and then carried under.

Beneath the Powder Tower you look upwards to its blackened tracery. Gothic leaf-mouldings caress the stiff classical window frames; serene gothic kings judge from the solemn thrones of the Caesars, and medieval angels sweetly play the instruments of Renaissance Prague – a diversity of styles so harmonious as to collapse all Christendom into a single thought, a germ of eternity, which has yet to sprout into time. Prague is a Christian capital, whose Archbishop, old and weary though he is, has refused to compromise, preferring a perpetually dwindling priesthood of believers to the dog-collared communists who, as members of *Pacem in Terris*, hide once again behind that suspicious little word. For what kind of peace is this, that each day sends a man or woman to jail for the old Archbishop's sake; in which to join privately for prayer, to belong secretly to a religious order, or to spread the gospel in one's place of work, are crimes more heavily punished than robbery or rape? Yet they are crimes of which half the country is guilty. This woman, for example – Eva Zelená, the wife of Jan – who walks with troubled countenance beneath the Powder Tower, and hurries down twisting cobbled streets, half-blocked by scaffolding, to the radiant church of St James, that masterwork of Panetius, where flowers of rococo glory climb on a gothic trellis to the sky.

Light fills the regiment of domes like a dance of angels, and

Eva looks up as she enters, her broad pale face milky in the lower darkness, and her blue eyes fixed like a child's. Crossing herself, she hurries to a pew near the gilded pulpit, and kneels as if in prayer. But she does not pray. Instead she reaches beneath the pew to a box that has been fixed to it, and lays hold of a crumpled paper: *Informace o církvi*, secret bulletin of the underground church. She glances over her shoulder before attending to it. Soon she is lost in her reading and does not notice the figure who enters, crosses himself and kneels for a while in prayer. Nor does she see him leave; nor does she notice him watching her, as she sits for a while in the *Jugendstil* café beside the Powder Tower, stirring her glass of Turkish coffee, and writing in her notebook those thoughts of the day which trouble her, and which she has learned to keep to herself. Only when she glances briefly upwards to the great clusters of brass and porcelain that shine their festive light on the almost empty interior, does she sense his presence. He has the shabby elegance and the unkempt hair which catch her attention; but she knows that it is Oldřich Hromádko even before she has turned her still eyes full upon him, aware of him less through sight than through a faint tremor of tenderness that seems to begin in her fingertips, and then spreads through all her body.

Eva breaks into an open smile. 'Oldra!' she cries, and 'Eva!' he responds, for he too is part of the play: though what a strange role is his, and how hard it would be for Eva, should she decide – as from time to time she has come near to deciding – to allow herself to love him! Yet in this strange world where every belief is controlled by an impersonal government, love alone seems free, and only through love can our characters make the tiny space that is theirs.

Though space for what? Perhaps Oldřich knows; Jan too has an inkling. But Eva? Eva knows nothing.

THE SEMINAR: AN OPERA

Dramatis Personae

JAN ZELENÝ, a dismissed scientist, about forty: baritone.

EVA, his wife, about thirty-five: soprano.

Their three young children, JIŘINA, KAREL, LENKA: two treble, one alto.

MARKÉTA, a pop-singer, and Jan's mistress, about twenty-five: soprano.

OLDŘICH, a well-known dissident, about forty-five: tenor.

MRS NOVÁKOVÁ, a prole: mezzo soprano.

Interrogators: bass and counter-tenor.

Chorus of Students: SATB.

Chorus of Policemen: SATB, the upper parts falsetto.

Dancers: Dr Forster, 'Margaret', 'Eva', Policeman, five students.

The action takes place in Prague, in the eighties.

Prologue

A silent theatrical prologue accompanies the overture. We see a dimly lit railway station, and a bustle of silent, anxious people. Jan is looking distractedly at the departure board: Vienna is shown, so too is Budapest; otherwise Czech and Slovak stations. Police in uniform are checking people's papers: with them are security officers in leather jackets and jeans. Jan seems unable to decide whether to take the train. Noticing the policemen, he takes some papers from his pocket and hurriedly drops them into a litter bin. The police pass him by; as soon as he has gone, however, a plain-clothes officer returns, takes the papers from the bin, leafs through them, and throws them back with a sardonic smile.

Act One

Scene 1

(Prague: the interior of a flat: run down, but many traces of Habsburg elegance and Gemütlichkeit. *On the left a door leading to a balcony; at the back another door, leading to a bedroom. To the right, separated from the main stage by a partition, which could be imaginary, or the effect of lighting, is the entrance to the flat, and next to it the door to the kitchen. For the most part the action takes place in the main room of the flat, which bears all the marks of the Central European dissident culture: arrays of books which are read only fleetingly and in moments of distraction; a gramophone, with a well-kept shelf of records; sticks of ugly furniture of a post-*Devětsil *design, contrasting with the elegant cornices, doors and window-frames; a desk with some papers arranged neatly on it; a couch, an armchair or two, and space for people to sit or crouch on the floor. A crucifix is prominent on the wall, along with one or two Christian-seeming lithographs, in the bathetic bad taste of 'catacomb' religion, and above the door, in a gesture of bravado, the motto of Jan Hus:* Pravda vitězí: *Truth prevails.*

Jan is alone at the desk. He is staring anxiously at the void, his hands clasped before him.

Music: Melancholy, ancestral, Slavonic, in the manner of Mussorgsky's 'Bydło'.)

JAN: Steps to nowhere,
  Steps I climb,
  I, a stranger in this land of mine;

  To trudge forever
  With my pack of things
  Climbing the stairs of vanished kings:

  A stumbling petitioner
  Who cannot be heard,
  Persistent, pedantic, and absurd.

(He gets up and crosses to the balcony; the music lightens, while retaining its ancestral character.)

And you, Prague,
You who cannot change
Though they destroy you utterly –
Propped in scaffolds
Like a fainting prisoner
And calling to me; always calling:

Asking me to live
Like the decent citizen
Whose habits hang in your archive;
To join myself to bitter men

Who once believed 'let truth prevail'
And knew the truth thereafter. No –
Don't ask me, or I fail . . .

(Eva enters from the kitchen, and looks sadly at Jan.)

EVA: What is it, Jan? Why
   This brooding, why these hours apart?

JAN: Not brooding, but preparing. *(Looks at watch)* Hey!
   In half an hour the seminar will start!

EVA: Oh Jan, this self-deception!

JAN *(sharply)*:   So you call
   My life in question, do you, Eva?

EVA: Oh no, Jan.

JAN: Let me finish!
   'Progress', 'Peace' and 'Victories'
   All are falsehoods, none believed.
   And yet we answer lies with lies;
   So they vanquish truth in spite
   Of us, and we're deceived.
   And if I fight
   The lie, it is myself, you say,
   That I deceive: myself
   That I deceive!

(He stares angrily at Eva, who shrinks from him.)

EVA: Oh words, Jan, always words!
   We miss you, miss your love and care!
JAN: A charming fantasy!
EVA: I should not need to charm
   My husband, nor to covet   *(duet)*
   Like a child his kiss,
   Although I love it
   So! If only you'd be warm!
JAN: Such a charming fantasy!
EVA: Do you think I mind your spoiled career?
JAN *(angrily)*: It's no career to be a slave,
   To parrot nonsense to a room
   Of apparatchiks, to close
   The minds of those who'll one day govern us.
   My place is here, not prisoned
   In a false professor's gown,
   But speaking freely in
   This seminar, where seeds of truth are sown . . .
EVA: And other seeds . . .
JAN: Again and yet again
   You mention it!
EVA: I know Jan, it was only once, only the one
   Fresh girl who flattered and who made
   A fool of you.
JAN: Why don't you understand?
EVA: I fear this thing
   Surrounding you,
   This strange enchantment . . .
JAN *(defensive)*: Listen Eva, when they sent for me that day
   To the Rector's office,
   I had no choice.
   'Stay with us and prosper,' so they said;
   'Defy us, and we'll supervise your ruin.
   We're thorough. We lift every stone;
   Wife, mother, father, child:
   We'll turn them all against you, and destroy them

In destroying you. Is it worth it?"
Well, Eva, is it worth it?
EVA: Whatever they might do
I bear . . .
JAN *(ignoring her)*: Then let us act as two,
Defending truth!
EVA: Not truth! It's you:
It's Lenka, Karel, Jiřina –
Nothing else is true!
JAN *(melodramatic)*: Eva, I have failed you, failed myself.
Plato's arduous path to things above
Is one I cannot tread; instead I delve
In shoddy mystery, and call it thought –
You're right, I cannot be what Plato taught,
So let me be content with what I have –
EVA: Oh may you be content with what you have *(duet)*
The fragile gift of love!
*(She takes a step towards him, but seeing his frozen expression
hesitates, and then quickly withdraws into the kitchen. Jan buries his
head in his hands for a moment, and then looks up as though waking
from a dream.)*
JAN: The fragile gift of love! That's not it,
That's not it at all! They told me: you are no longer
A professor, but plain Dr Zelený: the failure that
You would have been but for us. Would your poor gifts have
Earned you, in some easier place, such eminence?
Would you, in some capitalist haven – to which, by the way,
You're free to emigrate – carry the pretence of scholarship?
It is your choice, Professor. Become what you are: a nothing!
And then you, Markéta, you came to me, with that other
Gift of love!

Scene 2

(The stage revolves to reveal a park. Slogans everywhere, claiming the victory of socialism, 'Peace and Friendship', 'Forward in Brotherhood with the Soviet Union', and so on. A few people in drab Central European costume, with mournful proletarianised faces, scurry about with their foragers' shopping bags. Sometimes they exchange whispers; mostly they are eerily silent, moving along the paths like dead leaves before a breeze. The trees are bare, with a few spring blossoms just beginning. Centre left is a park bench: Jan walks towards it; another figure enters behind him, and the audience is left guessing as to whether Jan is being followed. The other figure stands until the following conversation has begun, and then disappears. Enter Markéta hurriedly.)

MARKÉTA: Dr Zelený! Dr Zelený!

JAN *(turning)*: Ah! It's . . .

MARKÉTA: Markéta.

JAN: Of course, Markéta!

(They shake hands, a slight embarrassment; troubled erotic music.)

MARKÉTA: I'm so glad I've met you in this place
  Where we can talk! So glad that I can tell you . . .

JAN: Shall we sit down?

(They sit, slightly apart, on the park bench.)

MARKÉTA: You've given me so much!
  Until I found your seminar,
  I lived as if
  I'd been conscripted to a foreign army
  And those beside me, like those I had to fight
  Were just as much my hidden enemy –
  Oh, Dr Zelený!

JAN: Yes, you are right,
  It *is* like that.

MARKÉTA: The poet says our lives are bound
  By walls, on one of which is painted – see! –
  A door, which only the foolish suicide
  Imagines he can open. Yet behind

Us is another door — turning we find
A friend who from his courage made a key!
JAN: If only I deserved your flattery!
MARKÉTA: You do Jan — Dr Zelený —
JAN: no, Jan.
MARKÉTA: You do Jan! Yes! Although I do not see
    My neighbour, although I look in empty eyes
    And find no answer to my silent plea,
    I think of you and all my songs are cries
    Of joy!
JAN *(moved):* You are a singer then?
MARKÉTA: I sing
    In nightclubs sometimes, sweet forbidden songs,
    Songs of freedom.
JAN: Such a thing
    Needs courage too.
MARKÉTA: No, I am not strong
    Like you: I'm caught between myself and me,
    A butterfly in slides of glass.
JAN: Let's hear you.
MARKÉTA: Now?
JAN: Why not? The people've gone,
    And see, the night is falling, we're alone.
(Markéta looks at him for a while, and then suddenly stands up and clears her throat to sing. The song is sentimental, sub-Beatles, with a strummed accompaniment, like the songs of the 'Plastic People of the Universe'. Jan listens in rapt admiration.)
MARKÉTA: Oh Mr Security,
    Please take your eyes off me!

    You're a cat
    And I'm a mouse
    So how can I be free?

    If I sat
    In my small house
    You'd use your master key.

Oh Mr Security
Please take your eyes off me!

I'm a mouse
And you're a louse
And still I can't be free:

I scratch and scratch
The itchy patch
And know you're biting me!

Oh Mr Security,
Please get away from me!
(She looks around shyly, and then sits down in the same place.)
JAN: That's wonderful: the Jazz soul of Bohemia!
MARKÉTA: Nonsense, Jan, it's rubbish. I'm a fool
  To sing it to you. I feel small
  Beside you. It's not jazz but such as you
  Who are our nation's soul.
  Oh Jan, you know your role –
  Be true to it: be true!   *(duet)*
JAN *(moving closer)*: I will be true, I will
  But show me how!
MARKÉTA: Come with me to Smíchov, to a crypt
  Where I have prayed for you and wept
  Amid my friends. We're open there,
  And innocent, and brave.
  At times we stage a play of miracles,
  And people come in secret to our catacomb
  To know that they are saved . . .
JAN: Markéta, this is foolish, they will hear –
MARKÉTA: And if they do? Oh Jan, I have no fear,
  So long as you will join me. We can shield
  Each other, and step firmly on the path
  That you have shown.
(She rises and extends her hand.)

JAN: Markéta, dear, I yield ⎤
  To you.   ⎥
  (He rises also, and seizes her hand.)   ⎬ *(duet)*
MARKÉTA: And I to you and all you're worth!   ⎦

(They kiss, the music rises to a climax, and, as they saunter off left, we see Eva, walking in the park: the figure who might have been following Jan earlier is now following her. She looks curiously after the couple and then, seeming to recognise them, is horror-struck and turns away. But there is doubt in her face.)

EVA *(uncertainly)*: Can it be?

(The stage at once revolves back to the time and place of Scene 1.)

Scene 3

(The flat again. Jan is awakening from his reminiscence.)

JAN: Was it Markéta I kissed that day, and so many days
  Thereafter? Or was it myself, mirrored in her admiration?
  No: I *was* strong then, and so were you my darling.
  Where are you now? Why did you disappear?
  Did Eva cause this change in you? Or was it fear
  That we had gone too far, linked our friends
  Too firmly, and endangered them and us?
  Or was it *they* who took you: let it not be so!

  But yes, I was a hero then, your drunken love
  Caused drunkenness in me, and God too shone
  In our embraces: God in whom I scarce believe
  Made real and wounded in adultery!

(The children enter from the bedroom door. As children tend to be in communist states, they are quiet and well-behaved, in a tip-toe, eery manner. They stand meekly before their father, who at last looks up.)

JAN: Karel, Jiřina, and little Lenka!

JIŘINA: We've come
  To say goodnight.

JAN: Goodnight. *(Kisses them)*

KAREL: We've learned
A song for you.
JAN: A song for me?
(The children shuffle to attention and begin to sing. The following is based on the folksong 'Veselé dievča', which Martinů sets on p. 7 of Nový Špalíček.)
CHILDREN: If I had a bright red frock
I'd be married every Sunday;
If I had a new red smock,
I'd be promised every Monday.
Every Sunday, every Monday!
JAN *(sadly)*: Every Sunday, every Monday!
To bed now children; and don't forget your prayers!
KAREL: Prayers are bad.
JAN: Who told you that?
JIŘINA: Our teacher;
She said that prayers are what the others do —
JAN: What others?
CHILDREN *(looking at each other and then reciting)*:
The enemies of the people
And of socialism!
KAREL: Are you one, Daddy?
An enemy of the people?
(Jan looks at them silently, with a sad smile, and then nods. They go off singing.)
CHILDREN: Every Sunday, every Monday!
(Exeunt.)
JAN: An enemy of the people . . .
(As Jan sits brooding, there is a soft knocking at the door, and we see Eva opening it. The students enter with gentle smiles and whispered conversation over trudging, Slavonic music as in the opening of Scene 1. The students are a mixed bunch: quiet adolescents with long hair and sandals; a few sad professors with Central European beards and waistcoats; indeterminate people in the drab, mass-produced clothing of communism, and here and there a plain-clothes priest or nun, recognisable by an air of supererogatory poverty. All

remove their shoes on entering, and are quietly deferential each to
each. Jan greets them, as the music substitutes for conversation.)
THREE STUDENTS *(coming forward)*:
    Have you heard the news? News of our Markéta?
JAN *(starting)*: What news of her?
ONE STUDENT: By the church in Olomouc,
    Rudolf saw her, leather coats
    Surrounding her. She gave no sign:
    He got away –
JAN: And she?
ANOTHER STUDENT: We must suppose
    She'd been arrested; for what, God only knows.
CHORUS *(spontaneously beginning to pray)*:
    Lord have mercy on our sister
    Help her in her hour of need;
    Fold her in the arms of Easter
    Make her faith a shining sword,
    Proof against the world's disaster
    In those hands that serve the Lord!
JAN: Proof against the world's disaster
    In those hands that serve the Lord!

    But why, Markéta, why no word?
(Jan is troubled, distracted, as the students move quietly into place
for the seminar. He seems to have little interest in the typewritten
manuscript of Schopenhauer which he takes up from the desk.
During what follows the chorus hums occasionally, broken or
whispered snatches. They too are more interested in the fact *of the*
seminar than in anything they might learn from Jan, whose mind is
elsewhere.)
JAN: Today we'll study Schopenhauer –
    I have him here in *samizdat*,
    And some of you have old editions . . .
A STUDENT: Let his meditations
    Help us to regain our own:
    All that's ours is broken, torn,

Scattered like leaves before our grasp!

CHORUS: Scattered like leaves before our grasp!

JAN *(gestures upwards to the suppositious microphone)*:
Quiet please, quiet!

(He takes a pace, flicks through the book, lets it hang by his side.)
Renunciation of the will,
Cultivation of the mind –
Must we assume that this is all
The wisdom that he left behind?

Read on . . .

(There is a sudden loud ringing of the bell – unusual since until now the students have knocked quietly, in a conspiratorial way. All are startled and look up with expressions of fear. Hastily they gather up their books and papers. Eva opens the door, and in the background we see her greeting Oldřich.)

EVE *(soaring, lyrical)*: Oh, it's you!

(Oldřich enters rapidly. He is an impressive character, self-assured, with the uncompromising, slightly self-righteous air of the hardened dissident. The students are clearly awed by him.)

OLDŘICH: Forgive me that I'm late.

JAN: Ah Oldřich! We were reading Schopenhauer.

STUDENTS: Oldřich Hromádko! In our seminar! That's great!

JAN: Shh!

OLDŘICH *(humorously)*:
Shh! Schopenhauer! What wretched stuff!
This man who never had enough
Of sorrow for his cosy appetite!
Read a page of Calderón,
And the worst things seem alright:
Study Plato, live alone,
What disaster then can harm
You, what great passion spoil your calm?

(Suddenly serious):
Well we know the world has altered:
Solitude's an open boat,

Culture nothing but a halter
Which they've set about your throat.
JAN *(embarrassed)*: Let's turn again to Schopenhauer . . .
OLDŘICH: Forgive me, what I said was premature.
(He sits down, but the students' eyes remain fixed on him as Jan
tortuously tries to formulate his thoughts.)
JAN: The question is, what harmony
Can be induced in *me* by these reflections?
How can thought compose what tyranny disposes?
My friend is right – all inner peace supposes
Outward justice, truth – and law: the source of health
In every state!
CHORUS: And whence comes law, comes
Justice?
(Oldřich jumps up again.)
OLDŘICH: I shall tell you if I may.
(Secretive): In the still reaches of the human heart
There sounds the little bell of sacrifice –
Hearken to it, make yourself a part
Of our communion – the church
Invisible of all believers, all
Who turn aside the world's temptation –
This is the source of law, obey its call
Then order grows around you and within.
CHORUS *(sympathetic)*: And order grows around us, and within.
A STUDENT: Surely not in Vilém here, the swine . . .
VILÉM: What do you mean, you salamander!
(They fight playfully.)
JAN: Quiet please, be serious!
OLDŘICH: Yes, be serious!
If Dr Zelený allows, I'll share
Some thoughts that have been troubling me.
JAN *(resentfully)*: Feel free – the students here
Admire you, and I'm curious . . .

*(It is apparent that Oldřich is the principal object of the students'
attention.)*

OLDŘICH: We who sweat instead of weeping,
 Who have no use for chill philosophy,
 Who have no love for useless tears —

 We need to brush against disaster
 So faith in us be sword and shield.
 We have no love for useless tears.

 Faith for us is lack of wisdom,
 Faith goes blind in search of truth
 Like a matcheting explorer;

 And in hand-to-hand encounter
 We give all so truth is won.
 We have no love for useless tears.

 Philosophy is dignified,
 Like a precious mausoleum.
 Quiet it is in there, and holy,

 But with a sense of life departed,
 Life departed and undone.
CHORUS: Quiet it is in there and holy,
 But life's departed, life's undone.
(excited): Let faith to us be shield and sword:
 Bring us to that last encounter,
 Where the truth is our reward.
JAN *(aside)*: This is so much empty clatter
 So much undeserved applause!
*(Jan goes to the balcony and stares out over Prague. Suddenly his
voice rings out, rising above the chorus.)*
JAN: Ah Markéta! Markéta!
 In losing you, what did I lose!
*(The scene comes abruptly to an end, and the stage revolves to
reveal:)*

Scene 4

*(The kitchen of the flat, with its door into the living room. The sound
of the chorus can still be heard, a passionate, melodious, but distant
humming. Gradually during this scene the chorus first becomes
hymn-like and then lapses by degrees into a spasmodic hum or
whisper – a 'melancholy, long, withdrawing roar', over which
Jan's voice can occasionally be heard.*

*Eva is preparing Central European canapés, from poor scraps of
food brought by the students. There is an air of poverty and carefully
husbanded resources. Eva is alone and preoccupied.)*

EVA: Oh, Jan I sense your outline, grey and dim,
   A flicker in the incandescent stream
   Which floods my heart and mind: this jealousy!

   My thoughts of you are only memories,
   Seeking you always in that vacant place
   Which love had made – pathetic fallacy! –

   Though once you sat there, dear, drab dingy thing,
   Balancing hesistant words along
   The edges of your mind;

   That was your life, the life that I had joined:
   Modest, decent, futile, sad and kind.
*(She returns to her work. A burst of humming as the door opens and
Oldřich enters. Eva looks up with a start, and stops her work.)*
EVA: You always come. I was expecting you.
OLDŘICH: Always? Yes, Eva, always. But now
   There's something on my mind.
EVA: I suppose it must be Jan.
OLDŘICH *(looks searchingly at her)*: He worries me,
   He's changed, and puts at risk
   Not him and you alone, but others too,
   Who seek him out and flatter him.
   Forgive me – I am fond of Jan,
   And that is why this posturing offends me.

EVA: I know!

OLDŘICH: You know; you've seen that glazed
  Theatrical look, that air of
  'Take this precious thought, partake of it,
  And think of me!'

EVA (*bitterly*):   'Partake of it
  And think of me!'

(*There is a silence between them, in which the humming chorus is briefly heard, and Jan's voice rising above it.*)

JAN (*off*): I would question that! Question that!

OLDŘICH: Ah well! It's his life, and
  Perhaps I have no right . . . except . . .
  I worry too for you, dear Eva.

EVA: Why for me?

OLDŘICH: You know my meaning.

(*Oldřich launches at once into a brisk aria.*)
  You know these helpless dissidents,
  Their inconstancy, their lack of sense:
  Anxiety and isolation,
  Desire for some new consolation;
  A view of home that's sentimental
  Weak, demanding, and unmeant – all
  This, and then the lack of caution
  Which swells his feelings in proportion;
  Thinking, 'Eva, wife, it's you I want,'
  He sticks his fingers in some other . . .

EVA (*screaming*):   Don't!

(*She hides her face in her hands, and Oldřich approaches her.*)

OLDŘICH: I'm sorry; but believe me,
  This life is not for you,
  And not for Jan . . .

(*He takes a crucifix from beneath his shirt and shows it to her.*)

EVA (*gasping*): You joined *them*?

OLDŘICH (*pointing upwards*):   Have a care!

EVA (*awed*): They say that Václav Bořivoj was found
  With burn-marks over half his body . . .

OLDŘICH: Václav now is happy: think of him
  And ask yourself, why flutter in a cage,
  Provoking them, and doing nothing?
  A choice now lies before you: stay with Jan
  And save him from his posturing,
  Or else . . .
EVA: What else?
OLDŘICH: Be bold. Be brave. —— Don't close
  The door; don't live as prisoned birds
  Must live: I love you, Eva, fly to me!
EVA *(stands quietly as he approaches)*: I'm married,
  And my love's not free.
OLDŘICH: True love is blessed in all its forms.
  Don't throw away this chance.
EVA: A sea
  Of dangers lies before me: yet I long
  To sail on it, to find again the land
  Of love and fortitude, where I belong.
  A boat rocks in the shallows, and a hand
  Reaches towards me with a strong desire.
  Shall I trust those flashing eyes, that face ⎤
  Which stirs me to desire?   ⎬ *(duet)*
OLDŘICH: Ah come with me! ⎦
(Their love duet reaches a climax, and then stops abruptly, as Eva, turning away, picks up the tray of canapés.)
EVA: Love what is real; the rest is fantasy!
(She goes quickly to the door, opens it, and a wave of seminar-sound rises around them, leaving Oldřich speechless, staring after her.)

Scene 5

(The living room, later in the same evening. The seminar has dissolved into groups: the canapés have been eaten, the humming has dwindled, and Jan stands apart at the window. Eva and Oldřich exchange tender glances.)

JAN *(aside)*: Markéta! Ah, come back to me!
(The music, having subsided from the end of Scene 4 to a state of weariness, suddenly picks up. The following dialogue is chanted over a percussive accompaniment.)
VILÉM *(standing up)*: Well, that's enough philosophy,
    Let's relax!
ANOTHER STUDENT: I'm with you: curse this atrophy,
    Let's lace our meditation
    With a dose of slivovitz!
ALL: A dose of slivovitz!
(Bottles emerge, and Jan looks on disapprovingly.)
JAN: Have a care! Have a care!
OLDŘICH *(singing)*: Come now Jan, a moment's relaxation –
    A melancholy demon sits
    With his talons in your hair!
JAN: You're right, my friend.
OLDŘICH: A small suggestion
    Then: a side-show, if it fits
    Your mood. It's called 'The Seminar'.
CHORUS: Let's have it! Let's have 'The Seminar'!
OLDŘICH: Some help then: Václav, Julius, Broňa
    Magdy, yes, and you, and you . . .

THE SEMINAR: A BALLET

(Dancers step from the chorus at Oldřich's behest, and sit in a row at the front of the stage. In the following 'Faust Play' they simulate puppets, in the style of Theatre on a String. *Oldřich holds invisible wires above one of the dancers, who wobbles to his feet, to take the part of Dr Forster.)*
OLDŘICH: Here's Dr Forster in his studio;
    The place is Cracow, and the time is now.
    The devil's speech he overhears –
    The speaker is himself, is what he fears.

(Dr Forster dances sadly; suddenly he stops to listen.)
   A knock: three students –
   (Oldřich lifts them with invisible wires.)

                     'We've been sent
   By M., our local chief of Solidarity,
   Who seeks philosophy, a seminar,
   To fight against the system. It's not charity
   He wants. He offers splendid terms – in short a
   Beautiful and eager Slava's daughter
   In whom you'll find *eterna femina* . . .'
(He lifts her from the ranks of students, and she begins to faun on Dr Forster.)
   While she, already lost in wonder there,
   Will soon be parted from her underwear . . .
(Titters from the audience.)
   'So will you sign the contract?'
   Yes, of course.
(The puppets dance together, and form themselves into a seminar.)
JAN *(anxiously)*: You bring the dead, the dead
   Before me, and you call this comedy?
EVA: How true to life, how clever – oh, how sad!
OLDŘICH: But listen to the hidden melody . . .
(The chorus begins to hum: perhaps the hymn with which they prayed for Markéta, or something similar which reveals their rising tension and disquiet. Oldřich sings above it.)
OLDŘICH: Secretly the heart tightens
   On its precious things;
   The unseen ghost, which frightens
   Us with iron rings

   Of darkness now is master here,
   Cancels laughter and forbids
   The ordinary mystery,
   Quickly rids

   The world of what it meant
   And quiet, intense,

Gives empty sentiment
In place of sense.

(Dr Forster dances; turns over the pages of a book; is distracted, fearful; glances always behind him, as the seminar wilts away, sharing his suspicions and seeking solitude. Only the Gretchen/ Markéta figure remains, making distant gestures of sympathy.)

And now this M. of Solidarity
Who offered lust
Must claim his wage: a parity
Of payment; dust for dust.

(The puppets now hide the Gretchen figure, and Dr Forster dances in pursuit of her. Oldřich lifts from the floor another puppet, who assumes the form of a policeman. Soon Forster and Gretchen are dancing again together, attempting to include the others in their dance. The policeman follows them stealthily, until, seizing his opportunity, he snatches the Gretchen puppet and takes her away with Punch-and-Judy violence. Forster, in despair, returns to his desk. Now Oldřich lifts up a final puppet, and the music begins to work to a climax.)

OLDŘICH: But who is this now? Sadder woman –

JAN: Oldřich, you go too far.

CHORUS *(anxiously)*:   You go too far!

(The phrase becomes an ostinato, which continues from this point until the end of the act.)

OLDŘICH *(turning to Jan, as the dance resumes)*:

But live in truth we must – this was the choice;
And truth that's merely forged by man is vanity.
So Forster cannot hear the only voice
That calls to him from realms of sense and sanity.

(The wife puppet approaches and is ignored. Forster returns to the seminar, and stirs the puppets into frenzied dancing. The motivating force of the drama is always the invisible wires pulled by Oldřich, which represent his magnetic personality, and the students' immediate response to it, knowing exactly what he means.)

JAN: This is more than I can bear!

EVA: Please stop now!

CHORUS: Stop, you go too far!

(The children, awoken by the noise, enter from the bedroom.)

CHILDREN: Daddy! Mummy! Oh!

OLDŘICH: So now he must act rashly, trouble starts.

(All the above voices are now interspersed throughout the climax. Forster takes the crucifix from the wall, and holds it above the puppets, who are magnetised by it. Jan gets up angrily, snatches the crucifix from the Forster-puppet and returns it to the wall.)

JAN: Enough now of this vulgar mockery!

EVA: Yes, enough.

CHORUS: Enough, you go too far.

OLDŘICH: See how it ends.

(The puppets now form a conspiratorial circle, with Dr Forster, dancing defiantly, leading them. The Policeman comes to the outer ring of it, and is stopped by the wife.)

OLDŘICH: She offers to protect him
Guard his house: but not for long –
Rejected, she must also now reject him
And force on him the sense of doing wrong.

(Other voices added as before.

The wife, spurned by Forster, retreats in injured resentment. Into the gap that she has left, steps the policeman.)

So now he hates himself, hates her;
His friends he hates and all the world.
Fate comes unresisted: a whirr
Of wings and then:

(The Policeman rushes forward and is about to grab Dr Forster when there is a violent knocking on the door of the apartment, which breaks open to reveal a party of secret policemen, who stare mockingly at the terror-struck assembly. The music suddenly stops on an atrocious chord.)

OLDŘICH: the flag of silence is unfurled.

(A quiet pizzicato chord. Curtain.)

Act Two

Scene 1

(In the manner of a prologue. The dialogue here is spoken above a ruminative viola accompaniment, to which other parts are added, as the scene brightens. The living room of the apartment. It is morning, and bright sun streams in from the balcony. Eva is preparing the children for school.)

JIŘINA: When is Daddy coming home?

EVA: Soon, I'm sure.

LENKA: It's been three months already.

EVA: He'll be home
The sooner then.

KAREL: Where is he? I know where:
In prison.

EVA: Who told you that? For shame!

JIŘINA: Teacher told us yesterday. She said
He is the people's enemy, and we'll all
Be punished and I'll never be allowed
To go to university.

EVA: How cruel!
Don't listen to her.

LENKA: But is it true?
Is he in prison, Mummy?

EVA: He's gone
For questioning, that's all. And as for you,
Stop listening to silly stories. He'll soon
Be back with us.

KAREL: But Daddy said himself
He is an enemy of the people.

CHILDREN: An enemy! He said he was.

EVA: Where's your apple
Lenka, and your books? You're ready now?
Then off you go — forget your teacher's story.

CHILDREN: Is he Mummy? Is he?
EVA: Off you go!
   Of course he isn't: go along now, hurry!
(She ushers the children out and then returns, sadly meditating. She sits at the desk.)
EVA *(self parody)*: Of course he isn't!
(Serious):   If I could see you now!
   If I could be with you and comfort you!
   I too am an enemy, my crime is yours
   And greater, for I failed you.
   Oh Jan, I did not see
   That each man takes his own unsettled path
   To truthfulness. I did not love you well!
(She picks up a letter from the desk.)
   One letter they allowed
   To show you in the censor's eye.
   You ask me there to pray:
   To what, to whom? You do not say –
   Nor do I find an answer in my heart.
(She stands up, her jealous mood returning.)
   And is this too a fantasy, to go
   On bended knees, your folded hands just so –
   Not to worship, but to be
   Worshipped yourself, in sympathy?
   Ah Jan!
(Remorseful, she drops the letter on the desk and clasps her head in her hands. The door-bell rings and she looks up, startled. After a moment's hesitation she wipes her eyes, smartens herself and goes to open it. Her middle-aged neighbour, Mrs Nováková, stands flushed on the threshold, with a slightly self-mocking look on her face.)
MRS NOVÁKOVÁ: Good morning, Mrs Zelená!
EVA: Good morning, Mrs Nováková!
MRS NOVÁKOVÁ: You know I've always been
   A good neighbour to you, Mrs Z.,
   I don't repeat no gossip,
   Don't listen to what's said –

EVA: Thank you, Mrs Nováková –
MRS NOVÁKOVÁ: Don't thank *me*, it's only nat'ral.
    We've got to stick together
    Otherwise your actual
    Bigwigs have it for the asking –
    Talking of which, could you
    Help me out with just a little thing?
EVA: How can I oblige?
MRS NOVÁKOVÁ::   To cut
    The story short, the same old trouble.
    Not a drop of liquor in the flat,
    The in-laws due for lunch, and double
    Queues in all the shops. A bottle's
    All I need: for myself, a tot'll
    Do, for them a glass or two.
    Vodka if you've got it –
    If not, slivovitz.
(Joy enters the music, and parts are slowly added, moving towards an unexpected and radiant climax after Mrs Nováková's departure. Eva goes to the cupboard briskly, and takes out a bottle of vodka.)
EVA: Here – Wyborowa Vodka,
    And I hope it suits.
    Don't you think of paying,
    We've no need for it.
    Enjoy it – that's enough.
MRS NOVÁKOVÁ: Wyborowa! Just the stuff!
    How good you are, how good you are!
    I won't forget!
(She takes the bottle and goes. Eva, suddenly lightened, almost happy, turns to the balcony, opens the French windows and breathes in the morning air.)
EVA: Sunlight on the rooftops –
    Those little points where angels dance;
    Whatever life has done to us,
    Still we have a chance:

Yes, still we have a chance!
(She puts on her coat and goes out quickly.)

Scene 2

(The same, some months later. Jan, entering the flat alone, stands bewildered in the doorway. He crosses to the dresser, takes some papers from a drawer, shifts through them, and then flings them back, with a gesture like that of the police 'minder' in the Prologue. Musical reminiscences of the seminar and Dr Forster.

Eva enters from the bedroom. They look at each other for a moment, and then wearily resume distant and distracted postures.)

JAN: Where are the children?

EVA: With their granny.

JAN: And why with Granny?

EVA: Must you ask again?

JAN *(suddenly out of control)*:
    Again, again and yet again!

EVA: How can I
    Bear it? Perhaps I can, since I'm insane
    As you are. But they: why must they suffer
    This contempt for us, contempt for them?

JAN: Contempt for them? Say rather . . .

EVA: For whom then?

JAN: For their father.
    For their father, who betrayed . . .

EVA *(claps her hands to her ears)*:   Enough!
    I've heard enough!

JAN: No, listen, I've not said
    It well, not told it properly, not half
    Of it . . .

EVA: Again you'll tell it? How I dread
    These monologues.

JAN: No listen, let me tell
    The feeling of it – all that then befell . . .

(Eva sighs, and falls onto the sofa. Their position and gestures suggest a ritual that takes place each evening, and which can never reach its climax.)

Scene 3

(Some months earlier.

The stage revolves, and discloses the inside of a prison. A cell with a bare lavatory bowl in one corner; a few bunks, a pail of water, bare walls scratched and stained with the marks of previous occupants. High up on one wall an air vent and, at one end, a door, with a peep-hole in it, opening on to a corridor which is visible to the audience. Both corridor and cell are lit by bare bulbs hanging from the ceiling. The scene opens with a clatter of terror-struck music, as the seminar is brutally herded with truncheons down the corridor, and flung into the cell. As the lamentation dies down, Jan detaches himself from the chorus and walks slowly forward to address the audience and Eva, who is still sitting on the sofa, somewhere in semi-darkness at the front of the stage. Jan speaks quickly over the ominous music (repeated notes in the bass, tremolando violas, obsessive figures cast adrift in the upper reaches of piano, xylophone, vibes and celesta).)

JAN: For two days they kept us, men and women in neighbouring cells.

Nobody told us our crime, and when we asked for news the warders laughed.

(We see the women taken out and herded into another hidden cell. Warders enter with food buckets, the contents of which they pour (as was occasionally practised in Czech prisons) over the floor. The members of the seminar shy away, extend beseeching hands, and are greeted with silent laughter. From time to time during the ensuing scene one of them will take a slop from the floor and eat it, driven by hunger.)

JAN: We comforted ourselves with hymns. Oldřich led us,
    always calm, always strong, always with a smile for
    each of us. And I hated him.

OLDŘICH AND CHORUS: Lord have mercy, Christ have mercy!
   Hospodine, pomiluj ny!
(The music of the old Czech hymn sounds through the orchestra.
Oldřich's voice soars above the others, full, confident, warm, while
Jan stands silently, with bowed head.)
JAN: Then they took him away —
(We see this happening)
                       and silence fell.
(Sings):
    They turned to me, those frightened faces,
    And I looked down at frozen tears
    Scattered on the cell's cold basis
    Like fallen stars.

    Their faith cooled. Oh, what had I taught them?
    Only to laugh at absent power;
    But power was present now, and power had caught them:
    This was its hour!
(Warders enter and brutally, with truncheons, take away a handful
of inmates.)
JAN *(speaking)*: One by one they left for that other place,
    for questioning, for freedom or a worse despair.
(Sounds of distant beating, and cries — as in Scene 1 of Janáček's
From the House of the Dead. *The cell empties as Jan slowly*
returns to it.)
JAN: At last I was alone: The cell was cold now
    With another coldness.
    My teeth chattered, and my limbs hurt
    As though knives, not bones, were sheathed in me.
(A warder tips food on the floor, kicks Jan, and then goes out.)
JAN: What are you doing now, my Eva?
    If I could see you secretly,
    Look with you, my Lenka,
    At your book of pretty birds,
    The lark, the red-start and the hopping wren,
    And there behind, the black cat slinking,

Eyes aglow . . .
(Moves forward slightly, troubled by a new vision.)
                    Eyes, eyes –
Eyes that mark you out
For daily mishap
Endless provocation
And – perhaps –
The final hesitation
As you turn from me who caused your hurt
And give yourself in weariness to them!
Lord protect you!
(Suddenly the voice of Oldřich is heard.)
OLDŘICH'S VOICE: Lord protect you, Jan Zelený!
JAN *(looking up in surprise)*: Oldřich!
OLDŘICH'S VOICE: Speak to the grill above you, and I'll hear.
JAN *(directing voice upwards)*:
    Where are you, Oldřich, tell me, where?
OLDŘICH'S VOICE: Just next to you, divided by a wall
    That does not separate: fear nothing, Jan!
JAN: Help me to bear it, help me to recall
    My faith!
OLDŘICH'S VOICE: Faith's the gift
    Of God, and not of man.
    Recall the love of Eva, whom you cast adrift
    And when you weaken, learn to hate
    The weakness in you, which they share.
JAN: Ah – Eva – then I'll learn to hate
    The weakness in me, which they share.
*(Jan comes forward to address the audience, and the scene behind
him fades into utter darkness. Now he stands alone, transfigured,
and the world around him is nothing but the sounds which impinge
upon his memory. The music returns to the idiom of the opening bars
of the scene.)*
JAN *(speaking rapidly)*:
    I heard them open his cell;
(A clank of iron, and brutal, ordinary noises.)

My loneliness was deeper still.
I heard his return;
(More clanking, the thud of a body, and groans.)
                     I felt his pain.
How ashamed I was that once I hated him
For showing me myself. Now I saw how fine
He was, myself a worm. I would accept
What terms they offered me, while he – he kept
His purity, his grandeur. And his voice
As day by day he dwelt upon the choice
That lay before me – reminding me that I
Had you, and could rebuild my life, while he
Had God alone – was full of resignation.
And then, the night before interrogation
He cried out in another tone –

OLDŘICH'S VOICE *(in the darkness)*:
When your turn comes, Jan, remember me!
All that man has is faithless, untrue,
Unless he loves where love is asked for,
Unless he hates where hate is due!

JAN: Astonished by the hatred in his voice
I joined with him at last, rejoic-
ing in his weakness, glad for the vengeful
Feelings that we shared: he *was* no angel!

*(With those last words Jan returns to his cell, now lit by half-light,
and we see him singing with the invisible Oldřich, his fist raised in a
futile gesture of defiance.)*

JAN AND OLDŘICH: All that man has is faithless, untrue
Unless he loves where love is asked for,
Unless he hates where hate is due!

Scene 4

*(The interrogation room: lit by a single bulb above a wooden table,
across which Jan and the interrogators face each other. There*

are two interrogators: one a bass, the other (number II) a counter-
tenor — following the normal communist practice of combining
threats with wheedling sympathy.

   Policemen stand against the walls in semi-darkness; others occupy
the middle space, and seem tensed in readiness. Behind the interroga-
tors there is another table on which a tape-recorder has been placed.
Each interrogator has a glass of water before him, a notebook, and a
pencil with which he plays.)

INTERROGATOR I *(laughing)*: . . . Please, not your version!
   I've heard it all before, so many times,
   And yet, it never ceases to amaze me!
   Human rights and international laws:
   Covenants, accords and articles!
   As though you came before us on some legal nicety,
   Appealing to a technicality!
POLICEMEN *(stepping forwards)*: Appealing to a technicality!
INTERROGATOR II: Please, Dr Zelený, try to see your problems
   From our point of view: try to help us.
   Permit me, then, to summarise your case.
   Three years ago you saw another man promoted
   Before his time, yourself demoted,
   And he a mediocrity.
   So then? Forgive me, but you're no Socrates
   And, sensing this perhaps — at any rate,
   Full of a disappointed hate
   For what you called 'the system', you offered
   To sign a foolish document, so forfeiting
   Your job and all your hard-won freedom.
   Deep you sank then, deep and ever deeper
   To the breeding place of anti-social vipers
   The muddy place we stir from time to time.
POLICEMEN: The muddy place we stir from time to time!
INTERROGATORS I AND II:
   You suddenly revised your view of life:
   You made a god of failure and of strife
   And called it truth. And in truth's name

You stood against realities, hoping to claim
Failure as success,
Despair as resignation, mad excess
As noble courage; worshipping your self-made god.

JAN: I am a Christian, obedient to Christ alone!

INTERROGATOR II: Don't make me laugh!
Man's gods are but himself writ large
And so with you: this demiurge
Called truth or Christ: it was a lie
Falser than any ideology.
Leave this burning altar, stop these games
Which feed your wife and children to the flames!

POLICEMEN: Which feed your wife and children to the flames!

JAN: How dare you mention them!

INTERROGATOR I *(suddenly furious)*: Don't answer back!

INTERROGATOR II *(restraining his colleague)*:
One moment please! Because of our unceas-
ing thankless work the people live in peace.
Your children have full stomachs, schoolbooks, shoes:
And yet you greet your children's suffering,
When teachers tell them of their father's fault,
With affectation of surprise. Offering
No comfort, but compounding the assault,
You drag them with you to a phoney martyrdom
And so increase our people's righteous odium
Of you and all your works. While you, you blame
The system, and blame us who tried to save them!

POLICEMEN: Ha! Ha! Ha! Blame us who tried to save them!

INTERROGATOR I: You've spread hostile propaganda,
Poured scorn on state, society and party;
You've fraudulently practised as a teacher,
And worst of all, you've joined a
Secret church, along with a notorious traitor.
For that, ten years at least:

Ten years harsh reality!

INTERROGATOR II: But truth to tell, a person of your quality
Needs treatment that is less haphazard.
For you, we'll use another method.
We'll offer terms. No punishment
If you will sign this document.

POLICEMEN: If you will sign this document!

INTERROGATORS: The others told us you'd be glad to
Testify against this Hromádko –

JAN *(starting up)*: Against Oldřich! Why, you bastards!
(Policemen step forward.)

INTERROGATOR I: Give him the treatment!

INTERROGATOR II *(holding up a restraining hand)*:
Sign and you are free.

POLICEMEN: Give him the treatment!
(falsetti) Sign and you are free.

JAN: Oldřich, I hear your voice still calling me!

OLDŘICH *(off)*: When your turn comes, Jan, remember me!
*(The two interrogators consult in a whisper, while Jan, standing by
the table, sings to himself)*:

JAN: All that man has is faithless, untrue,
Unless he loves where love is asked for,
Unless he hates where hate is due!

*(The interrogators suddenly come forward together, with resolute
expressions.)*

INTERROGATOR I: Since you won't cooperate,
We'll bring you down to earth!
*(He beckons to a pair of bruisers, who come forward threateningly.
Jan cowers in fear.)*

INTERROGATOR II: No, I know a better way
Of showing him reality!
(He waves the bruisers away, and goes to the tape-recorder.)
Remember this?
*(He switches on the machine: we hear the humming chorus of the
seminar, and Jan's voice singing, 'I would question that! Question
that!')*

POLICEMEN *(mocking)*: Hmmm! Hmmm! Question that!

INTERROGATOR II: And where was Mrs Zelená then?

In the kitchen, thinking of your infidelities.

(Another tape, of Markéta singing her pop-song: impatiently the interrogator speeds the tape forwards, to the love duet between Jan and Markéta. Jan starts up and is seized from behind.)

VOICES OF JAN AND MARKÉTA:

Markéta, dear, I yield

To you!

And I to you and all you're worth!

(The sound of kissing, amplified, and promptly taken up by the policemen.)

POLICEMEN: Kiss! Kiss! I yield to you!

INTERROGATOR II *(switching off the tape)*:

Patience, Dr Zelený, patience. I too

Find that scene embarrassing. Let's turn instead to

Mrs Zelená, and Oldřich Hromádko.

JAN: What do you mean?

INTERROGATOR I *(laughing)*: You'll hear!

(The tape is changed — or perhaps another machine is played — and we hear Oldřich and Eva in the kitchen.)

EVA: Shall I trust those flashing eyes, that face

Which stirs me to desire?

OLDŘICH'S VOICE: Ah, come with me! *(trio)*

POLICEMEN: Ah, come with me!

(Superimposed in Szymanowskian polytonality until the chords scrunch abominably.)

JAN: Enough! Enough!

(The interrogator abruptly stops the tape before the final climax of Eva and Oldřich's love scene — and it should not be lost on the audience that, in doing so, he conceals the fact of Eva's resistance to temptation.)

INTERROGATOR I: You'll sign?

JAN *(bows his head)*: Oh God! Oh God!

INTERROGATOR II: We don't need your signature:

Who would accuse us of a forgery?

We offer you a chance
For self-discovery.
Such is the work of all philosophy.
Socrates it was who first defined it —
The gentle role of midwife
To another's thought. The pain of birth
Is not the midwife's doing: our task
Is just to hasten what will happen anyway.

POLICEMEN: Just to hasten what will happen anyway!

(Interrogator II pushes the paper towards Jan, who looks at him with hatred.)

INTERROGATOR I: OK. He's had his chance.

(The policemen advance threateningly.)

POLICEMEN: He's had his chance.

INTERROGATOR II: Such self-deception!

POLICEMEN: Come with me!
   I yield to you!
   Kiss! Kiss!
   Oh come with me!

(They close in with tender sadism.)

INTERROGATORS: Let's hasten what will happen anyway.

JAN: I'll hasten what will happen anyway!

(Stands up suddenly, holds back the policemen with a defiant gesture.)

JAN: So let me hate, then, let me hate
   Where hate is due!

(He makes as though to receive the first blow, but completing the gesture, picks up the offered pen and quickly signs.)

Scene 5

(We are back in the living room of the flat. It is evening of another day, and Jan and Eva are sitting just as they were at the end of Scene 2. The above recapitulation has clearly taken place many times since

that occasion. Jan and Eva are silent, not looking at each other. At last Jan speaks.)

JAN: So I did denounce him! I deserved their mockery,
   And the mockery of every one!

EVA *(sighs):*   How exhausting!

(She gets up and puts a record on the gramophone. It is an instrumental arrangement, for jazz combo, of Markéta's pop-song. The music tinkles vapidly through the ensuing scene – as in the last act of Lulu. *Jan frowns, as though trying to remember something.*

   A gentle knock. Eva opens the door to one of the students, who returns a book, takes another from the shelf, signs for it in the ledger which Eva dutifully, but wearily, fetches for him. The student goes towards Jan, hesitates, looks at Eva, and from her look divines that he should go. He leaves quietly. Another knock, and the same ritual. An older student now enters, let in once again by Eva. He goes to Jan, holds out his hand, is ignored, and turns, bewildered, to address his remarks to Eva.)

STUDENT: I saw her today; she came to see me,
   Our Markéta . . .

EVA: Your Markéta!

(She turns away, and begins to dance lugubriously to the music.

   The student looks from one to the other, finds his looks unreturned, hesitates, and then steps forward nervously, addressing no one in particular.)

STUDENT: Yes she's back – back from where they sent her.
   She said: prepare the way, tell him
   'Under the earth this spring, new sap
   Is flowing, under the earth
   A mother's arms unfold.'
   She said you'd understand.

(Jan is silent; Eva continues weirdly to dance.)

STUDENT: That's what she said. What message then?
   Or is there no reply?

(Jan stays silent. Eva takes the record off the gramophone, and with a humourless laugh goes into the bedroom. The student stands for a moment.)

STUDENT: Oh God! Oh God!

(He goes out precipitately, leaving the door ajar. The lighting changes, and Markéta enters, as in a dream. By degrees, however, we realise that it is not a dream. She is sombre, slow, as though transfigured.)

MARKÉTA: Jan? Are you alone?

JAN *(starts, but does not look at her)*: Alone!

MARKÉTA: Can we speak?

(Jan gestures upwards to the unseen microphone.)

JAN: Oh yes, let's speak!
    After all, they've yet to hear the last act
    Of our drama.

MARKÉTA: Yes, there is one fact
    They need to know, and I alone can tell it.

JAN *(rising and turning to her fully)*:
    Markéta!

MARKÉTA: No Jan, I will not kiss you,
    As I longed to kiss you once.
    Having kissed, I miss you:
    All else you took me for's a lie.

JAN: Are *you* a figment of my vanity?

MARKÉTA: *(lyrical, with love remembered and restored)*:
    Don't say that Jan, not your vanity –
    Don't blame yourself for my disgrace
    Which wasted you. Listen –

(Her tone changes, and she narrates quickly, half-speaking, half-chanting, over a Les Noces accompaniment, urgent, rhythmical, percussive and dry.)

                    When I left
    It was the cops who took me,
    As you guessed. But not to jail –
    To sunny California,
    Spying in a nest of exiles, and well paid.
    You were my worst assignment. The one I had
    To ruin utterly, to lead,
    For love's sake, to the riskiest things,

And feeling love myself, betray
With all your friends.
(Lyrical: the antistrophe to the previous expression of love):
                        Ah don't forgive!
There is no mercy due to this deceiver,
Only listen till I leave here –
(Dry once more.)
In that polluted world I come from
Even there at times a cold
Spring sun can shine:
That sun was you, and in my heart
I longed to bring you nearer, make you part
Of my corruption, redeem myself
In undermining you, and yet
At last to save you too.
I did not know they'd go so far,
And wound you in the tender part
That I'd protected.
When I heard, I knew
That I must see you,
And confess . . .
(She breaks off in emotion.)
JAN *(cold and amazed)*: Thank you, now I know.
    That you ruined me, I might forgive;
    But Oldřich! Did you have to ruin *him*?
MARKÉTA *(earnest)*: You trusted Oldřich?
JAN: Trusted and betrayed him,
    Who loved where love is asked for . . .
MARKÉTA: Ah Jan! And whom did Oldřich love?
JAN: He loved my wife, as I had never loved her;
    He loved the truth and God –
MARKÉTA: Oh God above!
(Eva enters from the bedroom, eyes the couple for a moment, and comes slowly forward.)
MARKÉTA: Listen Jan, it's Jan that's Eva's lover,
    And as for Oldřich, it's Jan, not he,

That was betrayed. Oh they were clever,
Putting that bastard in the cell next door,
Convincing you that he – their agent –
Was the victim. Oh Jan, you poor
Deluded fool –
JAN: No he wasn't!
I'll not believe you!
MARKÉTA: Alas he was,
And that's the other thing I came to tell –
*(Jan looks at her for a moment and then turns sharply away, coming
face to face with Eva. A* Rosenkavalier-*like trio ensues.)*
EVA: And now I understand that force
Which turned me back from him; the spell
Betraying the magician!
JAN: And now I understand the force
Which drew me close to him: the skill   *(trio)*
That turned away suspicion!
MARKÉTA: Please, both of you, believe what I have
                said:
What I have done, the same thing Oldřich did!
*(Jan, without glancing back at Markéta, goes quickly into the
bedroom, leaving the two women to confront each other. Markéta
makes a move forward, and Eva raises a hand to restrain her.)*
EVA: So you've done what you came to do:
You who lived by falsehood showed me truth.
MARKÉTA: Not falsehood only. What I felt was real –
EVA *(with a dismissive gesture)*: And why should I believe
This new unlikely story: that Oldřich too
Was one of them, or rather, one of you?
MARKÉTA *(bitterly)*:
Ah Oldra, if you knew him!
EVA: So that was it!
So you and he – and you and Jan! The fit
Is perfect: let's hope you swine betrayed
Each other –
MARKÉTA: OK, I've overstayed

My welcome. Go to Jan, he's yours,
And as for me
(She gestures upwards to the microphone)
                    I'm finished now, of course,
And one day soon – but there, it wouldn't do
To think a traitress killed herself for you!
(A light dawns and Eva starts forward with a gesture.)
EVA: Markéta!
(Markéta turns quickly and goes out.)

Scene 6

(The bedroom, which also serves as a study. The children's room, a kind of conservatory, filled with the light of a street lamp, adjoins the bedroom. Jan, alone on the bed, sings a disordered fragment of his 'loyalty duet'.)
JAN: When your turn comes, remember me!
    Love where love is asked for,
    And hate . . . and hate . . . no . . .
(Enter Eva, who kneels beside him.)
JAN: Well Eva, perhaps I'm someone after all.
    That they should use so many clever ploys
    To ruin me.
EVA: Forgive me, Jan, this fall
    Away from you. This truth you sought,
    We have it now, if only you'll permit
    The love I offer you, with all my heart!
(Jan enters a state of exaltation and, almost ignoring Eva – on whose head, nevertheless, he places a condescending hand – sings):
JAN: Ah yes, I see it now – that you alone were true,
    True in your doubt, and in your jealousy!
(A light goes on in the conservatory. The children come in, in white night-dresses, a visitation from a bright and unpolluted sphere.)
CHILDREN: Mummy! Daddy! You woke us up! You woke us up!
KAREL: Do you want to hear our song?

LENKA AND JIŘINA: Hear our song?
JAN AND EVA: Sing it then! Sing it then!
CHILDREN: A doctor called Adam, he
    Left the Academy
    All for a reason
    That nobody knew.

    To teach they forbad him, he
    Wasn't to madden the
    Students with reason-
    ing that was taboo.

    But when they said 'Adam, he
    Is the class enemy
    And he speaks treason,'
    He ceased to be blue;
    He ceased to be blue, be blue, be blue,
    Because it was true, was true, was true!
JAN *(laughing)*: And who taught you *that* song?
KAREL *(knowingly)*: Not the teacher!
JAN: Ah so! A playground
                                       seminar!
*(Eva and Jan join in the song. The stage revolves quickly, to reveal
the station, as before, with a train announced for Vienna. Markéta,
anxious, enters and looks up at the departure board. A police minder
is following her, and watches as she searches in her bag, brings out
several passports, and seems to select one of them, throwing the others
into the litter bin which Jan had used. Two leather-jacketed secret
policemen approach. One of them is smiling, and Markéta gives
herself up to him at once, with a gesture of defeat.*

    *The song of 'Doctor Adam' returns, the stage revolves back again,
and as the hilarious family reach the end of their chorus, Jiřina
suddenly arrests them with a commanding gesture, points upwards to
the unseen microphone, and ostentatiously says 'hush!'. The music
bustles quickly to a close.)*

                     Finis

Scarcely has the curtain fallen on our opera than another curtain is raised. Smiles are breaking across features which for years had been sealed by hatred; people are greeted who yesterday where shunned; the fog of deception swirls away and into the empty citadels of power there come – with diffident steps and hushed whispers of amazement – those 'enemies of the people', the only ones whom the people trust.

Is it a miracle? There are those who think so – Eva, for instance, who each morning offers her thanks to the blessed Agnes of Bohemia. Her children's teacher, too, is convinced of it, and now volubly utters her faith, entertaining the classroom with sweet improving stories of the saints. How proud the children are of the name of Zelený – the Zelený whom the teacher had condemned as an enemy of socialism, and who is now adviser to the Minister of Education. Each Tuesday his famous seminar takes place in the university, and often the television cameras are there; he is visited by foreign journalists and scholars; he is written about in the new newspapers, as the saviour of Czech philosophy. Almost every night his voice can be heard on the radio, offering opinions on the issues of the day; and in the street he can hardly walk for a hundred yards without being accosted by a fellow citizen and warmly shaken by the hand.

Eva too is proud of him, though they meet more rarely now. For Jan is too busy for his old commitments, and besides is much occupied by the question (which takes, for him, a metaphysical form) of a particular pair of pale grey eyes. Alena is a student, and in her unblemished face Jan has discovered a strange appeal to his conscience, an injunction to live anew and totally. And so it is, he thinks, for all who have suffered. To such people angels are sent, messengers in human form, whose purpose is to turn sorrow to wisdom, and to give form and meaning to a life in tatters.

Eva does not know of Alena, but she guesses – guesses and forgives. Too much is happening; nobody has time or thought or energy for those old emotions. Eva too has her sorrow; and if truth were told it is greater by far than Jan's. But she has her own way of overcoming it. Her life is given – not to Jan, but to his children; not to Jan's ideals, but to the Civic Forum which embodies them, and in whose local office, once an Agitation Centre, she spends her busy days. It is thanks to Eva that letters are written, telephones answered, meetings announced and posters hung. It is Eva who welcomes visitors, draws up agendas, records decisions and sees that they are carried out. She soothes all rivalry, calms all anger, moderates ambition and forges alliances. It is because of Eva – who knows nothing of politics, except that it is the work of human beings – that her local branch of the Civic Forum fills so many public offices. It is only right that she should be publicly congratulated for her labour by Oldřich Hromádko, the famous ex-dissident and symbolic leader of the young.

The religious orders have been revived, and their property has been returned to them. It is in a monastery on the outskirts of Prague that Oldřich – who has refused all office – now holds his court each Sunday. Young people come to seek his advice. For there have been many vocations, and sometimes it is hard to know whether the call of one's country is competing with the call of God. Oldřich speaks kindly and clearly to each of his visitors; all that he says is treasured, and all that he advises obeyed. For did he not serve both God and country, in those difficult years when so many others betrayed them both?

Sometimes – for such is the turmoil of this new Bohemia – Jan, representing the Minister of Education, meets Oldřich, a leading spokesman for the Church. They spend an hour together over a glass of beer – a small indulgence permitted by Oldřich's Order. They do not discuss the past. Once, however, Oldřich – with a peculiar expression of tenderness which sticks in Jan's mind like a stab of jealousy – makes a strange remark. 'The things they made us do to each other, Jan!' They both fall silent. And then, with a shrug, Jan speaks of other matters.

Who knows exactly, looking back over that time of lies,

what part his neighbour played, or whether he himself was guiltless? Far better to forget, to let truth and falsehood dwindle together. Jan has so much to do, so many plans and schemes and hopes, so many opportunities, and such confidence in those soft grey eyes which guide him. Why should he brood on other mysteries? Besides, he admires Oldřich, admires most of all that splendid gesture of renunciation, made just when so many were claiming their reward.

And so the tide of history rolls across Central Europe. The doors of all the churches stand open, even the little church in Smíchov, whose erstwhile secret priest is now a bishop in Moravia. At the hours of Mass the bells of Prague ring out in sympathy; and around them the nation listens, hearing half-forgotten meanings, and dreaming its half-forgotten dreams. Jan dreams, Oldřich dreams, and Eva tries to dream the new reality. In the world's eyes they are heroes, the ones who saw the nation through. And in their own eyes? Each remembers Markéta, whom nobody has seen.

Thirty
Points

30, Colborne Road
London N15
30th September 1985

Albright and Sigorski, Solicitors
15, The Mall
Southwark
London SW1

Dear Sirs,

I am seeking legal advice on the following:

1.   Recovery of property: two paintings and a sketchbook, presented as gifts to an architect.

2.   Recovery of fees, paid to the same architect, for draughting lessons which never took place.

3.   An outstanding application for admission to the Lutyens School of Art and Design. The Post Office claim no knowledge of the address, which is impossible since the architect teaches there.

4.   The Greater London Council, which failed to return designs submitted to a competition. (The project was for a multi-cultural arts complex, though I would have rather built a church.)

5.   Once he said to me – we were in his office and he was showing me his designs for Holy Trinity – that he would divorce his wife if it made me happier. I told him not to be silly, that marriage is sacred and in any case I had no rights. Actually, what were my rights?

6.   The designs for Holy Trinity were no good. You cannot

express religious feeling in modernist forms – they are too abstract, too impersonal. Their meaning is that there is no meaning. My own designs for Holy Trinity employ a bold mixture of gothic and classical styles, executed in freestone and marble.

7.   A psychotherapist, for suggesting that my crisis was a religious one (at the time I was wondering whether to become a Roman Catholic) and that I should advertise for a boyfriend in a left-wing magazine.

(When I first met him, how mild he seemed, his hands pressed gently together on the desk like a folded tulip, his head leaning to one side in repose! He was waiting for me to speak, as I waited for him. It was not that an angel stood in the room then, but that the room stood for a moment in an angel. But why did he rise up so high, those eyes so large of a sudden, so blazing with pride and defiance?)

8.   Westminster Cathedral, for not replying to nearly five hundred letters I have written (this may be an exaggeration) regarding instruction in the Roman Catholic faith.

9.   Father Mark Grayling of St Aeldred's church, for not listening to my confession. Also for imagining that when I described God as the architect of the world, I was speaking of some sensual emotion. My aim was to transcend the sensuous, to rid my life of clutter.

(Though it is true what St John of the Cross says, that Satan stations himself with great cunning on the frontiers between sense and spirit.)

10.   I would have shown him my designs for Holy Trinity, except his arrogance deterred me. Those sinful hands of his, leafing through folder after folder as though disclosing the works of God!

I don't say all of it was rubbish. There was a house he invented once, with ogee arches, and a courtyard behind. It was divided by a staircase, with two light-filled bedrooms, one his, one mine. They opened on to a landing where all the vectors of the house cascaded and joined.

But the public buildings were criminal: arrogant, contemptuous like himself. Those sheets of glass and steel, those slabs of concrete – defying God's commandments. He should never have been awarded the commission for Holy Trinity. The Kingdom of heaven is formed in another way – from arduously chiselled links of stone.

11. A German poet for beating me up four years ago. Does it matter that this happened outside the jurisdiction?

12. A private citizen, who wrote to me at home, at the time of my conversion, accusing me of witchcraft and threatening to call the police.

13. It was the third time we met when he first mentioned Holy Trinity. He spoke of it in a peculiar tone of voice, like a vision. 'All materials are sacred,' he said, 'even concrete and glass. Especially concrete and glass.' And when he said those words, they sounded like a fanfare of muted trumpets. I imagined a window of faintly coloured mica, and through it the unbreathing stillness, made for holy deeds.

He did not teach me isonometric drawing either then or on any other occasion.

14. Westminster City Council, who offered me temporary employment, and then a few days later cancelled the agreement, without explanation.

15. The first time he kissed me was in his office. The assistants had gone home, a kind of pink hazy light was oozing through the windows, and I was confused by the noise of some birds which were cooing and chattering in the courtyard. Across the roof you could see the spire of St Bride's, stacked like a pile of boxes, but neat and clean at the edges as only stone can be.

Not that I blamed him then: he was the victim of a greater force. Only why was he so insensitive? Why, for instance, when I needed encouragement, did he look at me as though I hardly existed, as though in any case I had no clothes when standing in his presence? Why did he not shield me from his glance? Why did he make such efforts to appear large and shameless – yes, shameless – before me, as though my eyes counted for nothing, and only his could see? I do not refer to those obvious and pleasurable transactions which occur between man and woman.

His kiss tasted of toffee.

16.   I should like to know what rights are accorded by the law to the one who confesses. Father Mark could have prevented a crime. Yet he chose not to do so.

17.   My landlord, for letting unauthorised people into my room during my absence. Also for writing to the private citizen complained of above.

17a.   I should add that there has never been any relation between the landlord and myself except a financial one, and that I, for my part, have always observed the strictest propriety.

17b.   Once he came to visit me at home. I heard him speaking to the landlord in the hallway, and hurriedly packed away my designs for Holy Trinity. I had just finished the arch of the North Transept, with its angelic figures symbolising the powers of light, and a swathe of recessed mouldings going deeper and deeper into stone like the knife of the Spirit into unresisting matter. (The arch leads to the temples of the Holy Spirit and of its works in this world. It was in the third of those temples that a crime had taken place. Father Mark knows about this.)

I received him quite correctly and offered him tea. There was no expectation on my part that he would behave as he did. Those eyes of his – pale porcelain blue, like the eyes of a Siamese cat.

18.   The mystery of the Trinity includes all other mysteries – the incarnation; the transubstantiation at the altar when a wafer dipped in wine becomes God himself; death, in which spirit and life fly apart although they are one; creation, in which God builds from himself the thing which is himself and also other; love, in which two persons become one substance; justice, in which the Holy Spirit restores the unity of a divided world.

How are three things one? As the hand, the touch and the pain are one.

18a.   To symbolise the Trinity in stone – it must be stone, for nothing else displays the hand of creation – this was my mission.

19.   Mental cruelty on the part of Father Mark Grayling; also my ex-psychotherapist, a private citizen, and Angela Hopwood, who refused to walk home with me when she could see that I was distressed.

20.   A church is a forest, a place of secret life, where light is trapped in dialogue with shadow, where invisible eyes observe and follow you. A church is God's mind, growing with vegetable stillness, a composition of planes and light, pervasive and unresistant like the Spirit, where man wanders in the company of things unseen. A church must be carved by a reverential hand, touched into life like Adam himself. Its first small flutter of breath must be shielded like a flame, fanned and fed until it lives entirely.

20a.   N.B. He could taste no happiness unless it were steeped in the sauce of women's tears. (Or is that too old-fashioned a phrase?)

20b.   The forest he took me to was full of violent colour – the scarlet berries of nightshade, the flame-coloured leaves and purple shadows, the copper-coloured spaces between the boughs, and flashes of kingfisher blue as the sky rushed to perceive us, like a great eye stationing itself in every clearing. He insisted. He was a creature of the wild, he said, a creature of the woods; and all of a sudden the yellow mist of birch-tops clouded over.

O Western wind, when wilt thou blow, that the small rain down may rain?

The wind was rushing in the leaves, and the rain flapped about my face like a wet cloth. I could not see him.

21.   The chairman of Holy Trinity Trustees, for not replying to my letter warning them against his sinful designs – even though they had asked for comments, and had expressly raised the question whether modern materials could be used to symbolise God's threefold majesty.

21a.   In a sense they can. For the Trinity, which embraces everything, shines through everything. Every human work speaks loudly of it. But to represent its highest truth – this is a task for holiness.

There must be, for instance, a temple of justice, a place where the evil of the world is rectified. In my designs this was to be the third chapel of the North Transept, flanked by Egyptian pillars at the entrance, but with a cloister-like circle of Corinthian columns within. At the centre the altar: a smooth granite block, with cuneiform channels to collect the blood of the victims and feed it to the marble cistern of the Spirit. I envisaged, too, a wondrous tapestry, which would hang about the altar from a cylindrical cornice, supported by Ionic columns in polished porphyry. In its rich fabric would be woven the story of man's fall. The serpentine forms that spring from the head of modern man writhe there in a tableau of temptation, sliding about the upright columns like the hand of a seducer on the thigh of a girl.

There had been only one other person ever, and with him I had severed all relations.

22.   The British Museum for wrongly describing the Elgin marbles as a triumph of the sculptor's art.

23.   Recovery of property – an essay which I wrote for him on the classical Orders, which he promised to read and never afterwards mentioned.

24.   Of his own free will he offered me lessons in draughting. I insisted on paying in advance, since I wanted the matter to be set on a business footing. Nothing stood between me and my future career, save only this. After a few lessons, he assured me, I would lift the ideas from my head and put them down on paper as though they were comic transfers. These lessons never took place.

25.   His weight on top of me was a weight of concrete. Yet he was made of glass. Going into his office I could see right through him. Only when he spoke did I know he was there. He regularly practised this deception.

26.   One part of the forest was sacred. Here the trees were small, orderly, grouped like temples, and the stones, where the moss did not cover them, had a moist and silvery sheen. I lay there, the birches arching over me, little brown birds hopping in the branches like angels in the spandrels of a choir. He pulled aside the curtain, and I was astonished at his dress – a robe of pink from head to toe, and at his waist a buckle of gold. He put the basket down beside me, and took from it bread, wine, a knife.

27.   Rockingham Galleries, Wimpole Street, for keeping three of my paintings (a triptych called 'Sacrifice') and for the despicable treatment received from one of their directors, in the public part of the gallery, and while several people were watching.

27a.   I would be prepared for him to keep the paintings, and also the essay. But not the fees.

28.   Father Mark, for offering cruel and facetious comments instead of spiritual guidance. When I described the crime to him, he suggested that I see a psychiatrist. 'I have been seeing a psychiatrist for two years,' I said, 'and she sent me to a priest.' His reply was: 'The scene you describe is a fantasy; no church has ever countenanced human sacrifice, and the idea that a priest should atone for his fault by exchanging roles with his victim – this is an enormity of Aztec proportions.'

28a.   Aztec proportions actually have a great deal to recommend them. My own measurements of Quetzalpapalotl's palace suggest the repeated and rhythmical use of golden section rectangles, not only in the laying out of the ground plan, but also in the spacing of triforium arches, and the perspective of the temple steps. I borrowed the idea for the second chapel in the transept of the Saviour.

29.   Bread and wine are united in the Presence. How it happens is the deepest mystery. In a world without holiness who can combine them? Yet to sunder them is easy, like emptying flesh of its blood.

30.   Also my parents – my mother especially – for mental

cruelty, wrong decisions taken on my behalf when I was growing up, and for not allowing me to come home when I begged them.

I have picked your name from the phone book. I do not know whether I am entitled to legal aid. Please advise,

Yours sincerely,

Imogen Copleston (Miss)

A Mistake

I T WAS not my door in the long corridor that I opened and, seeing a woman's blue camel-hair coat on the stand, and catching a faint whiff of hyacinth, I muttered 'a mistake' and began to withdraw. But I had no time to retreat across the threshold before a familiar shy voice said 'No, not a mistake. I've been waiting for you.'

'Mother!' I cried, and with a joyful impulse I stepped into the room and closed the door behind me. She was sitting at the desk, dressed for work in a short-sleeved blouse. On her face was the slightly enigmatic, though on the whole kindly, expression with which she greeted my little bids for independence. She was without her glasses, and her wide-open browless eyes were of an intense, almost unnatural blue, as though painted over by someone wishing to emphasise her better features. It was not my office in which she sat, but a bigger, brighter place, higher up the building, and the typewriter on which her fingers rested was of an older model that we no longer used downstairs.

'Sit down,' she said, pointing to the visitor's chair. 'No, don't kiss me. It won't be necessary.'

And she laughed, her old raucous laugh, of a woman who believes that she alone of all the world is risible. The chair was warm, as though someone had just vacated it, and the arm-rests seemed to cradle my arms like the hands of a rescuer. How agreeable everything was in this room! The spaces seemed larger, the furniture more comfortable and better arranged than in the corridor below. And the little reminders of the world outside – the prints of Oxford Colleges on the wall, the gay Venetian vase before her, in which a few pale tulips stood,

the bookcase with its Edwardian volumes of poetry – all bore
the mark of her anxious good nature, which could settle itself in
any place, and fill it with a fragile sense of home. Impulsively I
jumped up again, and began to pace on the Turkey carpet.

The view from this floor was especially harmonious. It
seemed as though our little town had been designed precisely to
be viewed from such a height, and was at last able to offer me
(who had lived in it grudgingly for forty years) a pleasing
prospect of ivy-clad houses, busy courtyards and churches of
yellow stone. I seemed to recall the prospect too, perhaps from
an old postcard – though how on earth it could have been
captured in those days, before the office tower existed (a tower, I
should add, which has spoiled the harmony of our townscape for
ever) I had no idea.

'How extraordinary to find you here,' I said; 'though come to
think of it, I heard a rumour that you might move in, now the
firm has expanded, and we have acquired the floors above. Of
course, it is typical that you didn't bother to tell me. I suppose
you were afraid of seeming pushy, afraid of encroaching, as you
put it, on my independence. Honestly Mother! As though that
mattered now! But then you were waiting for me, you say, in the
very room into which I have strayed, suffering from some post-
prandial confusion not unconnected with my habit (I regret to
say it Mother) of drinking far too much at lunch-time. Well,
you don't really expect me to believe you! On the other hand, it
is just possible that you have been following my movements
today. I must admit that it wouldn't have been difficult, me
being so sluggish, and – to be quite frank Mother – somewhat
depressed of late, taking such a long time to make even the
smallest decision, like for instance whether to have lunch at the
George, or whether to go instead to the Coach and Horses
which you have never cared for. No, it wouldn't have been
difficult to keep track of me today, nor to rush ahead without my
knowledge, to install yourself in the office into which I was
about to blunder – just the kind of impish trick you always play
on me. And no doubt with some fantastic plan, to tempt me

away from work – maybe to the bookshop at Haysborough, though as you know it's rather a sorry affair these days, with nothing but biographies of yesterday's men. Or maybe – for I can see a mischievous twinkle in your eye – you are planning something rather more ambitious: one of those jaunts to Oxford or Woodstock, to get a breath of old stone as you say, though how you imagine we could get there now that the Morris has gone to the Great Car Park in the Sky I don't for the life of me know . . .'

All this and more came out in a rush. And while the words were far beyond anything I had meant to say, constituting indeed a breach of the longstanding rule of silence between us, I felt them to be entirely natural. How often does it happen, meeting a familiar person by chance, and in circumstances which do not lend themselves to conversation, that you suddenly give way to the impulse to say everything in your heart? There had been so much I had wanted to express to her, and which, for one reason or another, I had never dared to say: not the great things (for who can say great things to his mother?) but all the little, gentle, joyful things which would cause her such pleasure, which she mutely begged to hear from me and which in my embarrassment I had always withheld. I wanted to tell her how beautiful she was, how beautiful she had always been, how secretly proud of her I felt – and not only of her beauty; of her intelligence too. For really, when she puts her mind to it, there is no one better than Mother at finding solutions. Take any problem – how to buy chicken giblets, for instance, how to get the best price in curtain material, how to write a business letter, how to resolve a labour dispute, how to conduct the symphonies of Beethoven (for Mother knows those wonderful scores by heart) – and she will give her queer, hesitant and impeccably conservative answer to it, utterly indifferent as she has always been to the world's temporary opinion. And I was proud of that too: her conviction, come down from recusant forefathers, that the good sense of the present may be in every particular the exact opposite of the truth, and that we had no better guide, when all was said and done, than the secretly enduring things, in which God has concealed his will. Not that she believes in God, any more than I do – at least, not in any literal sense. And that is a remarkable thing too, the almost religious vision we share, of a world entirely fallen, ourselves striving for righteousness, at odds with our times, and capable in our isolation of a kind of crazy joy, like the joy of the Credo, a private hallelujah, and neither of us believers!

I knew instinctively that this thought, which had just occurred to me, was running through her mind as well, that she even associated it with the very images which came tumbling into my consciousness: the sea at Brancombe, pouring green over blue, and rushing at the pebbles like a kitten at play; the little boarding house with the smell of magnolias, and its sepulchral suppers when we whispered and giggled like children under the stony eyes of the guests; and the long walk that day over the moors, the farmstead which was our assumed destination (though we needed none); the old couple, brother and sister, who welcomed us into the kitchen, who fed us from the dishcloth-flavoured bacon which hung in flitches from the beams, and who sang with us at the harmonium, hymns and parlour songs, our lungs straining in cheerful rivalry, until the sun began to slope towards the near horizon, and we stalked it home to the sea – how wonderful it was to remember this together, and to be once more enfolded in the oneness of the world!

I had sat down, but was so excited that I again leapt up before she could reply to my stream of questions, which were not questions at all, but invitations to the deeper silence that lay beyond this necessary flood of words. The view from her office delighted me. It showed the town as we had known it, every detail still in place, and I gestured to her vigorously as I described the scene. I had the impression that she rose slightly in her chair, as though tempted to join me at the window, but then thought better of it and sat quietly, enjoying my words. There was Hapgoods the grocers, with the Regency shop whose

torn canvas awnings were often carried away by the breeze.
There were the churches: the Parish church of sandstone, with
lancet windows, surrounded by its audience of graves; the
Methodist church, upright, classical, with yellow half-columns
strapping its walls; and the Catholic church, our church, in
Victorian freestone and flint, jabbing its stubby tower like a self-
satisfied thumb into the skyblue waistcoat of the heavens,
claiming discrete but exclusive ownership. And there was
Pelham Street, with our old house still standing, so clearly
visible from this angle that I could count every tile on the roof
and even, it seemed to me, peer through the windows and guess
at the life inside – for instance there was a woman, combing her
hair before Mother's lacquer dressing table.

I could make out the little paddock with Bill Maidstone's
ponies, a white fence surrounding it, and the shed painted in
circus colours as it always was. In fact, it seemed to me that I saw
the old pony, Scamp, who pulled Bill's rag-and-bone cart
around our street all those years ago – Scamp with his neolithic
neck, his vast bony indented head like a rhinoceros, and three
white socks on his dung-coloured legs. But of course Scamp was
dead: the pony was evidently another from the same stock, a
mortal instance of the eternal Form of Scamp. I beckoned
Mother over to comment on this interesting fact. Before I had
finished explaining, however, my eye was caught by another
detail – the allotment, our allotment, right there behind St
Hilda's Church of England Primary School, with the rhubarb
patch still sprouting and the cucumber cloches laid out neatly in
rows.

'Who do you think is working it now? No, don't tell me: it is
Jack Baines, who took it over when – when it happened and we
were rid of Father for ever. He had been wanting our allotment
for some time, I remember, on account of its being the sunniest
spot, just that little bit lighter, and less damp too, than the
patches along the road, and blessed, as you would say, with
those elder-bushes at the top, they're still there I notice, from
which old Jack could gather fruit for his home-made wine . . .'

Of course, it was a mistake to mention Father, however obliquely, and I was not surprised when, having several times made as if to speak, she now remained silent, her eyes turned down to the typewriter, and her fingers playing sadly and distractedly over the keys. I wanted to embrace her, to stroke her grey hair, to smooth her still youthful brow, to tell her how little those painful years mattered, how the good things were always with us, shining through the temporary clouds, and warming our spirits into joy. I took a step towards her, talking still, though God knows why, of Jack Baines, his vinegary wine and vinegary opinions (for Jack had been a Baptist preacher before his wife's death, and still retained, in his despair, a belief that God should be instantly informed of every wickedness), and with my heart full of tenderness and concern for her, of a desire above all to wipe away the memory of those sufferings to which I had been so helpless a witness – when suddenly my eye was caught by the Mickey-Mouse transfer on the black enamel side of the typewriter.

'Mother!' I cried. 'It's the same old typewriter! How crazy! They must have given you one of the new electric jobs, and there you go bashing away on your dear old Remington!'

I suppose it should have surprised me that she made no answer, but instead began to type, as though recording my words for future reference. But it did not. On the contrary, the clatter of the old machine conveyed me at once into a realm without surprises – a realm where all was foretold and un-changeable. I recalled those evenings at home, twenty years before, when she would work at the table, on the letters which came to her from Mr Crimshaw, the Estate Agent. I had found my first job, in the parcels department of our firm; I had also begun the course of legal studies which I was never to finish, but the rumour of which aroused an occasional faint interest at work, and which would, Mother assured me, eventually lead to promotion, if not to the sales department, at least to the office marked 'Contracts' where for a while I spent my days. Perhaps it was the sound of her typewriter, indeed, returning after so many years, which caused me not to say what I first had in mind, but to rehearse those old and unforgotten topics. For some reason it excited me to believe that my words were being faithfully recorded. For Mother is a brilliant secretary, who has no need for shorthand, and who can reproduce the most rapid conversation word for word, her fingers dancing on the keyboard like grasshoppers, her pale face divested of interest, and with a kind of child-like innocence, as though the torrent of another's words could sweep all the guilt and hesitation from her consciousness.

Knowing that she would not miss a word of what I said, therefore, and anxious to move slowly towards the point that we both desired – the point at which, after all these years, the defences would be lowered and our love would prevail – I began to debate in my mind what I should say to her. I knew she would want to hear about the office, my colleagues, my career, for, although I had made little progress of late, the promise of advancement had not finally receded. And I was eager, too, to explain my projects for the summer, which had sprung into being over lunch that very day: I had been given two months' leave, and was planning a trip down the Danube, from Vienna, via Bratislava and Budapest, and on through Romania, to the Black Sea itself. On the other hand, I recognised in her face and posture the signs of an old disturbance, and knew that, having fortuitously mentioned him, I must do what I could to exorcise the memory of Father.

For a while, therefore, I ceased to speak, turning back to the window, and staring at the houses and lawns, at the concrete roadways of the new estates, and at the intruding fingers of farmland, which probed the entrails of our town. I think my mother was speaking now; at least, I recall a rapid humming that must have been her voice, unless it were some machine, a tape-recorder perhaps, which she had switched on so as to occupy the temporary silence. In any case, I did not listen, so deeply was I sunk in recollection, so overwhelmed of a sudden by images of those years at home, when she and I kept vigil at our separate ends of the table, our eyes directed towards the chair beside the empty fireplace, watching the shadows of his humour as they drifted across his face.

My father was an accountant. At least, accountancy was his work, on the increasingly rare occasions when work engaged his attention. In his own mind, however, he was not an accountant at all, but a poet, a musician, a legal genius and a social reformer. Not that, objectively speaking, he had made much headway with those careers. A poem had once appeared in the local newspaper, describing the worm-ridden carcass of a bird. There were some scraps of music-paper in the piano stool, on which he had jotted the first bars of his 'Eternal Symphony'. Some old law books habitually rested beside him on the fireside table. And he had written countless letters to 'the authorities', as he persisted in describing the officials to whom they were addressed, complaining of the injustice of English society in general, and of his own position in particular. But those scrappy projects were mere hints of the vast ambitions that gave rise to them, and which seethed within him with such force that he sat shaking for hour after hour, overwhelmed by the thought of the sacrifice that would shortly be required of him. Sometimes he would cry out, calling for pen, ink and paper. When these were brought to him (and the penalties for disobedience were terrible), he would scribble hastily for a minute or two. Then, with a snort of disgust, he would abruptly cease, casting the pen away from him, and tearing the work to shreds with a violence that caused us to shudder. His bloodshot eyes would bulge from their sockets, his brow would become blotched with anger, and from his dry taut lips a strangled cry would emerge, a cry of grief and isolation, to which there was no conceivable response, save a mute and humble acknowledgement that the pain of the world was borne by him alone. How we trembled to hear that sound, the prelude frequently to days of silence, or equally to a sudden leap into the air, which he would beat with his little fists (for Father was a small man, and resented the fact that so great a spirit was trapped within such a constricted frame) as though striking down invisible demons!

Sometimes a tear would form in Mother's eye, though she would hasten to conceal it, for there was nothing he tolerated less than women's tears. Indeed, the sight of them could cause him to scream at the top of his voice and to call down punishments from heaven on those who, while enjoying the comforts of their dull routine, dared nevertheless to pretend to some personal disaster. And once the cursing had begun he would see little cause to temper it. Parties, priests and parliaments; presidents, popes and kings; councils and communities – all were berated for their habit of ignoring him. Nor would he confine himself to the more obvious symbols of power. He had, in his rage, a zealous eye for detail, a novelist's sense of the particular, which would cause him to scent out new and surprising enemies, and to hunt with invective until the prey was pinned down inescapably in some cul-de-sac of words. It was not enough, for instance, to denounce the prejudice of the Fire Brigade (which had failed to prevent the destruction of our shed when one day, in a fit of anger, he had decided to set light to it); he was compelled to describe, in his submission to the authorities, the exact words and gestures of the superintendent, who was a half-hearted member of Jack Baines's congregation, and with whom therefore Father had embarked on an altercation concerning the duties of a nonconformist believer. Nothing escaped his denunciatory passion: the man's uniform, his beard, the cast of his eye and the drift of his opinions – all were included in a document which endeavoured to summarise an alien existence and consign it to the rubbish heap of time. And here I should point out a peculiar feature of my father's mission in this world. He was an atheist: convinced and uncompromising. Yet he stopped short of saying so. Indeed, he spoke and acted as though God himself had authorised his attitude, granting him a private copyright revelation that all churches to date were impostures, that no worship or faith or obedience enjoyed the faintest whiff of heavenly approval, and that there was but one way to salvation, which was to pour scorn on other people's doctrines, to smash their idols and to sneer at their paltry efforts to do good. At the same time there was nothing he loathed more, in his victims, than religious doubt and compromise. He regarded himself as obliged to hold the rest of humanity to its superstitions, which he fervently mocked to those who subscribed to them, while rebuking their smallest departure from orthodoxy as a sign of a deep spiritual corruption.

Without having intended such a thing, I began to speak of those days – not so as to condemn the ghost that troubled us, but on the contrary so as to cower once again in its presence.

'We were poor then,' I was saying, 'and of course it didn't help matters that he constantly reminded us of the fact, sitting all day, jobless and unoccupied at the hearth, the fire never lit even in the depths of winter since we could not afford the coal, and only one ugly strip-light burning in the living room, beneath which we both had to work, you at your letters, me at my law, finding in the intricacies of contract a consolation which I could never explain to you. And at mealtimes, which he often refrained from attending, having decided to blame us for the surrounding disaster, and believing that the moral pollution of our presence was temporarily too great to risk for the sake of a little food – food which in any case he could easily obtain later, after he had sneaked back from the Coach and Horses and found his plate, which you always slavishly filled for him and put aside in the larder – at mealtimes, when he was present, it was necessary to beg for each scrap, even after it had been ladled on to the plate and the question of its ownership was to all intents and purposes settled. Notwithstanding he would lean across to remove a potato, a carrot, a sausage, giving a full account of its nutritive and financial value and of the inadequacy of one's title to consume it. Even then, humiliated in this way, you would withhold your reproaches, and merely look at him beseechingly from wounded eyes, so adding zest to his mistreatment, and leaving me in yet deeper despair, the sole cause and reason, as I saw it, of this catastrophe – I who was after all superfluous to nature's requirements, an unwelcome intruder into this web of persecution which you had established between you and, what is worse, an extra mouth to feed, as well as being in some obscure way the subject of your quarrel.'

I paused to look down once again at the streets below. A child on a bicycle was circling in the little square before the parish church and despite the distance I seemed to catch sight of every detail of his happy face, even the dewdrop on his nose, as he worked at the pedals, swinging from side to side and opening his small mouth in song. Suddenly I turned to her.

'I am worming into that world,' I shouted, 'seeing my disease in every crevice, and my disease is you – no, don't take that down, it came from nowhere.'

She looked up blankly. After a moment, during which I felt a trifle dizzy, I began again.

'And all the while that you fought with him, this peculiar battle in which you yielded everything, and yet retained the will and the need to go on, I was taking stock of my own situation, as a boy of indifferent talent, with no real hope of an education, and with a pressing need for freedom . . . No, cancel that, there is something else I meant to say. Yes,' I went on, 'he needed life around him, so as to absorb and destroy it. That was the reason why nobody in this town would employ him, and the reason too why he would not accept defeat, would not move elsewhere, to a place where his reputation was still unblemished, but instead was condemned to stay in his birthplace, dictating, negating and ignored, until death put an end to his futile energy.

'And one way or another the no doubt mad idea entered my mind that I had been brought into this world precisely to prove that – notwithstanding a nervous disposition, a sensitive and even artistic nature, and of course every conceivable psychic trauma – it is possible to live, as I have lived, an entirely normal life, to conceal, even from one's closest friends (not, I admit, that I have many friends) the ache of despair in one's heart and the floods of tragic poetry, to deny if need be under torture the possession of the faintest scrap of intellect, to perform the most ordinary tasks in the most ordinary office, eating and drinking with the most ordinary people in the most ordinary cafés and pubs, to submit one's soul to every kind of punishment from popular music, tabloid newspapers, television, to attract not the slightest hostile attention nor even the most fleeting spasm of curiosity. Only one thing was missing, Mother – the thing which is in fact the reward for this self-denying existence – I mean, the woman, the one with whom I was "going out", or rather staying in, the one who . . .'

I paused. To mention Helen was impossible. And yet I was tempted to remind her of that time when – the impossibility of a girlfriend having been established beyond dispute, so that the very mention of the female sex in my connection was enough to elicit guffaws of laughter from the chair beside the fireplace – I finally decided to invite Helen to meet my mother, which was, after all, only the most elementary precaution, and when I had been forced to bring her in secret to the back door, there to confront a frightened and unspeaking mask. But how could I refer to that episode, which led to nothing – or rather, which led only to Helen's flight from me (which was not after all so difficult, since she had committed herself no further than a half-hearted kiss), and which left my own condition in Mother's eyes unaltered? Far better, I realised, to have done with those days for ever.

'I suspect that you never really intended to leave him,' I went on, 'even in those moments when, with the most heart-breaking gestures, you begged me to come away with you. Do you imagine that I was pleased by such proposals? Not a bit of it. For suppose they *were* serious, and that you even had some specific plan in mind – rented accommodation somewhere, extra work to make ends meet, and such detailed provisions as would be necessary to change a sentiment of rebellion into a decision to act for yourself. In what position would this have put me – an eighteen-year-old boy, with my own plans, my own ambitions (for I had ambitions then) – suddenly to have found myself the sole companion, the custodian (because it would have amounted to nothing less) of a woman whose record in the matter of coping for herself was far from distinguished? It's not that I didn't love you; I was even prepared for considerable sacrifice on your behalf, perhaps so much as a year or two of my precious life, if I could see you settled and well at the end of it, with a God-sent guarantee that my duty was over and that you would henceforth lead your own life. But such a guarantee was unobtainable.

'Or suppose, on the other hand, that your proposals were not seriously meant – as in all probability they were not, given the vagueness, the culpable imprecision, with which they were presented and which seemed to transfer entirely to me the burden of providing a programme of action. What a torment would this be, that I should be placed in the position of judge over you, spectator of your weakness, who saw how far you were from any real understanding of your situation, how far you were from mastering, or even decently withdrawing from, the turmoil he had created and which was the source of all the events that truly impinged on us! You, who should have been my refuge in this storm, would appear then as a piece of storm-débris, a wreck – and what is more a dangerous wreck, unanchored and with many hidden angularities, against which I too could be shattered, and around which I must steer at whatever safe distance could be accomplished, weak and un-practised though I was in the art of survival . . .'

I continued, becoming more and more part of the words, feeling for the first time the force, the urgency, the necessity of uttering those truths which had been buried within me and which bore so directly upon our destiny. I mentioned the hesitations, the failures, the retreatings which had on countless occasions caused me, in my search for consolation, to cast myself adrift at the crucial moment, to contrive for myself, in the face of every womanly surrender, that sudden hugging need for solitude, that coldness of the eye and heart by which even the warmest female passion is instantly extinguished.

I mentioned too the petty jealousies at work, the absurd lapses in professional conduct which caused me, all unconsoled as I was, to ruin every chance that I encountered. I mentioned the growing resentment, even dishonesty, which spoiled so many of my dealings with others and which caused them, I suspected (though how just this was towards people against whom I had not the slightest reason for rancour and indeed who would often embarrass me with their sudden kindnesses, offered in the teeth of a most obstinate detachment, I do not know) to look down on me and even to pity me for the weakness which I perceived in myself and which I lacked the will to cure.

She typed at fever pitch, snatching paper from the drawer, tearing it soiled with ink from the machine, and throwing it on to the desk before her. Tears of grief and loneliness gathered in her eyes and dropped in tiny splashes on to the keys of the typewriter. I longed to cease my accusations (which of course were not really accusations, but only descriptions of how things were and had always been, offered as foundations for the future good behaviour which I knew she willed in her heart as much as I did); I longed to speak to her in quiet tones of those days of happiness (and there were many days) when things were well between us and he, confined to hospital, cast only the weakest chains across our thoughts in the quiet living room. I hastened with my words, therefore, speaking faster and faster in the hope that I might finish all that was distressing. Soon, surely, I would embark on those warm and grateful thoughts which had never been expressed, perhaps never entirely felt, but which would triumph now over all our disappointments. I longed to tell her that I loved her, and forgave in my heart what little there was to forgive. And with my head on her breast I would explain the great gifts she had granted me, which I had never known how to appreciate but would certainly appreciate henceforth; and mingling our tears we would ask each other's forgiveness and grant it to the furthest reaches of our undistinguished natures.

With this end in view I began to change from subject to subject, leaving behind the memories of Father, the frustrations at the office, the women who had succeeded Helen and who could never compensate for the loss of her, sifting through every detail of those years in search of the moments of tenderness – moments which lay smothered by the débris of our doubts.

'And another thing,' I said – and this time I was certain that I had lighted on the matter required – 'which I ought to have mentioned years ago, although strangely there never seemed time, so far as our relations were concerned, for the real reproaches – the reproaches, I mean, which go straight to the heart of what we are and so lead nowhere, not even to forgiveness but at best to a kind of raw, wounded toleration – another thing, which was my first day at Grammar School, when you insisted on coming with me, a fact shameful in itself though just about tolerable had you kept a sufficient distance as the other parents did; and then, as we were all assembled in the playground, in our itchy uniforms, eyeing one another with a kind of exploratory contempt, and about to enter through that severe gothic arch to our first assembly, you bent down, took hold of my shoulder and, with a handkerchief that you had knotted up and moistened in your mouth, rubbed a spot of dirt on my nose. Surely it would have been better then to have no nose – certainly better to have no mother, intent on polishing it with her own saliva!'

I had raised my voice as though in anger, though God knows it was only the gentlest feelings that inspired me. I had even advanced towards the desk, and begun to lean on it, thrusting my face in her general direction and squeezing my palms against the wooden edge. Only then did I notice, however, that she had ceased her work, and was shuffling the papers together into a bundle.

'What are you doing?' I cried.

It seemed for a moment that she was in breach of her professional duty, had no right to leave her desk in the midst of this dictation, was indeed deliberately trying to frustrate me, not only in her actions, but with the futile tears that accompanied them and which were designed precisely to arouse pity and compunction, and so to prevent me from the task which I had set myself and which, for the sake of our future, should be accomplished as soon as could be.

She made no reply but, taking the blackened papers from the desk, and thrusting them into my hand, went quickly to the coat-stand, gathered her clothes and rushed from the room.

'Where are you going?'

I followed her into the passageway, and was in time to see her enter the lift. But the doors closed, and I watched the light descend, lower and lower, to the very bottom of the building. I was surprised to discover that we had been on the fourteenth floor; it had never occurred to me that the tower stood so high. It was now imperative to catch up with her. I ran to the stairwell, and bounded into the abyss, two steps at a time.

'Yes Mother,' I shouted, 'I am the scourge of God, the avenger; I am come from spheres of glory, and judgement is mine!'

They were my father's words, full of bombast and mocking laughter. They were all around me, the air was full of them – those absurd and sublime resolutions, which he was careful never to translate into deeds. It was another subject I had neglected to mention, and I ran after her in a frenzy, hoping still to discuss it. Then I paused on one of the landings, looked out over the modern streets on this side of the town, and came to my senses. I was overweight, and in no state to pursue her. Already a minute had passed since she had entered the lift, and my only hope was that she would forget what I had done to offend her – for God knows, I had intended nothing but kindness – and make her way to Pelham Street, where we could talk things over as we always did, beneath the ugly strip-light in the living room.

Just as I was becoming certain that the same idea had crossed her mind, and that I should see her again in a moment, I realised of a sudden that my hope was quite ridiculous. For I had sold the house four years before! This all-important fact had quite escaped me, even though I vividly recalled the transaction, the letters, the lawyers' offices, the fragile simpering of the purchaser, Mr Philips, as he received the title deeds. I thought for a moment: yes, it was certainly four years ago, a year after her death, and a month after my demotion, when I had been forced to sell my only asset, our only asset, and move to lodgings in Gresham Street.

My thoughts hovered inconclusively around these old bones of fact. Then I recalled the papers in my hand. It occurred to me that it was an answer to my words, and not the words themselves, that she had typed on them. But the sheets of paper were blank.

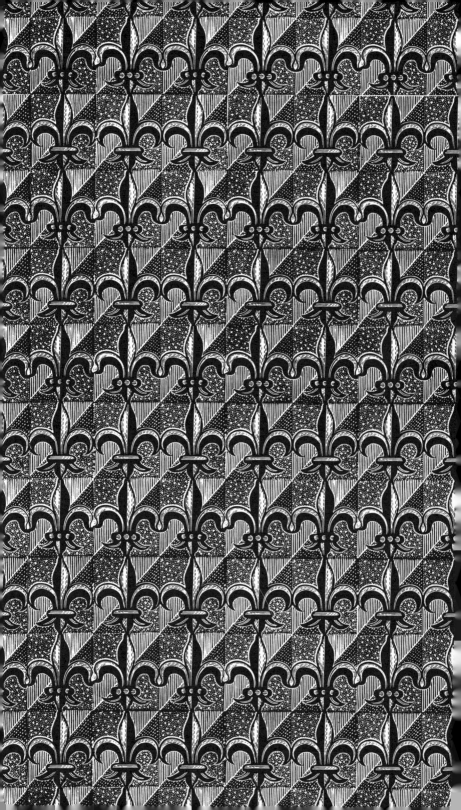